W9-CCF-896

RAMSEY CAMPBELL

THINK
YOURSELF
LUCKY

This is a **FLAME TREE PRESS** book

Text copyright © 2018 Ramsey Campbell

All rights reserved. No part of this publication may be reproduced, stored in
a retrieval system, or transmitted in any form or by any means, electronic,
mechanical, photocopying, recording or otherwise, without the prior written
permission of the publisher.

FLAME TREE PRESS
6 Melbray Mews, London, SW6 3NS, UK
flametreepress.com

Distribution and warehouse:
Baker & Taylor Publisher Services (BTPS)
30 Amberwood Parkway, Ashland, OH 44805
btpubservices.com

Publisher's Note: This is a work of fiction. Names, characters, places, and
incidents are a product of the author's imagination. Locales and public names
are sometimes used for atmospheric purposes. Any resemblance to actual
people, living or dead, or to businesses, companies, events, institutions, or
locales is completely coincidental.

Thanks to the Flame Tree Press team, including:
Taylor Bentley, Frances Bodiam, Federica Ciaravella, Don D'Auria,
Chris Herbert, Matteo Middlemiss, Josie Mitchell, Mike Spender,
Cat Taylor, Maria Tissot, Nick Wells, Gillian Whitaker.

The cover is created by Flame Tree Studio with
thanks to Nik Keevil and Shutterstock.com.
The font families used are Avenir and Bembo.

Flame Tree Press is an imprint of Flame Tree Publishing Ltd
flametreepublishing.com

A copy of the CIP data for this book is available from the British Library
and the Library of Congress.

HB ISBN: 978-1-78758-063-3
PB ISBN: 978-1-78758-061-9
ebook ISBN: 978-1-78758-066-4
Also available in FLAME TREE AUDIO

Printed in the US at Bookmasters, Ashland, Ohio

RAMSEY CAMPBELL

THINK
YOURSELF
LUCKY

FLAME TREE PRESS
London & New York

For Mark and Nel, with love – we survive...

CHAPTER ONE

"Hello?" It was the last word they ever spoke, but by no means the last sound they made.

CHAPTER TWO

"It isn't even in the paper," Emily said, and patches of her small neat face flared pink. "They don't want some people to be heard." Helen tilted her head as if her sympathetic grimace had pulled it awry, and Bill ducked towards the gap under the window of the currency desk. "Who's they?"

As his long thin face offered its habitual smile Helen retorted "Anyone who makes a joke of that kind of thing."

David felt anxious to head off an argument. "Emily, can we help?" Andrea raised her broad face as if she meant to head off any disagreement with her pointed chin. "Just by leaving it, David."

"He was on the phone, Andrea. He didn't hear," Emily said and told him "I was saying a friend of my dad's was attacked outside his house. He was punched in the face when he was only trying to defend his daughter. She was being stalked on her way home from school by a man who lives across the road in what's supposed to be a care home."

"There are too many of them out on the streets," Helen said and twirled a finger like a mime of drilling her close-cropped red-haired scalp. "Nobody cares enough."

"They blamed her and her dad and let the man off," Emily said as her face grew more thoroughly pink. "They said she should have phoned the police, and her dad's a community policeman. Only the police said it would be his word against the man's, and the man would have his social worker in court."

"Antisocial, more like," Helen said. "Working against the rest of us who know how to behave."

Andrea emitted a cough to put a full stop to the discussion and stood up to take an armful of holiday brochures to the racks. "Well, we've all got work to do," she said.

David wondered if she meant to make sure his parents weren't brought into the argument, but he suspected she was only being managerial. He might even have called it officious, since just now his and Emily's and Helen's work consisted of waiting for their phones to be answered by anything more than an automatic response. He watched Andrea file the brochures – Winter Wonders, Spring Forward, Summery Summaries, Crucial Cruises – and then unlock the door as though hoping to attract custom. All she let in was a gust of February air and the trumpeting of a busker outside the railway station down the hill. "Lucky," David murmured.

"Watch out, girls," Bill called. "You've got our Dave talking to himself."

Andrea's glance made it plain that she didn't welcome being called a girl at thirty, even if he had two decades on her. He was one ahead of Helen, and Emily was half his age, a few years short of David. "I'm just saying we're lucky to have jobs," David said, only to feel that something else had been in his mind.

He heard a living voice on his phone at last as Andrea returned to the counter. The tour operator couldn't help him except by providing another number, which offered him a trio of numbers to select from, and another and another... Five minutes after that an advisor made it clear that David couldn't book extra leg room for his customers on the Maltese flight until next week. He called them and apologised on behalf of Frugogo, and was replacing the phone in its plastic trough when someone came into the shop.

His sharp face looked drawn taut by enthusiasm. His greying hair trailed at various lengths over the shoulders of his tweed jacket, which was equipped with shiny leather elbows that reminded David of a teacher at his old school. Before David could think why else he seemed familiar, the man came over to him. "David," he said loud enough to be addressing every listener. "Didn't know you were this close."

David's uncertainty earned him a reproachful blink to go with a vigorous handshake. "Len Kinnear," the man said like rather more than a reminder. "I gave you my bill in the street."

Andrea contributed a cough. "It didn't use to be like you to owe anything to anybody, David."

"My handout, love," Kinnear said. "A flyer for my bookshop. That's We're Still Left, just up the hill. We're about empowering the people and giving them a voice."

"I should think most people have one of those," Helen said without enthusiasm.

"I'll tell you who's got one if he's let, and that's our David here."

"I didn't know anyone wasn't letting him," Andrea said.

"You'd know, would you, love?"

"If anyone here would," Bill said not quite low enough to be unheard. David was acutely aware of her silence, the kind he recognised all too well from their months together. "Anyway," Kinnear said, "remember the invite. Seven o'clock Friday above the shop."

"What's that for, David?" Emily was eager to learn.

"We aren't just a bookshop, we run a writers' group," Kinnear said. "All Write."

"All write as in you think everyone's a writer?" Helen said.

"They will be now the web's democratising it at last. That's the new culture, only some of them need to be told." When Andrea cleared her throat, a high sharp sound, Kinnear said "Just say you're coming Friday, Dave, and I'll be out of your face."

Although David knew why Kinnear wanted him, he wouldn't have called it a reason. Before he could answer Kinnear said "Give us a shot, eh? If you find you aren't for us, no bother at all."

Not least to be rid of him David said "I expect I could give it a chance."

"A glass of plonk says you won't be sorry. Now here's some real customers instead of me." Kinnear held the door open and observed "As somebody was thinking, about time."

David couldn't help feeling vindicated when the young couple came straight to him. He sold them a fortnight in Kefalonia while Andrea fixed a man up with a weekend in Prague, and then she turned to David. "I'll have to say he was right in a way," she said, "your friend."

"Right how? Not about me," David felt compelled to establish.

"We need to promote ourselves like him, however we have to. We're competing with the internet as well. Any ideas from anybody, I'll be listening."

Emily parted her pink lips, but only to say "Why does he think you're a writer, David?"

"It was just a mistake," David said. He was as ordinary as any of his colleagues – if anything, more so. He turned to his computer terminal but couldn't ignore his own thoughts. What was troubling him? Not just Andrea's oppressive interventions, not Bill's heavy humour, not the way Emily and Helen had inadvertently reminded him of the work his parents did. The busker outside the station produced a fanfare that might almost have been mocking David's inability to pin his feelings down. As the computer keys began to clack beneath his fingertips he had a sense that he'd let something out he should never have said.

CHAPTER THREE

Who's next? It's Mr Accident, marching back from the shops with a paper rolled up under his arm. Maybe he thinks it makes him look like a soldier with a stick. With his droopy face he reminds me of a dog that's fetched one. "Stick it in your gob," I say, but he's too busy looking for traffic before he waves me out of my drive. "Stay right where you are," I tell him.

He hitches up the paper and then lifts that arm from the elbow like a robot to shove his ear wider, though it's already big enough to poke a fist in. "Er…"

"Don't worry about it. I'll be there before you know and then you won't need to hear."

It's the work of a moment. I've been distracted by our neighbour, who has come out of Binbag Manor to dump more garbage in her bin. He's in the middle of the road and hasn't time to dodge. I thought I was tramping on the brake, but it must have been the accelerator. I floor a pedal as the car lurches out of the drive, and it stalls inches short of Mr Accident, who staggers backwards and almost trips over the kerb. "Good God, what are you trying to do?" he cries and appeals to Mrs Rubbish. "I didn't even wave him out and he nearly ran me over."

"I'm truly sorry about that." I am that it was only nearly, and I add "I didn't mean to."

"You want to be more careful." Mrs Rubbish shuts the bin with a thump like a warning not to open until it's being emptied, and then she jerks her head back as if it's being tugged by her bun of straggly brownish hair. "Whatever have you done to your car?"

"He bumped into the gateway last week," Mr Accident says as though it wasn't because he waved at me and distracted me into waving back at him. "You can't afford to let your attention wander when you're driving. It's not safe."

She gives me a maternal look, though at least there's no love in it. "Honestly, what are you like?"

"Not like you, I hope, and the same goes for him."

She seems ready to ask what I'm muttering – she's tightened her face so much it reminds me of the bag, which wasn't much paler or more lumpy either – until she hears a groan of machinery along the road. The binmen are approaching, which is the highlight of her week. "Better move so you aren't in their way," she says.

"Time I was clearing out my gutters," Mr Accident says and marches off as she returns to the doorway of her manor, where the antique door may be all of ten years old. The dumpy house is the same as mine but desperate to look different from the neighbour that's its other half. As I drive away she's waiting to make sure the men whose lives are garbage don't strew the roadway with bins. I've seen her watching from her window in case anybody dares to drop rubbish in one of her bins, and if they try she knocks so hard on the glass I always hope it will crack.

The sound of the wagon gulping down the garbage seems to have brought more rubbish into the streets. A woman runs to contribute a bag of turds to someone's bin, and she's in such a hurry that she's left a lump on the pavement – presumably her dog's, not hers. A teenager shoves a laptop deep into a bin, as if he wants to make sure nobody can find out what he's been watching, unless he's just ashamed that the computer isn't the latest model. A toddler screams while his father jams a pedal car into a bin, and the screams grow even louder as the plastic cracks. "Having fun playing dad?" I remark, not that I know much about fathers – actually nothing at all.

The wrecker doesn't seem to hear me for the screams. I'd make sure he didn't like it if he heard. I feel as if I'm swarming with unfinished business all the way to the shops. The winding roads aren't wide enough for cars to be parked opposite each other, which means a lot are on the pavements, even though they could be on a drive. That must be how the owners stake their territory, along with adding bits to their houses as though this can fool anybody into thinking they're less identical. They might as well wear masks to convince people they have souls, whatever those are. They wouldn't convince me.

The shops overlook a stretch of gritty concrete strewn with lager cans that somebody's been scrunching to demonstrate their strength. As I park the car one squashed can flattens under a wheel with a tinny clank. The shops aren't so much a parade as a token line-up – Better Bets, Ho's Traditional Fish & Chips that are mostly kebabs and pizzas and Chinese food (there are samples outside, both uneaten and the opposite), Bonus Booze… The general store at the end says it's Open All Hours, which means just those that suit the Slowworm family, who can't even find the time to change the window display, magazines years old and packets of food no less pale with years of sun. "Is anyone alive in here?" I wonder as I let myself in.

Only Slowworm is. He's behind the counter spread with newspapers and sweets, more of which are in racks lower down for children to grab and whine about to their parents or whichever temporary version is in charge of them. "What can I get you today?" he says before I've even crossed the grimy threshold.

He's peering at me as if he can't quite make me out. He might try taking off the crumpled canvas hat he always wears. He's yanked the brim down to his overstated eyebrows, and the hat looks as though it's cramming his broad flat face together. "What's on offer?" he's goaded me to ask.

"Offer." Once the dull echo dies away he complains "Sounds like you want the supermarket. Us small shopkeepers can't afford to muck around with prices."

"I wouldn't say any of you was that small." I might add that doesn't include his brain, but instead I say "So long as you enjoy serving the public."

"Serving the public. I'd enjoy seeing a few more of them."

"More of them." I can play at echoes too, but I don't think he even notices.

I amuse myself by wanting to know "Don't you enjoy seeing me?"

"Seeing you." He can't quite echo me, and I wonder how much of his resentment has to do with that. "I'll like it when you tell me what you're getting. Words don't pay the bills."

"Let's hope you do." As his face betrays his struggle to decide how insulting this is I say "I've just come in for cigarettes."

"Cigarettes. Better stock up before they're against the law. Pretty soon they'll be something else we're not allowed to mention."

"I thought you said you don't think much of words."

"Don't think much." Before I can congratulate him on acknowledging some of the truth he says "What brand?"

The warnings on the packets behind him are bigger than the brand names. They look as if they're advertising death, which comes close to making me grin. "You don't sell Fatal Fags, then."

"Fatal Fags." When his face catches up with the notion of a joke he makes a stab at banter. "Not got those."

"Or Lumpy Lungs."

"Lumpy Lungs." If he means to sound amused it doesn't work. "Not them either."

"Poison Puffs? Ashtray Breaths? I know, C & C. That's Coughs & Cancer."

"None of those." He's growing so annoyed that he forgets to echo. "If you've just come in for a laugh— "

"I wouldn't dream of it. Give me twenty Players and I'll think of the game later."

He doesn't know if I'm still joking. His face loosens somewhat when I hand him the cash for a packet of King Size, with the chance of a free gift of a tumour big enough for a king. I'll take the consequences, except they've no chance in the world of catching up with me. I strip off the cellophane and leave it crackling like the start of a fire on top of a local newspaper that I could be in. "I'll let you have that," I tell Slowworm. "We don't want any more rubbish on the street, do we?"

I linger in the doorway to watch him pick up the cellophane and pull it off one hand with the other, then wave the fingers it has stuck to. As he starts tramping on the cellophane to dislodge it from his fingers I lose interest. I can always save him for another day, and I use my lighter on a cigarette while I head for the car. The oily taste of nicotine, the bite in the throat, the hint of dizziness – they all feel like sensations I'm remembering rather than experiencing, hints too meagre to add up to even a foretaste of satisfaction. After another ineffective drag I sprain the cigarette in the dashboard ashtray. The stuffing of tobacco that spills from the torn tube puts me in mind of a soft toy that has been ripped limb from limb. That isn't even a memory, and it leaves me more frustrated still.

My dustbin lies full length across my drive with its mouth gaping like a dead fish. Maybe the binmen left it like that, unless someone passing by thought it would be a hoot to tip it over, or just a way of spending a few seconds of their life. I leave the car in the middle of the road while I right the bin and trundle it behind the house, but nobody drives up for an argument. I don't need one of those for motivation. I back the car into the drive, where a scrape of paint on the gatepost would give me a reminder if I wanted one, and stroll along the road.

Mrs Rubbish has left her vigil now the weekly garbage ritual is done, and nobody else can see me either. The moans of the hungry truck are several streets away, and the streets are deserted under a sullen sky that dulls the colours the houses have been daubed with, shades like stale makeup where they aren't childishly garish. If the culprits haven't gone out to work I expect they're watching television or more likely on the internet. I feel as if I'm surrounded by an electronic mind that swarms with random thoughts. How much of my day happened as I've told it? All that matters is this will. I've reached Mr Accident's house.

It's well out of sight of mine, around more than one bend. With its carriage lamp sticking out of the shallow porch of plastic wood it looks as if it wants to be an inn, unless it's wishing it were in a street a lot more historical than this one, where a caravan squats in a neighbouring drive and half a car is littered all over another. His house makes me think of a child wearing a bit of a costume in the hope it will let them pass for a character. It has no more chance than him, but where is he? I'm enraged to think I've given him time to finish with his gutters. I dodge around the house and find him perched at the top of a two-storey ladder.

I'm glad my rage hasn't deserted me, but then it never does. I watch him poke at the gutter above his head like a bird searching for insects to crunch. The trowel he's holding dislodges a sodden wad of leaves, and as he flings the blockage onto the concrete outside the house he sees me. The ladder wobbles and the gutter gives a plastic creak as he grabs it with his free hand. "What are you doing there?" he gasps.

"Just going for a walk so I'll feel better."

"Forgive me, I didn't realise you were ill."

"Forgiveness is no fun, and I don't mean that kind of better." I take a step towards him before enquiring "And what are you up to? Doing somebody out of a job?"

"Pay a man to do a job you can do yourself and you've cost yourself twice over."

I should have known he'd go in for homilies. He lets go of the gutter and rests his hand against the house while he squints at me. "What kind of work do you do? We don't seem to know much about you, Mr…"

"You'll know enough." I can tell he's hoping I've no job so that he can lecture me about it. "I wonder what you'd want to say I am," I muse aloud. "Just call me Lucky, and a collector if you like."

"I will if it's appropriate. What do you collect, may I ask?"

"Let's say payments that are due." I'm at the foot of the ladder now. "Today I'm after payment for an accident," I advise him.

"I wish you joy of it. If people paid up when they should there'd be no need for your kind of profession."

"I'm glad you agree," I say and take hold of the ladder. "You carry on with your good work. I don't want any help." I plant one foot on the lowest rung. "I am."

"I've already told you I can do this by myself. Please just leave it alone." With a grimace that quivers his floppy jowls he adds "And me, if you don't mind."

"I mind," I tell him and climb another rung. "I'm only doing what you asked for."

There's a loud clang below us. He has dropped the trowel, and now he's staring at it as though he should have kept it for a weapon. "What are you playing at, you lunatic? Get off my ladder."

His situation has caught up with him at last. That often happens, and watching the delay can be half the fun. "I keep telling you what I'm doing," I remind him. "Collecting."

He slaps the wall under the gutter with both hands and stifles a cry. "Collecting what, you—" Apparently he can't think of a strong enough word, unless even in these circumstances politeness won't let him discharge it. "Get off there this instant," he says as if he imagines I could be a child, "or you won't like the consequences."

"I'm glad you've brought those up. That's exactly why we're here. Don't tell me you've forgotten what you said to Mrs Rubbish not half an hour ago. Someone scraped their car and all because of you distracting them."

There's recognition in his eyes at last, and it's on the edge of fear. "If you're after compensation you must know this isn't the way—"

"It isn't just the car. It's never just that kind of thing. It's everything you are," I say and scurry up the ladder to tug at his ankles. This time he can't keep his cry to himself. As I dislodge one of his feet from the rung they're desperate to stay on, he lunges upwards to clutch at the gutter.

I couldn't hope for better. I'm down the ladder in a moment, and in another I've snatched it away. It clatters at full length on the concrete as its owner dangles from the flimsy gutter. "Help," he screams. "Look what he's done. Christ, someone help."

He's saying more than he needs to, as so many of them do. You'd think they've taken a vow to use up all the oxygen they can, but he won't for much longer. I watch him struggle to haul himself up and find a handhold on the roof. His hand slips off the wet tiles, and the gutter emits a creak that sounds as if it's splintering. I might enjoy watching him dangle and wave his helpless legs for however many seconds he has left, but my instincts send me to the back door, since it's partly open. As I hear a choked gasp and a long loud creak I let myself into the house.

I can't see anything worth noticing. A day next week on the calendar beside the coffin-sized refrigerator is ringed in red and marked GREAT-NIECE'S CHRISTENING. That'll be missing a guest, I'm guessing. I prop my elbows on the edges of the metal sink and peer between the slats of the plastic blind. Pretty soon a flailing shape falls past the kitchen window. I don't see it land, but I hear it. You might think somebody has thrown a bag of rubbish on the concrete – pottery and useless meat. The large flattened slap will be the bag, and the crunch could be a piece of pottery that's sticking out of the top of the sack. I crane over the sink to make sure nothing is about to move except the contents of the piece of pottery, which has produced quite a spill. "We need you, Mrs Rubbish," I murmur, but the sight isn't sufficiently interesting to detain me. I make my way along the hall, past a lonely yellow vacuum cleaner with a furry upper plastic lip, and out of the house.

CHAPTER FOUR

"Here's our favourite waitress," David's mother declared.

"Our favourite chef," David's father said.

"So long as you're having a good birthday, Susan," Stephanie said, "I don't care what you call me."

She was wearing her chef's apron that said **MICK'S**. The candle on the cake she was carrying lent an extra radiance to her face – round chin, pinkish lips ready with a smile, snub nose, brown eyes with a glimmer of green beneath eyebrows whose height seemed to anticipate a surprise. Her auburn hair was tied back from her high forehead but had grown a little dishevelled, no doubt by the heat in her kitchen, which had left a bead of perspiration bejewelling her hairline. Once she'd set down the cake she led the song. "Happy birthday—"

"Who's having one of them?" Mick protested and trotted weightily to the Bothams' table, mopping his wide fleshy forehead. "Nobody told me."

"David's mother Susan is, and this is his father Alan. You know David."

"Not a comp, are they? You know you've got to clear freebies with me in advance. There's still plenty of my mates that haven't eaten here yet." As all the Bothams gazed at him he urged "Go on then. Happy birthday—"

By the time he finished singing along he'd mopped his forehead twice. David couldn't see much reason, unless Mick's bulk was constricted by the dinner jacket and dress shirt and bow tie he seemed to think a manager should wear. The photographs on all the walls showed that he'd been less podgy as a footballer. "Steph been keeping up our standards, has she?" he said.

"It was exceptional," David's mother said. "You've found yourself a treasure, Mr..."

"Call me Mick," the manager said but was visibly peeved not to have been recognised. "Mick as in Mediterranean Mick's, because we give you a mix of stuff from over there. She's good at all that food, no argument. I don't care where you come from if you do what I want, same as if you were ace with the ball on the field we never bothered what colour you were or if you could speak English."

"Thanks for the appreciation," Stephanie told him.

"No sweat, girl. Go ahead and cut the cake and bring these their coffees and liqueurs if they're having them. I've sent Jess and Rio home before they start squawking about overtime, so you can clear up in the kitchen, can't you? I'll be doing it out here."

Apart from the Bothams' table he would have nothing to clear. They were the last remaining diners in the restaurant, which had never been more than half full. As Stephanie headed for the kitchen, having dealt each of the Bothams a slice of cake, David's father said "So what made you choose Stephanie for your enterprise, Mick?"

"She came cheapest."

David's parents opened their mouths as if they were about to perform a reproving duet, until Stephanie sent them a quick wry smile from the kitchen doorway and put her finger to her lips. Nevertheless David's mother murmured "Nothing like being valued, is there?"

His father wasn't quite so muted. "And that was nothing like."

David saw the manager hunch up his shoulders as he might have prepared for a clash on a football field, and then he shambled into his office behind the bar. "Well," David's mother said and let the word gain weight. "Just you make sure she knows she's appreciated, David."

"I do."

"Hang on to her, that's what we're saying," his father contributed. "I don't mind telling you we didn't think Andrea was any great loss."

It was apparent to David that they'd all had a good deal to drink. He felt it was best to keep his thoughts to himself, but his silence earned him an injured blink. "Don't listen to us more than you want to," his father said. "Maybe we're so used to sorting people's lives out that we don't know when to stop."

"If they're sorted that's what matters."

"Too often they aren't, is that what you're saying?"

"I wouldn't." Since both his parents were gazing at him David couldn't help admitting "Some of the people at work might, but they wouldn't have meant you."

"What were they saying, David?" his mother said as if she were coaxing a child to speak.

"Just about someone's friend who was attacked by somebody in care. The friend was a community policeman and he was trying to defend his daughter."

"Sounds like – who is it, Susan?"

"Benny Moorcroft." She was plainly annoyed with having divulged the name as she said "He's one of my cases, David."

"But you wouldn't have defended him if it had gone to court."

"I'm afraid I would. He's been on cannabis since he was seven years old. You'd be psychotic too if you were him. People like him never had a chance at the kind of lives we have."

"Let's not spoil the birthday," David's father said.

"I didn't mean to," David said, though he wasn't sure that the remark had been aimed at him.

"You haven't," his mother said, knuckling the corners of her eyes. "Thank you for a lovely meal."

At least they weren't doggedly offering to pay, which would be worse than a rebuke. Once when he'd taken them out for dinner they'd ended the occasion by insisting, before he'd learned not to question their work too closely if at all. He was relieved to see Stephanie approaching with cappuccinos and grappa on a tray. "And thank you just as much, Stephanie," his mother said loud enough to be heard in the office.

"We'll have you both over very soon," David's father told him once they'd all finished their drinks. "We promise not to bring up work."

Mick emerged from the office as David's parents left the restaurant. He was clearly less than pleased that David lingered when he'd paid. "I'll wait for Steph if you don't mind," David said.

The manager's face sagged, especially the mouth. "Not been saying she's not safe with me, has she?"

"She'd have no reason, would she?" Having taken the silence for a denial, David said "We'll be going back to her place or mine, that's all."

"Lucky you." With no enthusiasm Mick said "Get you anything?"

"I'm fine unless you've something I could read."

Might this sound like a gibe about literacy? The manager hunched one shoulder and then the other as he lurched into the office, to reappear with Liverpool's daily newspaper. "Here's our news," he said, thrusting the jumble of pages at David. "If it's not beneath you lot from across the river."

David might have pointed out that the paper reported stories from his side of the Mersey as well. It was turned inside out with the football pages uppermost instead of at the rear, and the rest of it wasn't even in order. David set about putting it right, glancing at stories as he did. Football, football, monstrous interest rates on loans, police raids on cannabis farms, care homes shutting down for lack of funds… All at once a story caught his eye, or rather the photograph that illustrated it did.

MAN DIES IN LIFT. While his face was no larger than a picture in a passport, his obesity was plain. His name was wholly unfamiliar, but something didn't seem to be. It must be the struggle to place him that was turning David dizzy; he felt as if the contents of his skull were drifting loose. He raised his head to gaze at the empty restaurant, which hemmed him in with squares and rectangles checked blue and white. Just now it looked like a parody of domestic life or else of travelling abroad. His head wavered drunkenly, and then he shoved back his chair and dashed for the Gents, where the black tiles on every side gave him the impression that his vision was deserting him. He stumbled into the nearest cubicle, where he just had time to flush the toilet before falling to his knees and heaving up his dinner. He had to flush again to cover up his sounds. Stephanie mustn't think it was the fault of her cooking, even if he had no idea what was wrong with him.

CHAPTER FIVE

"What's stopping us now?"

"You just did."

I may as well not have answered him. He's simply complaining, not inviting anybody else to speak. The train had almost shut its doors when he waddled along the platform and gave the nearest one a flabby thump. If I were the driver I'd have put on all the speed I could and never mind how close the late commuter might be – the later the better. When the doors flinched away from the puffy puffing character, who is bagged in a track suit that I'm sure has never ventured anywhere near a track or any other exercise, he dumped himself on the seat across the aisle from me. The seat opposite him is occupied as well, not just by his feet in fat trainers that must have started out white but by a plastic bag that smells of its hot contents. "Are we off yet?" he asks nobody except himself. "Always being held up. Third time this week, which."

He doesn't even make the sentence sound as if it isn't finished. He's using the last word like an overgrown full stop, leaving it to lie there like a block of verbal lead. He finds the floor with his feet while he rummages in the bag for a hamburger. The polystyrene bivalve squeals as he opens it, releasing more of the greasy stench. Chomping on the burger shuts him up, but only until he clears his mouth enough to mumble. "Too hot in here. What are they playing at? Can't hardly breathe. No air down here as it is, which."

The train has gone underground with a roar the tunnel traps around the carriage. Windows someone opened to tone down the fierce heat let in more of the noise. "Too loud and all," the muncher moans through another mouthful. "God, what a racket. Won't let you think, which."

"Do you go in for much of that? I was assuming you just talk."

I don't imagine he hears me. I suspect he mostly hears himself, and he's his own best audience as well, though maybe he was hoping somebody would take the hint and shut the windows to save him from standing up. He plainly has no plans along those lines, since his feet are back on the upholstery. His eyes are as dull as the dough of a bun, and the rest of his face is more evidence of what he eats – it has the texture of an uncooked burger and isn't much less round. I don't know if I'm smelling the food in his hand or in his mouth, if not both. The train is coming to a station, and I wonder if it's his, but he's stirring only to plant his feet further apart, presumably in case anyone thinks of sitting opposite. "Conway Park," he says a good deal less distinctly than the recorded announcement overhead. "No use to me. They don't sell my style of shoes in Birkenhead, which. Every sod's but mine."

"Which style is that? I can't say I'd noticed you had any, Mr Meatface."

I needn't have bothered asking. I can tell he'll be keeping up his commentary all the way to his destination. He's like a child who can't stop babbling, even while he takes another big-mouthed bite. "It's the arches," he complains, and a half-chewed chunk of burger lands on the seat he's facing. "Doctor says I've got to have the shoes to fit, which. Pity his lot can't pay for them if he says they're for my health."

Apparently talking isn't enough any longer, and it's time for a demonstration. He plants the carton on the other seat he's opposite and sets about untying the knot on his left trainer. The mammoth task involves hauling the leg towards him with his hands behind the knee and straining his top half forwards over his stomach. "Give it up, you bugger," he snarls. "Don't go messing me about. Just come here, you bastard. Bloody come here."

He's forgotten to say which for once. Eventually he captures both ends of the shoelace and gasps as he gives them a hearty tug. He treads on the shoe while he releases the foot along with an extra smell that the draught from the open windows can't disperse. "Ah, that's it," he moans, pressing his foot in its discoloured chunky sock against the seat opposite and wriggling his sluggish toes. "Next best thing to a rub off the wife, which. She could do it for a living, her. Don't like to think how she'd leave the house if she ever got a job."

I can't tell whether he's thinking about the state of the place or saying she's confined there, not that I want to know. Once his foot has finished squirming like an animal in a sack he stuffs it back into the trainer, puffing out more of the stale sweaty stink as he hauls at the tongue of the shoe with both hands. "Get in, you little," he pants. "Get where you're bloody told, which. Get right in."

"Need a hand, Mr Meatface? I've two here that want to go to work." He's too busy gasping and sweating and tugging at his shoe to hear me.

At last he triumphs over the trainer and succeeds in tying a sloppy knot. The impromptu pedicure has taken us past one underground station, and I wonder how many the other foot may call for. He seems to think he's made enough effort, however, and slumps back to dig in his bag for a packet of crisps, which don't prevent him from talking. "Here's the shops," he announces as the train halts at the first station under Liverpool. "Hordes of shoes, which. No time to look. I'm everybody's servant, me."

The crunching of crisps is as loud as his voice. Both seem to need him to keep his mouth open as much as he can, expelling a smell of cheese and onion to join the other aromas he's bestowed on the carriage, not to mention spraying the floor and the seats with crumbs and larger fragments. "Next one for me," he proclaims at the second stop. "Wife's sister coming up from London, which. Can't get the train to us herself. Wants meeting and her bags carried, and the wife's too feeble to help."

"I thought you said she couldn't leave the house."

He's already waddling to the doors as the train moves off. He has left more than his mark – footprints on the other seats, the empty plastic bag, the crisp packet unfurling like an artificial flower and surrounded by a generous distribution of its contents, the carton gaping to display the remains of the hamburger and bun still glistening from his last bite, the various smells he donated to the train. "Let's get her done with," he says, only to protest when the carriage lurches. "Watch how you're driving, you. Some of us are standing up here, which."

He continues muttering until we arrive at Lime Street, where the trains from London terminate. He plops onto the platform and plods towards the lift. By the time the train worms its way into the dark we're alone down here. The corridor leading to the lift is tiled as white as a morgue and full of his plump footsteps, not to mention the smells in his wake. I wait for him to reach the end and thumb the button. "Get yourself down here," he exhorts the lift. "Some of us need the lav before the train comes, which."

He's started to repeat himself before the lift settles into view beyond the midget window. As the doors crawl open I move close to him, and I'm behind him in the lift when he pushes the Up button. His moist thumbprint shrinks on the plastic as the metal cell creeps upwards. I don't know whether he can see my blurred reflection in the window of the door ahead of him, but he shakes his head as if he's trying to get rid of an unwelcome impression. His cheeks haven't finished wobbling when he swings ponderously around and finds me at his back. He clutches his chest, and his shoulders slam against the wall so hard that the lift shakes. "Sweet Jesus," he gasps. "Where did you come from? Trying to give me a heart attack?"

"I think you've been working on that all by yourself, Mr Meatface. And you didn't say which."

"What are you blabbering about?" He chokes as if he's rediscovered a lump of hamburger, and then he sucks in an open-mouthed breath. "Watch out what you're doing," he protests. "You'll have us stopped if you're not careful, which."

I've moved to stand with my back against the controls, but I haven't touched them; I'm only making sure he can't. "What would you like to talk about now? Any subjects you think you haven't done justice to?"

"Are you mad or what, you? What are you on about justice?"

"That doesn't even make sense, and you forgot your favourite word again.

Take your time. You've got all of it that's left. Call that justice if you like."

"I'll be calling someone all right if you keep on." His face is mottled grey and pink and red, more like his choice of food than ever. "Leave them buttons," he pants, "which."

"You had a lot more to say for yourself on the train, I must say. But you never talked about your crisps or your hamburger."

"Them's your problem, are they?" He's managed to regain some sense of his own rightness. "Want to mind your business, you," he says, "which. Think you're a cleaner?"

"You could say that. Say I'm cleaning up the world."

He doesn't understand, or else he doesn't want to. "Well, if you've finished talking," I say, "how long do you think you can hold your breath?"

"Long enough, which." Whatever this is supposed to mean seems to desert him, and he demands "Who says I've got to?"

"Who else is here?" I enquire and bring the lift to a shuddering halt halfway up the shaft. "How long now?"

"What've you done?" He flaps his floppy hands at the controls behind me, where the emergency phone is housed as well. "Get away from there," he gasps. "Get it going, which."

"Make your mind up, Mr Meatface. How's your breathing now?"

He gapes like a stranded fish. He looks as if he's searching for a breath before he manages to find one. "Help," he yells. "I'm in the lift. It's been stopped. Someone come and fix it, which."

I doubt anyone can hear him. He's still using too many words, and the last ones trail off, robbed of breath. I can't stand the sight of his open mouth, especially the fat greyish tongue coated with scraps of his recent snacks. "Help," he bellows before he has summoned enough breath, and then starts to cough. This turns his face even more fiercely piebald but seems unlikely to achieve enough, and so I plant my hands over his nose and mouth.

I have to brace my heels against the metal wall to pin him where he is. His thick lips squirm against my palm, rubbing crumbs on my skin. My other hand flattens his nose, which puts me in mind of a slimy snail with a shell that's close to cracking. I've covered his right eye, but the eyeball struggles under my fingers while the left eye bulges and reddens and rolls about as though it's desperate to escape. His fat wet hands tear at my sleeves and perform other antics in a bid to reach more of me. If it weren't for all this I'd be in danger of losing interest before I'm anywhere near finished. At last his hands twitch and droop, and a flabby shudder passes through him, and the tedious task is over. His swollen eyes grow dead as marbles while his body turns flaccid and seems to expand as it slithers down the wall to slump in a heap on the floor. I send the lift to the concourse level, where nobody is waiting outside or coming down the passage that leads to the main station. "Someone's passed out in the lift," I call as I leave the passage, and then I'm lost in the crowd.

CHAPTER SIX

"Is there anyone here who doesn't believe they're a writer?" Darius Hall said.

As David thought of raising a hand a woman called "We wouldn't be here if we didn't."

"So let the world know who you are." Hall's roomy bronzed small-featured face stayed bland as he said "Any other questions, anybody? Anything at all."

"Aren't you bothered by the competition?" another woman seemed to want him to confirm.

"You're just competing with the ruling class. Creativity has room for all of you. It's as big as your imagination."

When several people in the room full of mismatched chairs wrote down some of this a man said "Watch out, Mr Hall. They're pinching your ideas."

"You can't control an idea. You never know where one will end up. Just buy the books and that's reward enough for me."

"How do you get an agent?"

"Do you really want to give away a percentage of yourself? Maybe the electronic age will do away with that and publishers as well."

"You're published by one," a woman objected. "Don't writers need an editor?"

"Try thinking editing is bullying, just like criticism. And anybody saying you can't write, that's the worst kind. It's like gagging you, the way they used to do to women. Yes, lady at the back."

"When you read a book don't you criticise it in your head?"

"That's not the way to read a book. Read it for whatever you can take away from it. Send your mind places you didn't think it could go. If you can read a book you can write one. And if you can't read one you can still write."

Len Kinnear picked up a copy of Hall's latest novel from the trestle table loaded with his work. "I hope you'll all be buying this," he said and flourished it – *The Red and the Grey*, in which foreign squirrels united with the natives to defeat the disease that a government agency had created to discredit the immigrants. "I reckon we've all been inspired tonight. Let's do our best to measure up to Darius."

Hall met the applause with an oblique smile and a heavy-lidded blink and a deprecating shake of the head, and David felt worse than cynical for wondering if all this could be a response to Kinnear's last remark. Suppose Hall's advice was designed to ensure that no editor would help his rivals to improve? As David put the surely unworthy thought out of his mind Kinnear said "Start by remembering you're writers even if you don't think so. Maybe there's somebody that doesn't yet but should."

At first David was able to hope Kinnear didn't mean him – he wouldn't have been there if he hadn't given in to persuasion – and then Kinnear said "That's right, David, you're the man."

Hall gave David a long but inexpressive look. "David..."

"Botham," David had to say, and felt as if he were owning up in a classroom.

"I should look you up online, should I, if you haven't brought your books."

"You wouldn't find me if you did. I really—"

"I saw it in him the first time we met," Kinnear declared. "You've got to know that, David."

When David turned up his open hands – a magician displaying how empty they were, a suspect ready to deliver his fingerprints, a writer with no pen and nowhere near a keyboard – Hall said "Let's hear the story, Len."

"I was plugging the bookshop and I tried to give David a flyer. I'll tell you, you never heard the like. Everybody round us in the street looked like they hadn't either. He'd just come up from the station and he'd had, what were they, David, people trying to sell you insurance and get you to change your phone provider and hoping you'd had an accident at work so they could help you claim. And you'd missed calls while you were underground and when you rang them back they were all spam. So me and All Write were the last straw and David just let rip. Five minutes' worth of rant, it felt like, and I'm not saying in a bad way. Things I bet we all feel and never let out, but he did. Someone that was listening said he ought to be on the stage, but I'm telling him he ought to write it down for us all to read. That's another way of giving everyone a voice."

"Is that right, everyone thinks like me?" When David heard some murmurs of assent he said "Then someone else can write it, someone who's had more experience."

"You've had all you need. You've lived it," Hall told him.

As David took a breath – he was only there from being too polite to refuse, because he was too often too polite – Hall said "What you need to get you started is a title."

"I haven't got one," David said with a good deal of relief. "That's what you're wanting. Come up with one."

"Darius means now," Kinnear said.

Was the author amused by the notion? Perhaps he was by the entire audience. David would have been ashamed to own up to his suspicion, but at least his reluctance suggested a title, though he felt desperate for mumbling "*Better Out Than In.*"

"You oughtn't to have told us, Mr Botham," said the man who'd protested about people taking notes. "Watch out nobody pinches it."

David thought of using this as an excuse to say he couldn't write whatever was expected of him, and then he saw it was a pretext to escape. "I'd better go and make sure, then."

He stood up so hastily that he almost felled the folding chair. Hall sent him an unreadable look as David hurried to the stairs down to the bookshop. Only streetlamps lit the bookcases full of hardcovers that smelled stale, the shelves of nondescript glossy self-published paperbacks. All the way to the door David felt as if he was toiling through a medium composed of dimness and haphazard thoughts. He was never going to be a writer, he promised himself. Even Kinnear hadn't mentioned all of David's diatribe; he'd left out David's gripe about the homeless man who'd tried to sell him a magazine. If this left David feeling even more shameful, at least it guaranteed that he would never publish any of the thoughts he should have kept to himself. Better yet, he wouldn't have them. As he stepped out of We're Still Left he saw the roofless church across the road, the walls left standing as a monument to the blitz, and it put him in mind of a hollow prayer. He suspected that was how a writer might think, and he expelled the fancy from his mind as he tramped downhill to the station.

CHAPTER SEVEN

As she and Emily came back from the staffroom Helen said "So there's some justice after all."

"Send up the fireworks," Bill said. "They're going to pay us what we're worth at last."

His comic grimace failed to moderate the frown Andrea sent him from the currency desk. With a rueful grin he muttered "We can dream."

"Which justice was that, Helen?" David said.

"The man the police wouldn't take to court," Emily said. "He fell all the way down an escalator."

"He's making out he was pushed," Helen said. "Maybe he met someone nastier or crazier than him."

"Are we talking about Benny Moorcroft?"

The instant this was out David regretted asking. "How did you know that?" Emily said while patches of her face turned pink. "I didn't say who he was."

"I don't suppose you'll like this, but my mother is his social worker."

"I expect someone has to be," Emily said as if she was forgiving him.

"I'm saying nothing," Helen declared, "since she's your mother." As the unspoken comment lingered Andrea gave a pointed cough and tapped on the window of the currency desk with the back of her engagement ring. "You could make that the last word on the subject, David."

At least nobody had asked him about the writers' group. He was happy to forget the dilapidated room full of chairs that looked homeless, the battered shaky table piled with books their authors hoped to sell, Darius Hall assuring questioners that grammar and spelling were forms of oppression — ways of denying the downtrodden a voice — while publishers and booksellers were involved in a capitalist conspiracy... He might have amused his colleagues with some of the titles on sale — *The Yodelling Killer, No Ham for Mohammed*, a book of science fiction tales called *Stories Set to Stun* — but that seemed more mean-spirited than he liked to think he was. He turned away from Andrea and saw Stephanie watching him.

She would be on her way to work. She waved at him over a poster for a fortnight in Tunisia and then, having hesitated, came into the shop. On her way to the counter she put a finger to her lip as if enjoining silence or thinking how little to say. She leaned towards David to murmur "Can I just have a word?"

"He's already had quite a few," Andrea wanted her to know. "Stephanie, isn't it? Aren't you the cook?"

"I'm in charge of the kitchen, that's right. And you're, don't tell me." When Andrea didn't Stephanie said "I expect you have to be Andrea. Has David been talking about me?"

"I've heard him talking, yes." Not quite so haughtily Andrea said "The only reason I asked about your job was that I wondered if you have promotions where you are."

"Promotions." This seemed to antagonise Stephanie. "How do you think I'd get one of those where I work?"

"Promotions." When repeating the word in a patient tone failed to render it more eloquent Andrea said "I'm asking do you take advertising."

"I don't think the management can expect me to deal with that as well."

"I'm sure they make the important choices. Do you know them well enough to say if they'd go for it?"

"I know him better than I want to. Go for what exactly? You aren't very clear."

"I don't believe David and the rest of my team would say that. You don't get to my position by not being clear." As David and his colleagues stayed quiet Andrea said "I've decided we should print out our offers every week. Perhaps you can ask your manager if the restaurant will take them."

"I don't know how much longer I'll be there."

"If you're moving on I hope you'll still be able to help us."

"I'm waiting to see what the manager's planning. He seems to think I can handle the kitchen all by myself."

"Can't you? Some cooks manage. We're quite a large family, and our grandmother always did at Christmas."

As Bill risked a muffled chortle and a wink at Stephanie, she told David "Mick keeps threatening to let someone go."

"These decisions have to be made," Andrea seemed to feel provoked to say. "I'm having to consider some reduction in the personnel myself. Now please do have the word you came in for."

"I've had a lot more than I meant to," Stephanie said with a wideeyed highbrowed look, though not at her. "You've heard what I came to say, David."

"Give me a call whenever you need to," David said and reached across the counter for her hand, which was soft and chill. "Who's where tonight?"

"I'll make my way to yours if we close early enough."

He shouldn't hope the restaurant was sufficiently unsuccessful to give her time to catch the last train, though he wouldn't mind her working for somebody other than Mick. He kept hold of her hand long enough to let Andrea see that he hadn't let go because she was watching. As the door closed behind Stephanie, Helen asked the question that the silence seemed to consist of. "What were you saying about personnel, Andrea?"

"I shouldn't have let myself be provoked. I'm sorry I spoke."

"All the same," David said, "you did."

"I don't need you to tell me, David." When everyone continued watching her Andrea said "Unless there's a significant increase in sales very soon we may have to look at rationalising the staff."

"Rationing, you mean," Bill said and had to find a grin. As Emily's face grew pinker Helen said "Who will?"

"I hope we feel we're all part of the firm," Andrea said. "I hope we'd want to do everything we can for it, even if that means making sacrifices."

"Have you thought which one you're going to make?"

David thought of saying that, but it was Bill who did. "Let's hope it won't be necessary," Andrea told him. "I asked you all to think of ways we can promote ourselves."

"When did you ask that?" David wondered. "I've forgotten if you did."

"Who's in charge here, David? Here's a hint. It isn't you."

The silence felt like suffocation until Emily whispered "You don't need to let her talk to you like that, David."

"I don't suppose she would," Helen said not much louder, "if you hadn't been together."

"I'm staying out of it if you don't mind, Dave," Bill muttered. "Too many ladies."

"I hope you're all discussing how to improve things," Andrea said.

David was assailed by a thought more vicious than he would have liked to think he had in him. Not least in a bid to suppress it he said "How about you? Any ideas?"

"I'm asking nothing of the rest of you that I don't expect of myself." She gave this a moment for appreciation before saying "When I've printed out the offers some of you can distribute them on the street. Now that's enough of me, and let's hear from someone else."

David mimed pondering, only to find that he'd driven every thought out of his head. He gazed at the brochures in the racks, but their sunny images seemed too remote from him. He glanced towards the window in case the posters inspired him, even if he might as well have been trying to read them in a mirror, and saw someone watching him. As soon as their eyes met the man dodged along the pavement and came into the shop to thrust his large blunt wide-featured face at David. "Mr Botham," he said. "Frank Cubbins. All right."

Once David grasped what the last phrase had actually been he recognised the man. Cubbins had warned the speaker at the writers' group that his audience was taking notes. "Can I send you somewhere, Mr Cubbins?" David found he hoped.

"You never said this was your day job." Before David could judge what kind of criticism this was Cubbins said "You know what I told you."

"You needn't worry about me. As I said—"

"You let everybody know your title and now someone's used it online."

"I expect it was there already, but it doesn't matter. I won't be writing anything at all."

"You're a writer, are you, Mr Cubbins?" Emily said. "What do you think of our David?"

"If Len says he's the gear that's good enough for me."

"There you are, David," Helen said.

Surely she was being as ironic as he wanted her to be, and he trusted Bill was joking when he said "They'll know more about it than us." He wasn't going to be forced to articulate ideas he would rather not have. "Thanks for thinking of me, Mr Cubbins," he said, "but you won't be hearing from me, I'm afraid. Some people just oughtn't to write."

Did Cubbins wonder if this was aimed at him? He gave David a suspicious look before leaving the shop. "You need to decide which job you're doing while you're here, David," Andrea warned him.

"Didn't you hear what I said? I'm no writer and I don't intend to be. What have I got to write about? Can you imagine anybody wanting to read about someone like me and my life? I've got no story to tell. If everybody has a book in them, some of them ought to stay there. Mine certainly should, except there's no book. I'm just what everyone sees, and who's going to be interested in that? If my friends and the people I'm closer to are interested that's enough for me, more than enough."

"Sounds like you've quite a lot to say for yourself." As David pressed his lips together so as not to say any more Andrea said "I hope that's the end of your visitors."

When the door opened he was afraid Cubbins had returned, but the newcomer was a woman. She turned to the racks of brochures, and David went over to her. "Can I help you with anything?" He, was doing his best to feel relieved, because surely Cubbins had let him. If the title he'd given away at All Write was online, that was one more reason never to let out the thoughts that were better kept to himself – best never thought at all.

CHAPTER EIGHT

Just a solitary member of the staff is dealing with the public while her colleagues find the bags of sweets that occupy the counter worthier of their attention. You'd hardly know you were in a cinema except for how you have to queue, back and forth along a rope on stilts as if they don't want you to reach the pay desk until you're hungry for popcorn, not to mention hot dogs dripping so red and yellow you might think they'd caught a cartoon disease. At last the girl summons the raw-necked resolutely bald fellow who's been jiggling the front post of the rope to annoy the staff, and he stumps to the counter. "What's *The Braining*?" he brays loud enough for everyone in the lobby to hear.

"It's a horror."

"I know that." He should, since he has titles tattooed on either side of his neck – *Human Centepide* and *Serbain Film*, presumably favourites of his, though not so dear to him that he can spell them right. "What's in it?" he persists. "Can't be much when it's a fifteen."

"It's about a monster that steals brains. We've had people walk out because it was too much."

"Still only got a fifteen." His morose braying reminds me of Eeyore – no, make that Eegore, given his craving for horror. "Go on," he says like someone performing a charitable act for all the onlookers to remark. "Nothing else I want to see."

He doesn't notice that he's being followed upstairs to his screen of choice. The entrance is at the back of the auditorium, and I don't give him any reason to look over his shoulder. For the moment I stay several rows behind him, and he won't have realised he isn't alone in the cinema. Soon the lights go down, but not too far, and Eegore twists around to stare towards the projection booth. He doesn't see me crouched in the seat, or if he does my grin in the dimness means nothing to him, and he faces the screen when it lights up.

It's showing adverts full of perfect people even more manufactured than the wares they're touting. The people are so interchangeable that the adverts might just as well be merged into a single one, where the lovely youngsters use their latest phones to change their banks and get a loan to buy a car built by robots brainier than them and drive it with a glass that they never quite drink from in one hand, because the advert's telling them they have to be responsible with alcohol. All this rot brings in the flies – more of an audience, bumbling along the rows of seats or buzzing with phones in their hands – and I could think I've missed my chance, except that any one of them could be another.

There's a pair of girls who look like overgrown children, their tubs of popcorn are so gigantic. Scent mixed with the oily sweetish stench suggest that they've been playing with perfume and didn't know when to stop. More than one newcomer is so busy texting that he blunders to his seat as if he doesn't know where he is, except somewhere on the communications network. One cinema enthusiast demonstrates how he can take bites out of a hot dog as an aid to spitting and swearing at the phone in his other hand. A rat is foraging in garbage behind me – no, somebody's rummaging in a bag of sweets, if there's any difference. As the cinema trailers go off like a series of bombs, each one louder and more blinding, a man wide enough to use an extra ticket arrives at my row and squeezes into the end seat with a loud moist wheeze. He's still wheezing when the film comes on.

Once the credits have finished twitching and jittering around the screen – names nobody except their families and friends are likely to have heard of – a girl starts cunting about while she waits for the story, such as it is, to finish her off. Cunting about is how only women behave, not like wanking about or cuntishness, which anyone can get up to and usually does. Women like to call it multitasking, but cuntery's a better word. As a shambling creature that reminds me of some of the audience pulls off the top of the girl's head and grabs her brain, which at least proves she's supposed to have one despite the lack of any other evidence, a latecomer thunders down the aisle, spilling popcorn from a tub to squeak beneath his boots, and drops himself on a seat along from Eegore's. "What's happened?" he wants to be told.

"He scrunched her head," Eegore brays, "and he squoze her brains out and I expect he et them."

"Right." More forcefully the newcomer demands "What're they saying?" He's asking about the dialogue he and Eegore just blotted out by talking.

When Eegore sticks his hands up and wriggles his limp fingers to indicate how little use he is, Deafskull raises his droning voice. "What'd they say?"

"Try shutting the fuck up," a girl advises him, "and maybe we'd all hear." Her protest might mean more if she weren't waving her illuminated phone, and now she returns to texting or playing a game or maybe even reading about the film she paid to watch. That's how it goes for the rest of the show. Deafskull keeps asking what someone on the screen said and then what they were saying while he was, and Ratbag carries on scrabbling for sweets, and the girls dig in their tubs for popcorn that squeaks like polystyrene; maybe that's how it feels between their teeth. Quite a few people seem to prefer their personal screens to the one that's showing the film. As for Bladderblob – he's the fellow in my row, who puts me in mind of a balloon full of water – he makes a trip that must be to the Gents at least four times an hour. He comes back every time up the other aisle and sidles past me as if he's being dragged along the row. "What's that?" he complains when he almost stumbles over my feet, and "What the hell's that?" the next time. It wouldn't take much to trip him – just lifting my leg. Once he sprawls in the dark I could trample on his head and crush his face into the carpet. The only trouble is that someone might notice before I could finish.

The creature on the screen turns out to be collecting brains so that it can benefit from all their wisdom and become more human. I laugh at that and some of the audience do, though it doesn't prove they've any brains themselves – none worth a monster's effort to get to know them. The monster hunters are unimpressed too, and they blow it to bits. As the credits bring the lights on I linger in the darkest corner of the cinema to watch the audience. They've hardly started to straggle out of the screen, leaving sweet papers and bags and plastic tubs and trails of popcorn, when I make my choice.

There's an extra scene after the credits. A chunk of blown-up brain comes back to life and sets about growing into a monster. Eegore and Deafskull might appreciate this in their own morose ways, but they've gone. Just Bladderblob is left, waiting to be certain he doesn't miss even a scrap of what he's paid for, unless he's having to gather himself to heave his bulk out of the seat. The screen turns blank, and he lurches so abruptly into the aisle that his innards must be urging him.

The corridor outside the screens is deserted, but someone's in the Gents. He's touching the front of a hand dryer on the wall and then fingering its underside in case this sets it off. That doesn't work, and holding his prayerful hands underneath the white box is no help, any more than moving them away and bringing them back or skimming them beneath the length of it, first slowly and then slower before he wafts them so fast that drips spatter the tiled wall. None of his overtures persuade the dryer to stop imitating a lump of marble, but as he takes his hands away it teases him with a metallic sigh. He spends some time trying to identify exactly where his hands were when they triggered it, and when the effect proves to be unrepeatable he lets them drop, which earns him a hot breath from the dryer – just enough to tempt his hands back in time to miss it. He jerks them up below it and snatches them away, which isn't the trick, however fast or slowly he performs it. As the dryer celebrates his failure with another terse exhalation he waves his hands so wildly that he looks as if he's trying to rid himself of them. I'd be amused to do him the favour, but he stalks into the corridor.

He's driven Bladderblob into a cubicle, but from the sound of it or rather from the absence of any he's too shy to use the toilet while anyone's within earshot. Maybe that's why he had to visit it so often. "Hello in there," I call. "What did you think of the film?"

The silence means I've bothered him, but that's nowhere near enough. "You in the cubicle, I'm talking to you. Don't be bashful. Don't be a bashful Bladderblob. Let's hear your thoughts if there's nothing else to hear."

That brings a grunt and an even more thwarted version, more like a squeak. "That's a start," I encourage him. "Carry on, make yourself heard. You still haven't said if you enjoyed the film."

"Which film?" he growls, and I hear that he's facing away from the door. "What's it got to do with you?"

"Don't you even know which film you saw? The one with all the brains in.

Did you like the bits of it you stayed for?"

"Why's that any of your business?" he snarls, and through the gap beneath the door I see his feet shuffling in worse than frustration. "Leave me alone, will you. I didn't come in here to talk."

"It sounds as if that's all you can do, Mr Bladderblob. Just tell me what you thought was in the bits you didn't see."

"What are you calling me?" he whinnies and lifts one foot after the other in something like a rain dance. "What are you up to, you—"

Whatever he might have said is cut short by a high-pitched grunt that falls short of producing a result. He won't be seeing any while I've more to say to him. "How about the bits you didn't care if anybody else saw?"

"Will you shut up," he squeals and stamps a foot as if this may jerk his bladder into action. "You think you're hiding out there but I bet I know who you are."

"You will. What do you think you know?"

"Aren't you the idiot that kept asking everyone about the film?"

"I'm no idiot of any kind. I'm the watcher you couldn't be bothered to notice. Lucky, that's me. Mr Lucky on another mission," I say and fling open the cubicle door. "Let me put you out of your misery, Mr Bladderblob."

I could think I already have. He lurches forward, and his forehead meets a tile with such a spectacular crack that you might think at least one of them has splintered. As he staggers backwards I hardly need to trip him. He falls face down in the toilet with his neck on the porcelain edge, and the impact drops the seat together with its lid on the back of his head. He has just begun struggling to raise himself when I sit on the seat, pinning his shoulders with my legs and digging my heels into the small of his back. "Sorry, what was that again?" I enquire. "You need to speak up."

He doesn't seem to have much time for words any more. I can't hear any among the hollow muffled noises he's managing to make. He's putting most of his energy into his hands, which claw at the air and punch as well as slap the metal walls on either side and grope extravagantly in my direction without finding me. It looks as if he's reaching for the flush, and I guide his right hand to the handle and help him yank it down. His choked sounds turn into gurgles, and his vague enthusiastic gestures grow even more vigorous, but I have to capture his wrist again and use his hand to clutch at the flush a second time before he tires of his antics. He's succeeded in achieving what he came for, though on the floor instead of in the toilet. Still, most men do both. Once I'm sure he has come to an end I leave him kneeling like a penitent so ashamed that he's hiding his head. That's how he should have felt, but it's too late for him to know. As I reach the exit I see the inspection sheet on the door to the corridor. The next inspection of the Gents is due in less than five minutes. "They'll need a bigger bag for you," I tell Mr Bladderblob as I step into the empty corridor.

CHAPTER NINE

"Help the homeless."

The woman outside Central Station was selling the *Big Issue* as so many of the homeless did. Regardless of her smile the middle-aged couple carried on their conversation as if they hadn't noticed her, although they'd only begun it when they had. "Help the homeless," and a businessman flourished his briefcase at her, though David suspected it contained no copy of the magazine. "Help the homeless," and a man and woman who'd tried to hurry past on either side glanced up in unison at the station sign as if this might persuade her that they needed to establish where they were. David couldn't do that, since he was climbing the ramp out of the station, and he didn't have a case, let alone anyone to talk to. He'd just reached the cold sunless March street when the woman smiled at him. "Help—"

He remembered the behaviour that he'd been too ashamed to admit to Len Kinnear, not merely dodging one of her fellow sellers but grimacing at the man. Before she could utter the rest of her plea David dug out more coins than the price of the item and pressed them into her hand. "Keep it," he mumbled, "sell it to someone else," and hurried uphill towards the roofless church.

He hadn't bought a magazine for years, from Slocombe's or anywhere else. If he needed the news it was on his phone or his computer. All the same, he regretted not having the magazine to show another seller halfway up the hill. No doubt she thought he was as uncharitable as he'd tried not to be. Was he feeling guilty because he couldn't help them all? He felt guilty enough for two people, he thought, or at least that was how a writer might think. Just now he was most concerned to help Stephanie find another job.

He was twenty minutes early for work. He took out his mobile as he came abreast of the travel agency, and was ready to go online when the door swung open, wagging its CLOSED sign. "You aren't busy, are you, David?" Andrea said.

"I could be for a few minutes."

He was thrown by her disappointed look. "I assumed you were here for us."

"Andy…" He felt as if he was pocketing the phone to make sure they weren't overheard. "I didn't know you still felt that way," he said and did his best to appear sympathetic.

"Just come inside."

She turned away before he could see her reaction, but once the door was shut she swung around to face him. "You know perfectly well that's all over. I very much hope you do."

"Well, I do now. I thought I did already." This didn't alter her expression, which was blank yet expectant without offering any hint of why, and so he tried adding "Only I thought you—"

"You're well aware I'm with someone else, David, and you seem to be."

"I don't just seem. Steph's been good for me. I hope what's his name is good for you."

"Rex. He is, and I don't care to discuss it with you any further."

David knew that tone from their months together. "We wouldn't be talking like this at all," he couldn't help pointing out, "except for what you said."

"I hardly think you can blame me, David. Exactly what are you accusing me of?"

"I thought you thought I was here for us."

"Yes." When her stare failed to convey the meaning she apparently believed it should, Andrea gestured at the racks of brochures, the dormant computers squatting on the counter. "Us," she said.

"I think I'm a bit early. I was just going to—"

"The brochures we wanted are in." She pointed to a heap of parcels with a Stanley knife on top. "We need them in the racks before we open."

"That shouldn't take long. I'll only be a little while and then—"

"May I remind you who's in charge here, David."

"You aren't in charge of me. I know you liked to think you were." He might have left that unsaid, but now he had to say "You can't be in charge when it isn't time yet. I want to do something for Steph."

"If you let her take precedence over your work I won't answer for the consequences. And may I just—"

"Come off it, Andy. No need to talk to me like that. There's nobody else to hear."

Andrea let out a long slow breath before she said "I won't have anybody undermining my authority. I think you'd better take time to consider what behaviour is appropriate in the workplace, David."

"All right, I'll go and do that now."

He was feeling stupidly triumphant when she said "For a start, don't call me Andy here. In fact, nowhere at all."

"Is Ms Randall all right?" David retorted, but only once he'd shut the staffroom door.

A faint smell of coffee lingered in the windowless room, where the walls were covered with posters ousted from the shop. Five straight not unduly padded armchairs kept their distance from a set of thinner seats resting their brows against a bare table marked with coffee rings. David laid his phone on the table and saw his fingerprint fade from the screen as the Frugonet icon brought him online. Very soon it was plain that he'd had less of an inspiration than he'd hoped. No local jobs for chefs were to be seen – not even any within an hour's drive or further away either. By now browsing had taken hold of his brain, one site leading him to another that tempted him to several more, besides which he found himself following random notions that seemed to belong less to his own mind than to the electronic medium. No wonder they called it the net or the web; he could have imagined that thoughts he hardly knew he had were being trawled for, if not drawn in by an insubstantial trap. He'd regained enough of himself to resist when it occurred to him to make one more search while he was online. He felt absurd for doing so, but he typed *Better Out Than In*, and in a moment was rewarded with a site.

It was an anonymous blog that seemed determined to live up to its title. While it took the form of stories told by a narrator as if they'd happened to him, presumably they were meant to be satirical; they were certainly outrageous enough, not least in the ways the blogger brought them to an end. At first David had to laugh at the exaggeration of it all, but what kind of mind could produce such material? He blamed the internet for letting loose the contents of the depths of people's minds, those aspects of themselves they might never have admitted before it existed. If he were a writer, perhaps he might have said the dark matter that had been released was forming a new species of monster. He was reading a rant about the patrons of a cinema when Emily came into the staffroom. "What have you done to our Andrea?" she murmured, having shut the door.

"I've done nothing to anyone. What am I supposed to have done?"

"She's in a sulk, that's all. Putting out the brochures and looking like she thinks someone else should." Emily moved to stand beside him. "David," she added as she read the screen, faking shock that nonetheless pinkened her cheeks. "I didn't know you went in for that kind of thing."

"I don't." He'd reached what he assumed was the end of the episode of the blog, in which the narrator followed a cinemagoer into the Gents. "It's what that fellow from the writers' group meant," David said. "The title was already out there."

"Are you going to find out what happens?"

"Don't blame me if it isn't nice," he said and scrolled down the page. "I've seen what he gets up to elsewhere."

"I'm glad this isn't you, then. Nobody could say you aren't nice."

Emily's face grew pinker, though he couldn't tell how much of this was caused by the story that crawled into view. All at once the phone skittered across the table as his hand jerked. "Oh, David," Emily cried. "I see what you mean."

Perhaps she did, but she couldn't see his thoughts. He recaptured the phone and peered at the screen in the hope of having been mistaken, but what he thought he'd seen was there. His head felt hollow and unstable, and all he could do was convince Emily that he'd been shocked for the reason she had. "We don't want any more of that, do we?" he declared and broke the connection. "Let's give Andrea a hand," he said, gripping the edge of the table until the dizziness went away. "As you say, it's a good job this has nothing to do with me."

CHAPTER TEN

He opened his eyes to find Stephanie's face close to his. It felt like being wakened by the sun until she said "What's wrong, David?"

At first he didn't quite know where he was or when. It was Sunday, and neither of them needed to get up, but this fell short of reassuring him. "Why is anything?" he mumbled.

"You don't usually talk in your sleep."

At once he was a good deal more awake. "What did I say?"

"I couldn't make most of it out."

"I expect it wasn't worth hearing. Just me using up my breath." He would rather not have added "You said most."

"You kept telling yourself not to say something." Stephanie reached out to caress his face as she murmured "You can say anything to me."

"I know. I have." Since this was inadequate he tried saying "You can understand I'm worried for you and your job."

"Don't be too much. There are a couple of places that wouldn't mind taking me on if I'm available. They mightn't pay so much, though." Before David could respond she said "Do I need to be worried about you?"

"I can't see why," David said but wondered if he should. "I haven't caused you any more problems with Miss."

"Andrea, you mean." When Stephanie only gazed at him across her pillow David said "It wouldn't be your fault if I had."

"You're saying you have."

"None I can't laugh at."

"You can with me if you like."

"I will if I need to, then," David said and slipped an arm around her waist. "You know I don't like speaking ill of people. Speak ill and you'll be ill, my grandmother used to say her mother said."

"I just wish sometimes you'd share more of your thoughts."

"Suppose they aren't worth sharing?"

"If they're yours they are to me." Stephanie held his gaze while she said "You shouldn't ever be embarrassed. We ought to know all about each other."

"Maybe there's nothing you don't know about me." When he felt her waist grow slack against his arm he said "You know a lot more than Andrea."

"I should hope so, David."

Perhaps he needed her discontent to make him say "All right, I'll tell you why I think I was talking in my sleep. Did you ever have an imaginary playmate?"

"I had enough who were real."

"I had plenty of those, but I made one up when I was little." He had a sense of setting free the truth with no idea of the consequences. "I called him Lucky," he said.

"Oh," Stephanie murmured and stroked his back. "Does that mean you didn't think you were yourself?"

"No, I thought I was. I remember my parents kept saying we were, and I couldn't see any reason to argue. We were a lot luckier than the people they had to deal with every day."

"So why did you call him that, your friend?"

"Because he could do things I didn't dare and get away with them."

He saw a glimmer of naughty amusement in Stephanie's eyes. "You did them and blamed him, you mean."

"I wouldn't have, not the kind of things he did. I'm sure you wouldn't have wanted me to. He behaved like the children my parents talked about when they thought I couldn't hear."

"Well, you were a child yourself." Before David could decide whether she was offering this as an excuse or even wishing he'd misbehaved a little more, Stephanie said "Anyway, I thought we were supposed to be talking about—"

"We are." Just the same, it took some effort to say "He came back."

"In your sleep, you're saying."

"Not last night and not while I was asleep. Long before that." With a laugh that hardly sounded like his David said "You might say he was me as I didn't grow up."

"I might if I knew what it meant."

"When I turned adolescent I was afraid I'd start being like the teenagers my parents had to cope with, so—"

"Poor David. You ought to have been able to let go at that age." With a smile not entirely free of wistfulness Stephanie said "You could a bit more now and then."

"That sounds like a complaint."

"Don't let it spoil our day. Just forward it to the appropriate department. Anyway," she said to return him to his subject, "you were being a teenager."

"Yes, and so I wouldn't be the wrong kind I brought him back."

"Your friend Lucky."

"I wouldn't call him that. More like bad company. You'll laugh, but I must have been trying to make myself think he wasn't a childish idea, so I gave him a last name."

"What did you call him?"

"Mr Newless, and don't ask me why. It didn't seem to have anything to do with me." For no reason he could think of David wondered if this was the first time he'd ever spoken the name. "I ended up using him when I was tempted to do anything I thought my parents mightn't like," he said. "He caused all sorts of mayhem, but only in my head. In a while I convinced myself I was what they wanted, and that got rid of him."

"So why were you thinking about him last night, do you think?"

"What I've just told you about, that wasn't the last time I called him up."

"You're making him sound like some kind of demon, David."

"Well, he wasn't." David stiffened so as not to yield to an unexpected shiver. As he pulled the quilt around them both he felt like a child trying to take refuge in bed. "He was just something I made up," he insisted. "And I did again while I was at university."

"I'd have thought you would have broken out of yourself there at least."

"I had fun, don't worry. It's a good thing I did, considering how hard I worked as well and where I've ended up."

"We have to take the best jobs we can get, don't we, even if there's more to us?"

"There isn't that much more to me." He hoped Stephanie realised he wasn't saying the same about her. "The problem was," he said, "maybe I had a bit too much fun."

She made a joke of looking apprehensive. "What am I going to find out about you, David?"

"It was the only time I got into drugs."

"Well, they're out of your system now, and you needn't think I didn't.

I shared a few bongs back then and ate the odd mushroom."

"I did all that too. I even had a year on cigarettes. You wouldn't have known that, would you?" For a moment David managed to feel he was sharing a secret, but he was too aware of keeping another. "Only once I went too far," he said.

"You're back now, though. What did you do?" Stephanie murmured and inched closer.

"I don't think any of us even knew what it was called. Give us a pill and we'd swallow it if it was something new that was going round the campus."

"Maybe that's how we had to be to grow into who we are now. So what happened, David?"

"I still don't know exactly what it did. Maybe someone at the university designed it, but we never found out who. It wasn't around very long. Maybe whoever made it panicked because they were afraid of being found out."

"What happened to you, I was asking."

"I know." David was aware of fending off the memory. "A few of us took it one night in somebody's room," he said. "Everyone else was happy just to lie around and have visions, but it didn't work that way for me. I had to get out."

"You aren't claustrophobic now, though. I suppose some drugs can make you feel you are."

"It wasn't just that. I was trying to get away from what I'd done."

"You couldn't just let go and enjoy it."

"It made me feel I couldn't, so I wandered off the campus on my own."

The memory was growing as vivid as any of the visions he'd wished he hadn't had. The old buildings of the university had glowed like bones in a fire, but he'd seen that the new blocks lit by white globes on stalks were fossils of the future. As he crossed a road, the cars that glared at him with their great eyes had seemed poised to multiply their speed the instant he stepped off the kerb. He'd had to walk through far too many streets composed of display cases furnished with a selection of people, unless the images within the frames were arcade games, since the figures didn't move until he stared at them. Despite the January chill, he'd felt his sweaty feet squelch at every step. At last he'd come into the open on the far side of a stile, which was as cold as metal and transformed his hands on it into wood. The electric amber sunset of the town had faded from the sky he'd left behind him, and eventually he'd lain down in the middle of a field that frost had turned into enormous spiky half-buried ribs. He'd felt the skeleton splinter beneath him, and then he'd been aware of nothing except the sky, where the moon had sharpened the edges of clouds as it crept from behind them. "Where did you end up?" Stephanie said.

"Somewhere out in the country. I can't tell you anything else."

"Is that where you met your Mr Newless?"

"I didn't meet him. I never have and I wouldn't want to."

"Gosh, I've never heard you sound so fierce. I was only thinking you might have thought you did when you were out of your head."

"Not even then," David said, which felt like trying not to put the memory into words. He'd lain on the icy shards of the world and gazed up at the moon, the half that shone like snow and the rest that he couldn't be sure he was seeing, a rounded segment of the night like a denial rendered solid. The frigid light had gathered all around him until he'd started to believe that nothing was alive except him – that nothing else was even real. The notion had closed around his mind, eating away at his sense of his own reality, a threat that had terrified him so badly that he'd clutched at the only solution he could think of. "It's exactly what I didn't do," he told Stephanie. "I managed to imagine everything was happening to him instead of me."

"Did it help?"

"It must have." All the same, for a moment if not longer – it had felt like the rest of his life – he hadn't known where or even who he was. Until he'd succeeded in recalling his own name he'd felt as if he had left his body, which had frozen beyond his ability to revive it, unless the dead light had entirely erased it. At last he'd rediscovered the use of his muscles and had jerked the shaky puppet to its feet, and it had jittered slithering across the blanched field towards the false dawn of the town – the amber glow that, however artificial, had seemed less dead than the moonlight. As he'd run back to the room he'd set out from, the breaths in his ears had sounded like the world returning to life. When he'd fallen back into his chair nobody had bothered wondering where he'd been, and he'd found his insignificance unexpectedly reassuring. He must have been over the peak of the drug by then, since he'd been able to close his eyes and dream in great detail of countries he wanted to visit even though he never would. "It got rid," he said.

"Or you thought it had."

David shifted uneasily, and the quilt slipped off their shoulders as if somebody were tugging it away from them. "Why only thought?"

"Weren't you dreaming about him last night?"

"He's never in my dreams that I'm aware of." David was conscious of having far too much still to tell. "Do you want a coffee?" he found he would rather ask. "We ought to be moving if we're going for a drive before you've got to head for work."

"I'll come down with you. I'm guessing there's more to hear."

As he made for the stairs David was beset by a sense of how little his personality was apparent in the house. The spare room was playing host to all the superhero comics he had collected as a boy and was keeping as an investment, but otherwise the place didn't seem to have acquired much character in a lifetime hardly more than twice as long as his. The dark green fittings of the bathroom belonged to the previous owner, but the plastic switches and sockets on the walls looked like the opposite of history, while the plain pine banisters of the narrow staircase and the carpets with their blurred perfunctory pattern could be as old as the house. In the kitchen some of the dull metal surfaces marked by anonymous scouring came vaguely alive with his reflection and Stephanie's as she followed him. "Is there, then?" she said.

"I told you what happened at the writers' group," David said and turned away from her to load the percolator. "I shouldn't have let myself go at all. I felt as if they wanted to turn me into someone else."

"Nobody but you is all I want. Are you saying they made you write about your character?"

"I never have and I wouldn't want to. They got a title out of me, that's all. The first thing that came into my head."

"That doesn't seem very much to bother you in your sleep."

"It was like being at an alcoholics' meeting and having to stand up and speak." With an effort David said "Only that wasn't the end of it. Someone's used my title for a blog or some kind of fiction site."

"It must have been a better title than you thought, then. And if you were wrong about that—"

"I'm not saying anybody stole it. It's just a phrase people use. No, the thing is, what's odd…" He almost wished he were a writer after all if that would help him speak. "Whoever it is," he said and felt his breath falter, "he's calling himself Lucky."

"That's a coincidence, isn't it? I don't suppose it's very much of one, though, if you say the title's such a common phrase." Stephanie gazed into his eyes as if she was seeing someone far away and said "Why does it bother you, David?"

"I suppose I don't like the idea that anyone could have things like that inside them. He seems to want to kill half the people he meets."

"Don't we all have days like that sometimes?"

"I don't believe I ever have." He hoped she didn't take that as criticism.

"It's how he writes about them as well," he said, "as if he's eager to find the next victim. And he has too much fun imagining what he'd do to them."

"So who does he want to get rid of?"

"There was a shop assistant who carried on talking instead of serving a queue, and somebody whose car alarm disturbed him every night even though it was miles away, and a man who kept walking in front of him in a cinema while a film was on. That's all I looked at."

"They all sound like people we might like to strangle."

"Yes, but we wouldn't write about it, would we?" Talking about the material he'd seen had left David more uneasy than he understood. "We wouldn't write about doing worse to them," he said. "We wouldn't put ideas like that in people's heads."

A hiss at his back gave him an excuse to turn away. "Here's the coffee," he quite unnecessarily said, "and now I'll forget about all that if you don't mind."

They took their mugs upstairs and shared the bathroom before making a token breakfast of cereal. As they left the house Mrs Robbins emerged from its twin across the road with a bag of garbage in her hand. "Off to work, Mr Botham?" she called. "And the lady, of course."

"Not just yet. Going out for a drive."

"Well, you take care." Having shut her bin with a decisive slam, Mrs Robbins said "And the lady as well."

She retreated into her house as David unlocked the car. "I don't think I've ever felt less like a lady," Stephanie said with a rueful laugh.

"You're enough of one for me," David said and managed not to wince as he glanced at the scrape on the side of the car. Weeks ago he'd ground it against the gatepost, having instinctively waved back to a passing neighbour. "Thanks for the souvenir, Mr Dent," he muttered, but he oughtn't to blame Dent for his own carelessness. Still, he was glad not to see Dent hurrying to guide him out of the driveway, as the fellow insisted on doing whenever he had the chance. Now David thought about it, he hadn't seen the man for weeks.

CHAPTER ELEVEN

As David stepped onto the crossing at the fifth bleep of the green man he was almost deafened by the blare of a horn. He just had time to stumble backwards onto the pavement as a car hurtled at him. A woman cried out behind him, and the driver brandished the mobile phone he was using. "You nearly trod on my toe," the woman complained. "It's sore as it is."

"My fault," David mumbled, though he hardly thought it was.

When he ventured onto the crossing again a man at the front of the crowd that met him was ready with advice. "You want to watch out what you're doing, lad."

"I'm trying to give people a holiday," David said and reached for a flyer from the bundle in his hand, but the potential customer had gone. As the green man fell silent and flickered like a dying flame David made for the opposite pavement. He'd set foot on it when a cyclist sped onto the crossing, almost knocking the leaflets out of his hand. "Mind the fuck out," the rider counselled him on the way to veering through the crowd.

"Forgive me for walking on the pavement," David said, but nobody seemed amused or even sympathetic. At least he'd made people look at him, and he took the chance to hand each of them a Frugogo flyer. "Everyone's a customer," Andrea had told him, though in the words of the head office, when she'd sent him forth. He was heading along Church Street in the wake of the cyclist, though the road was meant to be reserved for pedestrians, and turning up his collar against the vicious March wind when a discarded Frugogo handbill followed by another fluttered past him.

Might people keep the leaflets if he said something as well? As a young couple emerged from a department store he held out a flyer. "Are you thinking of going away?"

"We're going, mate," the man said, and his partner called back to David "We've gone."

A pair of oldsters looked more promising. "Are you going away this year? Because—"

"She is and I hope she's coming back." In case it wasn't clear why his eyes had grown even moister the man said "The hospital."

"I'm sorry I, I'm sorry." As a phalanx of young women wheeling toddlers in buggies came towards him David said "Have you booked your holidays this year?"

"How many do you think we get?"

"Try having kids and see how much they cost."

"Do we look like we can afford one?"

He had to dodge out of their way as they bore down on him, all three resuming conversations on their phones despite the wails of their brood. He seemed to have run out of questions, and so he didn't speak when he peeled off a flyer to hand to a woman on her own. "If it's about God I've got one," she said.

"It's nothing to do with God. It's—"

"Then you should be ashamed," a grey-haired man said and shook a pocket Bible at him. "Sinners like you are what's wrong with the world."

"My God, all I'm trying to do is make people aware of our holiday offers. I don't think that's much of a sin."

"Taking His name in vain is one, my friend." The man ensured that the capital letter was audible by emitting it with a wheeze. "Try making them aware of Him," he said in the same way, "and you'll do some good."

"That's what I'm trying to do as it is."

"He is all the holiday we ought to need. He brings more peace than any holiday."

The woman had departed at speed, but a few amused bystanders were lingering. "You look like you need one yourself," a man called, and a woman told David "If he's thumping you with the book, give him one of your screeds. Fair swap."

As the evangelist left him a testamentary frown David handed the woman a flyer. The preacher set about haranguing the crowd from the middle of the street, and David was moving onwards when a Frugogo leaflet sailed past him and flapped up an arcade of shops. He couldn't see who had consigned the flyer to the wind, but as he left the arcade behind, a man darted out of it. "Hold on there," he shouted. "You with the papers, hold on."

He marched into David's path and stared up at him. His large eyebrow-heavy face looked like a bid to compensate for his shortness. "Is that yours?" he said and jerked his head to indicate the errant handbill.

"It was."

"It's still your responsibility."

"I didn't throw it away. I'd blame whoever did."

"They aren't here and you are. In any case you need to show me what you're carrying."

"Take one by all means," David said, holding out a leaflet. "We've got offers to suit everybody. Grab whatever takes your fancy before someone else does."

"Not your advertising." The man lowered his eyebrows as if he suspected David of facetiousness. "What we've given you," he said. "The council."

"I don't think you've given me anything in particular. I don't live on this side of the river."

The man's head jerked again, and David saw it was a tic rather than an indication. "Leafleting requires a permit," the man said. "Kindly show me yours."

"I don't have one with me. If you'd like to contact our Bold Street branch—"

"Then I'm afraid I must ask you to desist at once."

"Look, the firm sent me out to do this. I'm just trying to get on with my job. I don't think you can say I'm doing any harm to anyone."

"For a start you're causing litter, and in any event we can't have unauthorised promotions. Our streets would be overrun with nuisances to the public."

"I've come across a few of those recently." Just too late David realised that the man might think this was aimed at him, and so he pointed at the evangelist, who was informing everyone that their existence was a sin. "Have you told him he can say that sort of thing?"

"Some people still believe in sin."

It wasn't clear whether the official did. "Just let me hand these out, then," David said, "and I'll make sure we have a permit when I get back to the branch."

"That won't be possible. You've been given notice of the situation."

"Can't you forget about it for a little while?" When the fellow only stared at him David said "Can't you loosen up a bit this once?"

The man's head twitched as if David had struck him in the face. "If you attempt to distribute any more material I shall be forced to call someone."

"You say you're from the council." It occurred to David that he should already have said "How about showing me some proof?"

"I believe I've given you every chance," the man said and snatched out a phone. "You can take the consequences."

"All right, you've won. You don't need to call for backup," David said and saw another of his handbills flutter past him. "I'll even help you keep the street tidy," he declared and darted to retrieve the flyer.

As it reared up and slid out of reach, an action that seemed positively mocking, David heard a metallic screech, and an object jabbed the back of his right calf. "Can't you look where you're going?" a man shouted.

He was riding a mobility scooter, though he barely fitted into the seat. "Trying to cripple someone?" he demanded so vigorously that a wobble climbed his stack of chins and spread through his apoplectic face.

"Well," David said but wasn't quite able to leave it at that. "I think…"

"Let's hear it, mister. Share it around."

"I think if anybody's just been crippled it was me."

The council official made a sound that hardly needed him to add "We don't encourage that kind of language about people who are challenged."

"He used it first." David felt like a child telling tales, which roused him to protest "They're not supposed to drive that fast where there are pedestrians, are they?"

"We expect a little give and take, especially from people without difficulties." In case David wasn't sufficiently abashed by this the official said "Our mission is inclusiveness."

For a moment David felt as close to ranting as he had the first time he'd met Len Kinnear. "I'm going back to the branch to tell them," he said.

That sounded childish too. As he limped away his calf twinged at every step. People with clipboards were canvassing for signatures on petitions just a few yards away from charity collectors rattling plastic pots. A string quartet played Beatles numbers while not entirely out of earshot a guitarist performed quite a different tune, and midway between them an exhaustively gilded man with a carton at his gilded feet waited for someone to pay him to move. A girl held a giant flattened lollipop aloft – a placard for a restaurant, not Mick's. Vendors of political newspapers eyed the opposition as if they were tempted to picket or worse. Someone was selling the *Big Issue*, and somebody was selling the *Big Issue*, and someone else was too. Did all of them have individual permits? When David began to doubt this it was easier to feel provoked to hand out the Frugogo flyers, once he'd glanced back to make sure the council official couldn't see him. "Have a holiday," he said and wished he'd thought of it sooner.

He still had a handful of leaflets by the time he came abreast of the agency. He followed a customer in, though not until the man had shut the door in his face. The fellow marched up to the currency desk and leaned towards Andrea. "Hand over all your cash," he said, barely audible above the conversations at the counter. "Put it in an envelope and don't let anybody see."

David saw Andrea's mouth begin to work. As he took a limping step towards the man who was the wrong kind of customer, dumping the flyers on the counter to free his hands for whatever they might have to do, her lips squeezed out a lopsided smile. "Rex, honestly," she murmured.

"Less of that, young lady. Do as you're told or you know what to expect when we get home."

"Rex, please. Not here." She glanced at David and then fixed him with a stare that seemed intent on persuading if not warning him he hadn't heard. "What's the matter with those, David?" she said louder.

Rex swung around and stuck out his hand. He was stocky – David supposed Andrea might think of him as cuddly, perhaps generously proportioned – with skin pale enough to sell holidays in the sun. Wiry red hair sprawled above his wide rounded plushy face. His moist handshake felt padded but determined to be firm. "David," he said. "The David?"

"One of them."

"Why, how many of you have there been?" Without bothering to look amused Rex said "What don't I know?"

"I couldn't say. It sounds as if you know about me."

"Someone didn't leave you many secrets." Rex seemed bent on impressing or else daunting David with his grip. "Rex," he said by way of introduction. "Only one of me."

"I should think that's enough."

"Had enough, have you?" Rex said and let go of David's hand. "I can see why you might have."

"Maybe you're seeing less than you think."

Andrea cleared her throat, a noise as shrill as the clink of a coin in the metal tray under the currency window. "David, I asked you a question."

"I was getting on so well with Rex I didn't hear."

"That isn't like you, and there's no call for it." When lowering her voice failed to bring him closer to the window she said more sharply "Just come here."

"Maybe it's more like me than you ever realised. Maybe I've got secrets after all."

David wasn't sure he wanted this to be heard, especially by the customers at the counter, but Rex caught it. "Better do what madam says," he told David. "You don't want her telling you off or however she deals with you."

David wasn't sure if this was meant to mock him. Perhaps Rex assumed they had more in common than was the case, a notion David found equally unappealing. He limped to the currency window and ducked towards the gap beneath it while Rex loitered almost close enough to touch. "What were you asking?"

"Don't pretend, David." Andrea's voice sounded like a threat to allow everyone to overhear. "Why have you brought so many flyers back?"

"Apparently we need permission to give them out, and we're not supposed to otherwise."

"You were only doing what she told you, weren't you, David?"

Rex's version of sympathy made David round on him. "And what do you do, since we're talking?"

"I'm in advertising. I'm in ideas."

"Then I hope you've given Andrea a few, or hasn't she told you she's looking for some?"

"Rex," Andrea said, and a good deal less softly "We've discussed bringing personal matters into the workplace, David."

"I thought I was talking about work."

"No call for cleverness. You aren't being a writer now."

This enraged David more than he could have explained. "Would you like me to go back out?"

"I wouldn't, no. We can't afford to get the firm in trouble. I'll look into the position with the street, but meanwhile you'd better stay here." He felt like a child rebuked in public by a mother, not that his own had ever had much reason. As David lifted the flap in the counter Rex said "So Andy says you're a writer."

"Why did you want to tell him that?" Too late David grasped that Rex had her comment about cleverness in mind. "I've never been one," he assured Rex, "and I never will be."

"Stay randy, Andy," Rex said and winked at David on his way to the door.

David looked away from him and managed not to glance at Andrea as he logged on the terminal. Alerts were waiting to be dealt with – seats to be booked on planes, special requests to be cleared with travel operators, complaints to be followed up – and he began to type, so rapidly that it outran some of his thoughts. This was as close as he would ever come to being a writer, he vowed to himself. He would be happy to forget everything that had happened since he'd gone out to distribute the flyers. Certainly none of it could make him write.

CHAPTER TWELVE

"Pests."

The woman stares at the flyer I'm holding out and then at me. "There's a few of those round here right enough."

Does she think she's on my level and entitled to agree, or is she suggesting I'm one of the vermin infesting the streets? They're inviting you to sign up for the Feet For Jesus marathon or collecting for Stand Up For Insects. There's World Without Weapons with a web address that looks like a joke its supporters didn't realise they'd made, and there are memorial funds for people I'm certain you'd want to forget if you'd known them. "Please do treat yourself to a notice," I say into the woman's smug wrinkled face. "You never know when I'll be needed."

She pinches the sheet between a finger and an even stumpier thumb. "What use is this to anyone? Where's a number to call?"

PESTS EXTERMINATED   GET LUCKY. "Don't you worry," I tell her.

"I go anywhere I'm called for."

She does her stupid best to look as if she's understood at the same time as finding me unhelpful. "Are you in the book?"

"We're past those. I'm your future. Look for me online."

"You aren't making it too easy for anyone, are you?"

"I'm giving them what they deserve."

She can't be expected to grasp this, and so she tries asking "Just what do you do?"

"You'd have to see it for yourself."

She peers into my eyes and seems about to ask another question. Perhaps she sees something, or possibly not as much as she supposed she would, because she thrusts the flyer at me. "I don't want it, thank you. No use to me."

"Too late. It's yours now. You'll have to wait and see how it applies."

I let her glimpse the depths of my eyes again before I leave her in the crowd. The flyer flutters in her hand, and I'm amused to see the shiver infect all of her. Maybe she needn't fear me; it depends if I have time. She's less of a candidate than the motorist who nearly ran me down on the pedestrian crossing or the cyclist who had a crack at it on the pavement. Still, maybe I've still to meet today's winner, and so I carry on handing out my literature. "Pests squashed," I call and feel as if an evangelist who's ranting in the middle of the street is trying to blot me out. "Parasites rubbed out. No job too small, no job too big. You know which you are, madam."

I can see I'm not appreciated. They never do that till it's too late. Quite a few of my flyers are ending up on the street; it's a pity Mrs Rubbish isn't here to chase them. One sails into an arcade between a pair of department stores, and I'm looking for the next taker when a man trots after me. "Hold on there," he shouts. "You with the papers, hold on."

He looks crushed by his outsize head and overhanging eyebrows. "Are you all right down there?" I enquire. "Need a lift up?"

His head jerks as if it's trying to deflect the questions, though he wants me to think they're beneath him, which would mean they're pretty low. "May I ask what you think you're doing?"

"May you?" After a pause for him to open his mouth and twitch his head again I say "I don't see any reason why you shouldn't. Go on then, give it a shot."

"Just what do you think you're doing?"

"Right now I'm letting people know I'm here."

"Who are you supposed to represent?"

"You don't see anyone but me, do you?" I say and flap a flyer in his face. "I'm all you get and that's enough for everyone."

"So you're the man I need to talk to, are you?"

He's trying to sound big, but his lurching head doesn't help his image. "You'd be better off hoping you don't," I tell him. "Who are you meant to be?"

"I represent the council," he says in a voice too large for him. "That's a big job. Sure you can fit it in?"

His head jerks as if I've struck it like a punchball. "I'm here to determine if you're authorised."

"Somebody wants what I do, believe me."

"I'm asking if you have a permit to distribute advertising." Mr Twitch narrows his eyes as if his bristling brows have put on weight. "If you can't show it to me—"

"Don't trouble your head. It looks as if it's got enough trouble as it is. I'm authorised all right."

"By whom?"

"Do you know, I think you've met him."

Twitch the midget scowls up at me and then at my hands. "I'm still waiting to be shown."

"Wait away if it'll keep you quiet. You want to see someone about those fidgets, though. Shall I have a go at fixing them?"

His head jerks so hard it seems to shake his mouth awry, but I expect he's grimacing at his inability not to twitch. "I'm warning you, Mr, Mr—"

"There'd have to be a pair of me to make me Mr Mister. I tell you what, take one of these and see how much you can find out. See, it's coming for you," I say and stoop to retrieve the flyer that has drifted out of the arcade.

"Can't you look where you're going?" a man shouts, and I get out of just enough of his way as I swing around to confront him.

He brakes the mobility scooter again, though I'm sure he's more concerned about it than about me. He has stuffed as much of himself into the seat as he can, and he looks like a petulant toddler who'd have a tantrum if anyone tried to deny him his old high chair. His round face resembles perished rubber pumped red by a tube made out of several chins. "I'm exactly where I'm meant to be," I tell him.

He shakes his head as if he's trying to outdo Twitch, and all the chins compete with his face at wobbling. "Trying to cripple someone?" he blusters loud enough to be appealing for an audience. "Trying to get yourself killed?"

"That's the very last thing I have in mind. You wouldn't say it if you knew me better."

"Trying to cripple me, then."

"I'd say somebody's already done a sterling job."

Twitch sees the chance to remind me of his. "We don't encourage that kind of language about people who are challenged, Mr…"

That doesn't fit my remark too closely, but perhaps he has to stick to his script. "The name's on the page," I remind him.

This time he takes the bill I hold out as the one on the pavement swoops at the evangelist. "Mr Lucky, is it?" Twitch says. "I wouldn't count on too much luck with me."

"I've lived up to my name all my life, and I don't count on anybody but myself," I say and stare at Mr Sitdown. "You just need a self worth counting on."

"I'm sure this gentleman has," Twitch wants to be heard saying. "Especially when he hasn't had so much luck."

"Can't he stand up for himself? I thought they all wanted to be equal. Don't tell me, only equal in a different way. I'm not like the rest either. I make my own life."

"I'll thank you not to talk about me as if I'm not here," Sitdown complains. "Hear that, he doesn't want you talking about him. Mind you, I don't know if he's up to standing up. How about it, Mr Sitdown? What do you think of your luck?"

"I warn you, Mr Lucky." Twitch makes my name sound like a distasteful task he's required to perform. "If you continue to behave like this," he says, "I shall be forced to call someone."

"Bring on all the security you like. I've never had a problem with them. What's the charge? Chaffing the chairbound, is it, or crushing the cripple? Or do we have to say disabling the disabled now?"

"You're in authority round here, are you?" Sitdown has turned on Twitch. "Are you going to let him talk about the disadvantaged like that?"

"If it's such a disadvantage maybe you shouldn't drive like you want to cripple everybody else. Or is that your way of making everybody equal?"

"That's quite enough, Mr—" Twitch can't bring himself to say my name again. "More than enough," he says and fishes out a phone that makes his little hand look childish.

"Are you calling the police to give Speedy here a ticket?"

"We expect a little give and take, especially from people without difficulties. Our mission is inclusiveness."

"I'll be including somebody and that's a promise. All right, put away your walkie-talkie. No need for talkies, little fellow. Let's all be off for walkies."

Sitdown waits for me to start, as if he has some kind of official standing though he has no standing I can see, and then he speeds away with a mechanical whine that sums him up. As soon as Twitch stumps back into the arcade I return to offering my services with a smile, smiling because nobody knows how they'd earn them. I've handed out just a few flyers when a man reaches for one if not the entire handful. No, he's trying to gesture them back where they came from. "Pardon me," he says, though not as if he wants it. "Weren't you told you couldn't do that?"

He's holding up his Bible like a certificate of authority or else a weapon he wants me to fear. His face isn't much less grey than his hair, and the mass of wrinkles makes it look as if he keeps it in a string bag, which has tugged his thin pale lips so straight that they're incapable of taking any other shape. "I can't pardon you," I tell him. "I'm not what you'd call an angel."

"I asked for no pardon. I—"

"That's a bit of a fib, isn't it? I heard you ask and I don't forget, ever. Maybe it isn't a mortal sin, but you'd better remember you're mortal."

"I know all about sin, and I—"

"You've tried the lot, have you? Sure you've missed none? If you can really tick them all you ought to get yourself into the record books."

He isn't used to being interrupted. When he was haranguing everybody in the street he didn't relent for a second, however many wags and unbelievers tried to heckle him. Now his face seems to grow greyer still each time I cut off his babbling breath. "I'm talking about you," he insists. "You and your indifference to authority. You were told—"

"No need to remind me. I heard Mr Twitch. Go on, take a breath before you choke. I don't need any myself."

His face wriggles with disgust before resuming its default expression. "Every one of our breaths comes from God."

"In my case you'd be surprised. Anyway, let's finish with breathing. I've helped a few people do that in my time." Before he can react to this I say "Father Greygrump, should I call you? Am I getting a personal sermon, Padre Grizzlepiss?"

"God's word is for everyone." No doubt he thinks insults are part of the job or even one of the ways God tests him. "He gives us life," he says with a wheeze to render the pronoun respectful, "and instructs us how to live to please Him."

"I've got someone else to please," I say and flap a handbill at him. "The only one."

"That's you, is it? What you call luck can only come from God."

"He's cornered all the markets, has he? You'll be telling me next he sees everything we do."

"That is the simple truth, my son."

"I'm nobody's son." As I see Pastor Fogface think he's found a way to reach me with his preaching I say "He's better than a security camera, is he? Better than computers. What else do you fancy he can do?"

"He is the source of all creation. Accept that in your soul and—"

"He's not the source of me, and he didn't give that liability on the scooter much luck. Aren't you lot meant to help people? Maybe you should have told him to rise from his chair and walk."

"It is not given to us to perform miracles or interfere with God's work."

"You won't be any good at bringing back the dead, then. Getting rid of demons, is that you?" I see he's wearying of the argument – maybe he's imagining that it's the usual kind of confrontation he has to deal with – but I won't have him walking away when he's taken up so much of my time. "Let's go somewhere there aren't so many people," I say, "and we'll have the style of discussion I like."

"God will still be with us," he says and is matching my steps when I hear a familiar sound – a mechanical whinge. It's the sound of an electric motor. Mr Sitdown is back.

If I've any fault it's that I'm too readily distracted, too eager to light on the most deserving candidate for my attentions. Saint Godlybore or

Mr Sitdown? Whichever I don't choose I'll be able to track down later, if someone else hasn't caught my fancy by then. Sitdown scowls at me and scoots off through the crowd as if he can leave me behind, which is all the provocation I need. "On second thoughts I've had my dose of you, Godgob," I tell the evangelist. "Go and tell tales to your fidgety friend."

I have to hand out several bills before he takes enough offence to stalk into the arcade in search of Twitch. Meanwhile Sitdown has sped to the next side street and disappeared around the corner, but I'm there in time to watch him turn left into a narrower alley at the end. Beyond the alley is a street with traffic, and he whines across the pedestrian crossing as fast as any of the cars he stopped were travelling. On the far side of the road he has to drive uphill, which doesn't slow him down, since the street is deserted. At least, he thinks it is. Even if he had mirrors on his scooter I don't know whether he would notice me behind him.

I wonder where he thinks he's bound, but there's no point in waiting to find out. As a bend in the street cuts off the sound of traffic I move within arm's length of his ridged blubbery neck. I watch it quiver as he speeds past the back doors of restaurants and shops and the fronts of clubs that won't be open until after dark. I'm amused to think he may be driving fast and shivering because he's nervous, but it's time to give him more of a reason. "You can stop now," I say if not breathe in his ear. "Race over. You're at the finish." The scooter lurches as soon as I lean across his shoulder. One wheel stumbles off the pavement and lodges between the slimy bars of a kerbside drain. Sitdown's forehead glistens like the drain as he struggles around on the seat, which involves such an effort that I wonder if his panic has puffed him up, clamping him between the arms. "God almighty, it's you again," he gasps. "What are you up to? Soft in the head or what?"

"You recognised me, then. Just the almighty will do."

"What do you want?" His eyes are jittering in their sockets, but there's nobody else for them to see. "Look what you've made me do," he whines.

"Aren't you capable of doing anything by yourself? Not much use at all, then. Not even worth your weight in everybody else's tax."

I'm enjoying the sight of his contorted swollen neck, but now I move in front of him to let him look all the way into my eyes. He's barely glanced into them when he does his best to avoid them while he tries to shift the scooter. The wheels judder and the motor screeches, but that's the end of the response. "Careful," I advise him. "You don't want to be even more of a wreck, do you? Think of all the people you've still got to try to run down."

His blotchy brows squeeze out a few more drops, but I don't think that's panic – more likely the effort of making himself say "I didn't hurt you, did I? I'm sorry if I did."

"Just me."

"You or anyone," he says, but he's had enough of pretending to be penitent; Father Godsdrone wouldn't think much of him. "We've got rights too, you know."

"Which rights are those, now?"

"The right to use the street just like anybody else for a start."

"But that isn't how you use it, is it? More like a racetrack. As I said, you've crossed the line."

"I'll tell you what right we've got. The right to be alive."

"Just like me, were you about to say? You'd be in for a shock."

He doesn't quite meet my eyes. Maybe he's trying not to grasp my words as well. "Will you stand out of my way, please," he says as if he fancies he can leave me no choice. "I want to get going."

"Don't worry, soon you'll be gone. There, I've stood. I'll bet you're wishing you were able to."

I've moved back a step, and he struggles to send the scooter forward. The motor screams in protest, and shredded scraps of sodden newspaper fly away from the drain as the grid rattles in its socket, but the scooter doesn't budge. His brows bulge and stream with sweat as he throws all his weight against the right arm of the chair, away from the trapped wheel, and the motor shrieks on his behalf. At last its frustration whimpers into silence while his eyes and his forehead compete at glistening. "What a pain," I say as if I've found some sympathy within me. "Can't trust gadgets. Always best to rely on yourself."

He's glancing about desperately, but there's no help in sight. "It's a pity your friend Twitch isn't here to take charge," I say. "He'd bring some big men to sort you out. That's what walkie-talkies are for. Not many walkies for you, are there? Too many talkies, though."

I've amused myself enough. I'm furious to think I may sound childish, not that his opinion of me or anybody else's matters. "Would you like me to help you on your way?"

"You better had. You got me into this position."

Maybe he's so determined not to feel dependent that he greets any offers of help this way. "Stay there," I say and take my grin behind him. "Wait till I get a grip."

I enjoy a few moments of staring at the thick mottled stump of his neck. I can imagine how fingers would sink into it, like squeezing rotten rubber. His large suffused ears look firmer, and I seize them with both hands and drag them away from his head. "Come on, make an effort," I yell in the right one. "Don't leave it all to me."

The shock convulses his body and rocks the scooter so hard that the wheel springs out of the grid. As he clutches the arms of the chair he starts the motor, intentionally or otherwise, and the scooter surges forward. "Give me a ride," I shout and perch behind him on a ledge above the axle. "That's the least you can do when I'm getting you on the road."

I don't know how much he hears, because I've dug a fingernail into the hole in each ear. The depths feel clogged, as if his body has exuded samples of its blubber. The poking of my nails seems to madden him, driving him to put on speed in the wild hope of somehow leaving me behind. "Look what he's doing to me," he wails at the top of his voice. "Look, somebody. Stop him."

I could think of putting together a collection of exit lines, except are any of them worth preserving? I don't know whether I'm delighted or disgusted to find how easily manipulated Sitdown is. By thrusting my fingernail into his left ear I make him steer right in a frenzied bid to dodge the sensation. This sends him along a deserted alley towards a street with a promising amount of traffic. "I told you I'd get you on the road," I say. "They look like your speed."

I don't suppose he hears me. I'm digging my nails so deep that I imagine I'm scraping his eardrums. "Look," he shrieks higher than the motor did, and I feel as if I've poked his brain clear of almost all the words he ever knew. "Somebody look."

Nobody does until the driver of a speeding van notices him, by which point it's too late. I've given the depths of the holes a vigorous parting poke that sends Sitdown helplessly into the traffic. I hopped off the chair as it left the alley, where I linger to watch the van mow Sitdown down. A large metallic thump is combined with a softer thud, after which the van drags its prize quite a few abrasive yards before the brakes bring it to a hysterically high-pitched halt. I'm diverted to see how many ways metal and cloth and meat can be torn apart and rearranged together. As spectators start to get in the way I leave them to their observations. My interest has already dwindled – it always does – but I have Sitdown's final word to take with me: his last outraged howl of "Look."

CHAPTER THIRTEEN

"Go on." The thin stooped man wasn't so much holding the door open for his wife as jerking it to urge her past it. "Go in," he said as well.

Both of them were greying – well on their way to elderly if not beyond. She was taller than her husband or perhaps not just so bent. The skin that dangled from her throat seemed to pull her face down, even the edges under her eyes, except for her vague but determined smile. Her husband watched with resignation no less pained than affectionate as she collected a copy of each holiday brochure from the racks and brought them to the counter. "What can I do for you today?" David said.

"Come and sit down with me, Pat." Her husband had been loitering near the door, but now he trudged to join her. "We'd like to go somewhere," she said.

"Anywhere special?" her husband might have been asking on David's behalf.

"They've all been that mostly, haven't they? Now you mention it I wouldn't mind going back to one."

"Are you planning on letting us know which?"

"Don't be like that. He knows what I mean," she assured David and possibly herself as well. "What about the one we really liked, Pat? Where they put, you know, on the bed."

"Sheets."

"Not them, don't be silly. Well, them as well. But you know, the place where they sort of, when they changed the bed they made it like you said, special."

"How'd they do that?"

"Flowers." With a surge of triumph that made her clutch at his arm on the counter she said "They put flowers on the bed."

"There's a few places did."

"Yes, but this was our favourite, wasn't it?" When he didn't own up to agreeing she said "Where they had, you remember, that thing on the water we liked."

"A boat."

"Not a boat. You're just being a pig now, Pat. A you know, sort of flashing. We saw it when we came back at night."

"A buoy."

"Not a boy and not a girl either. Are you trying to show me up? This young man won't think much of you for it."

"He just wants to do his job if you'll let him, Daff."

"I don't see how I'm stopping him. I'm not stopping you, am I?" Having given his badge a rheumy squint, she seemed to feel victorious for adding "David."

"I'm here for you. For anyone who needs advice." As Pat sent him a look that could have been some form of plea David said "Were you thinking of a lighthouse?"

"That's exactly what. See, he knew it all the time."

David couldn't tell whether this meant him besides her husband, who said "We've seen a few of them."

"Well, this was our best place."

"There's been a few of them as well."

"It was sort of, you know, an island."

David was ashamed to think the words her husband said. "Only sort of?"

"I'm telling you it was an island. And I'll tell you what else it was, don't tell me." As it became plain that her husband was unlikely to, she said "It was, you know, you do know. That place in Greece."

"A Greek island," David said and tried not to betray any relief. "Can you say which one?"

"Have we been looking like we can?" Almost as aggressively her husband said "Maybe we can take your books home and carry on there."

"You're welcome to take them. But honestly, I'm here to help in any way I can."

"Maybe it's not your kind of help we need. Just get the Greek ones, Daff. Leave the others," Pat said, jerking the door back and forth to hasten her out of the shop.

David felt as if his thoughts were following them downhill. As he returned the abandoned brochures to the racks he could imagine Pat and Daff were continuing the routine — inarticulacy aggravated by incomprehension — that appeared to have overtaken their relationship. Could the husband really understand as little as he had? David didn't like to think he'd been pretending, let alone enjoying the pretence. As he went back to the counter Andrea caught his attention with a peremptory cough. "I need a word, David."

"Any in particular?"

"I've told you before about being clever." She stood up as an indication that he should follow her. "Could you not let the little one damage those, please," she said to a couple whose toddler had snatched a brochure from the lowest rack, and not much less sharply "If I'm needed out here, someone let me know."

David had barely shut the staffroom door when she said "I want to hear what you say happened when you were leafleting."

"Someone who said he was from the council told me I needed a permit."

"You don't remember his name, or didn't you get it from him?"

"I don't know why I would have wanted it at all."

"You didn't think to ask for any form of identification."

"As a matter of fact I did, but he wasn't showing any to the likes of me."

"You ought to have insisted. You need to be a bit more forceful."

"Yes, I've seen that's how you like your men." Of course he didn't say that; he didn't even think it sounded like him. "You mean," he said, "he mightn't have been from the council after all."

"I'm afraid he was, and he tells rather a different tale."

"You've heard from him, have you?" When Andrea only gave

a displeased cough David said "Any success with the name?"

"It's Mr Norville."

"Nervous Norville, is it? I bet they called him that at school." While David managed not to say this either, it felt too close to thinking like a vindictive child. "I thought if I needed a permit," he said, "you'd have given me one."

"You're saying I'm to blame." Before David could deny it Andrea said "Was there anything else to the incident?"

"Don't try so hard to sound like a manager. I won't be forgetting how else I've heard you sound." Thinking this made David feel as if he was committing rape inside his head, not least because she couldn't know he was remembering her moans in his ear. "He tried to make out I was dropping litter," he said hastily, "if that's what you mean."

"And were you?"

"I wouldn't call our advertising litter, would you?"

"That sort of comment isn't going to do you any good, David."

"I'm starting to wonder what will."

"Certainly not that kind of remark either. Did you drop any of our leaflets?"

"Some people did. I'm afraid that's what they thought of our offers."

"Unless it was the way you sold them."

"Or how they looked."

"If you had a problem with the format, David, perhaps you should have raised it before you took them to the public."

"I didn't say I had one. I'm saying maybe some of our customers did. And as for littering," David protested, "I was nearly run over trying to pick one up that someone dropped."

"Run over." Without relinquishing her incredulity Andrea said "Where were you handing them out?"

"Nowhere I shouldn't have been, believe me, but somebody was scooting around as if he owned the pavement."

"You're referring to the disabled gentleman, I take it."

"You've heard all about him as well, have you?" In too much of a rage to be careful what he said David demanded "What else does your Mr Norville say I did?"

"I understand you got into an argument, and he says you used discriminatory language."

"I didn't say anything the fellow on the scooter didn't. How many more words are we supposed to keep to ourselves? There are words I don't like hearing in the street myself, but I'll bet nobody's going to listen to me." David felt near to indulging in the kind of rant that had led Kinnear to imagine he could be a writer – the kind he'd vowed never again to let loose. "Seriously," he said, "what business is it of his?"

"It's our business. That's what you were out there representing."

"Not after he'd told me I couldn't. He's trying to have it both ways if you ask me."

"You aren't being honest with me, David. I'll give you one last chance."

"To do what?" Her attitude seemed so intolerably parental that he had no idea how childish his response might be. "I don't know what you're on about," he said.

"You want me to think you did as you were told."

"Wasn't I a good boy? Has somebody been telling tales?" The retort only left him feeling more ridiculous. "Look, we can both behave better than we are," he risked saying. "If you aren't happy with the job I did, just tell me what your problem is."

He had to watch her face withdraw all recognition of the past they shared before she said "The fact that you carried on doing it when you'd been told you couldn't."

"By someone who wouldn't show me his authority," David protested, and then anger overtook him. "He was spying on me, was he? Hid in the crowd and followed me, or was it someone else? The chap on the scooter or the man with the good book?"

"I don't know what you mean by that, David, and perhaps I better hadn't know. You were caught on the security cameras."

"So that's what they're for, is it? Making sure nobody's offered any holidays. Nothing worse is happening out there." Although it made him feel absurd he couldn't help complaining "Maybe they should keep an eye on how people ride around the streets. Before the scooter got me a car on a crossing nearly did, and then a cyclist on the pavement had a go. Third time lucky, you might say, except I wasn't."

"Are you saying you were injured? You should have taken it up with Mr Norville at the time. I'm surprised he didn't see."

"He did."

"What exactly do you mean? That he isn't to be trusted?"

"Someone isn't. You decide." Close to accusingly David said "Did you think he was?"

"I haven't met him. He reported the whole incident to our head office."

"Too scared to come in here and speak up for himself, was he?" David didn't need her look to tell him he sounded pathetic; there was nothing in him to frighten anyone like Norville or indeed anybody else. "So what are you going to tell them?" he said.

"Is there anything else you'd like to say in your defence?"

"I was just trying to help the business."

"I can pass that on." She seemed about to continue when someone knocked at the staffroom door. "Yes, come in," she called. "We've finished."

"Sorry if I interrupted," Helen said. "It's the couple with the little one."

"What's he being allowed to do now?"

"It isn't that. He'll be too old to go free when they travel but they're saying he should because he's young enough now."

"For heaven's sake, can't anybody deal with people any more?" Andrea stalked out to the counter and planted her hands on her hips. "Well," she rather more than asked, "where have they gone?"

"I told them Helen was right and they took their ball home," Bill said, losing the larger part of his grin as Andrea stared at him. "Went looking for their free flight, anyway. It's not like anyone will give it to them."

"Maybe they'll come back," Emily said, "when they find we're as good as anyone."

"We need to be better." Andrea watched Helen and David return to the counter as if she was causing if not urging this to happen. "I'm leaving you in charge, Helen," she said. "I want to see how our competitors are promoting themselves."

Nobody spoke until she'd left the shop, letting in a strain from an accordion down the hill. "What was wrong, David?" Emily said. "Or don't you want to say?"

"Apparently I've been reported for handing out our leaflets when we should have got permission first."

Her face turned pink on his behalf while Bill and Helen made their indignation audible. "You were only doing what you thought was right," Emily said. "When you think what some people do…"

David felt he was being invited to ask "Anyone we know?"

"Whoever's been using that title of yours for a start."

"I did say it wasn't my title." He would very much rather not have been reminded of the blog, and felt compelled to add "Anyway, they're only words."

"It's worse than that. I wouldn't like to meet whoever's responsible." Despite his reluctance David couldn't avoid saying "Worse how?"

"Words can hurt too, can't they?" For a moment he was able to believe this was all Emily meant, and then she said "They've been writing about someone who was in the news. If they can say that kind of thing I wouldn't want to think what they'd be like if you ever met them."

CHAPTER FOURTEEN

He'd met far too many people like that, David tried to reassure himself. Behaviour like that was all too common on the train – people who brought food and its smell into the carriage, and ate with their mouth open to share the sight and sounds with their fellow passengers, not to mention planting their feet on the seats and leaving behind the detritus of however many courses of their meal – but how many of them also took their shoes off and complained about the fit? How many talked to nobody in particular throughout the journey and let sentence after sentence trail off, dangling a lonely word? There was no point in trying to deny the truth. Whoever was responsible for *Better Out Than In* had in mind a man David remembered from the train just weeks ago.

His name was Donald Sugden, and he'd died in the lift at Lime Street. Now David realised why the face in the newspaper was familiar, though when he'd read the item at Stephanie's restaurant he hadn't managed to grasp that it was. Sugden was in David's local paper too, in the obituary section. *Beloved Husband, My Life's Companion... Much Missed Dad... Unfailingly Helpful Brother-in-law...* David was grateful to be distracted by the rumble of a bin across the road, where Mrs Robbins was trundling hers to the kerb to await tomorrow's collection, but when he lowered his eyes he found two images of Sugden – a recent photograph and a younger version – gazing up at him. Why should he feel guilty because someone had disliked the man enough to celebrate his death? Vicious comments were often posted online after people died, not infrequently by total strangers lent courage by disguise or anonymity. He would be dismayed to think that Sugden's family might read the blog, but surely nothing would attract their attention. He had to admit that he was more relieved that nobody would associate the blog with him. Apart from Stephanie, nobody knew about Lucky, and she seemed happy to believe the blog was a coincidence.

Couldn't it be one? Weren't all the entries about common forms of misbehaviour – shop assistants ignoring customers, car owners who couldn't be bothered to quell their alarms, cinemagoers who blundered in front of you when you were watching a film? That entry seemed to have even less to do with David, since he didn't care for horror films, especially not the kind the blog described, if the film even existed. Surely all he need do in order to reassure himself was read the rest of the blog. He was behaving too much like Andrea's image of him – timid, ineffectual, useless. In a rage he brought up the site on his laptop and chose the latest listing on the sidebar. "Pests," it said.

He couldn't help agreeing for a few paragraphs, until he saw that Mr Lucky wasn't just distributing pamphlets in the street but being warned off by an official with a jerky head. While the blog didn't give the man's name, David knew it all too well. He had to force his hands to relax, because they were gripping the sides of the laptop so fiercely that he heard the plastic creak. Long before he'd finished reading the entry he kept feeling he'd forgotten how to breathe. "What are you doing?" he said wildly, he wasn't sure to whom.

"Look." That was the last word, and he stared at it as though it had paralysed him. The room around him seemed to have grown less substantial than a photograph – the shelves of favourite books from his childhood and later, not to mention discs of old films he liked; the armchairs he'd saved when his parents were replacing their furniture, which just now felt too much like a bid to conjure up companionship; the big thin television screen as blank as his mind wanted to be. He was hardly aware of fingering the keyboard, but it brought him back to the home page of the site, where the unrepentant title along with the column of first words and phrases seemed to invite him to venture deeper into the blackness against which they hung. Perhaps it was a desperate attempt to postpone thinking that made him click on another phrase. Who's next? the words might have been daring him to discover. Mr Accident was, and soon David had to give up pretending not to know his real name. Mrs Robbins was in the blog as well, and Slocombe's general store up the road. David felt he was being hollowed out by everything he read. When Dent's gutter gave way and the man fell two storeys onto the concrete, David's hands clutched at the air as if he could catch the victim. He raised his eyes with no idea of where he was looking except anywhere but at the screen, and saw Mrs Robbins bearing yet another bag of rubbish to her bin.

For a moment he felt too guilty to think, and then he lurched to his feet and dashed out of the house. How could he look normal, as if he had some pretext for being in the street? His bin had to be one, and he grabbed the chilly plastic handle to trundle the bin to the kerb. "It's that time again, Mrs Robbins," he called, the only words he could think of.

"It keeps someone in a job."

"True enough, there's nothing wrong with that," David said, and also babbled "We're lucky to have one, those of us that have." He saw Mrs Robbins turning away, and was so thrown by having inadvertently used the blogger's name that he seemed to lose control of his voice. "Have you heard anything about Mr Dent round the corner?"

"Good lord above, what a noise. You'll be waking up the night shift." She gave her rebuke time to take effect before she demanded "What are you saying I should have heard?"

"Nothing at all," David was able to hope, "if there's nothing to hear." If she looked suspicious, surely that couldn't be focused on him.

"Then why are you asking after him?"

"I just thought I hadn't seen him lately. Nothing wrong with that, is there?" David immediately regretted adding.

"I didn't know he was a friend of yours."

"I wouldn't say a friend." This seemed unwise as well. "He's like you," David said. "A neighbour."

"It's a pity a few more of us don't care about them."

"I expect so." David was close to agreeing with whatever she said if that would move the conversation forward. "Anyway," he insisted, "as I say, I haven't seen him since I'm not sure when."

"You won't, either."

"Why?" Even if he had to be imagining any accusation, the word felt like an obstruction in his throat. When Mrs Robbins didn't answer at once he said "What…"

"He was cleaning out his gutters. He should have paid someone who knows what they're doing. We always do."

"I'm sure that's best," David said, which only postponed asking "What happened?"

"He fell."

"I'm sorry." He mustn't sound as if he was apologising, and he tried not to seem concerned in any questionable way as he said "Did anyone see?"

"See what, Mr Botham?"

"I don't know, do I? I wasn't there." Before she could question his vehemence David said "Did they see how he came to fall?"

"Nobody saw that I've been told." With a longer look at David than he cared for Mrs Robbins said "Someone heard."

"What?" He would have preferred not to be made to add "What did they hear?"

"They heard him shout and they heard him fall."

"I don't suppose…" David wished he hadn't said that, because now he had to say "You wouldn't know what he said."

"I didn't ask. How many other gory details would you like?"

"I don't like them at all. I'm just, I'm just concerned I didn't hear."

He had no idea if this made sense. Perhaps she could assume he meant he hadn't been informed about the accident. "Is it flowers," he blurted, "or a charity?"

"Is what? I don't understand you, Mr Botham."

"For the funeral, or have they had it already?"

"I hope nobody's that eager." Her stare might have been convicting David of the offence as she declared "He isn't dead."

"He isn't." In his confusion David almost said too much. "What is he, then?"

"He's in intensive care."

David hardly knew why he was asking "Do you know where?"

"I wasn't told. I expect I can find out if you really want to know."

David wasn't sure if he would like to learn why she was staring so hard at him. "Don't go to any trouble, but if you should hear…"

"I'll come over with the information." She let her gaze linger on him before she said "I don't mind saying you've gone up in my estimation, Mr Botham. I wouldn't have taken you to care so much about your neighbour when he isn't even close."

David felt he was being praised as somebody he wasn't, and retreated into his house. How relieved could he let himself feel over the news about Dent? As soon as he started to ponder it the relief gave way to bewilderment that could easily yield to panic. There was far too much he didn't understand or want to understand. The computer screen had turned blank to save energy, but he could imagine it was saving up worse revelations for him, hiding them in the featureless darkness that was the net. He was almost at the computer when he wondered if the worst was to be found elsewhere.

He found he felt oddly resigned as he took out his phone, unless his emotions had grown too remote to grasp. He sank onto the nearest chair and looked up the number, and poked the key to call it before he could change his mind. In fewer seconds than he was prepared for a woman said "Transport police."

"I wonder if I could speak to somebody about an incident I think you'll have dealt with."

"I'll need some details, sir."

"Of course. I know. What it was, a gentleman, he was, he died in your lift at Lime Street Station the other week."

"I mean we need your details."

"I'm not from round here." For a panicky moment David was afraid his phone might betray the opposite, but could she locate him by his mobile? He seemed to have no option but to blunder onwards. "I'm," he said and heard himself improvising desperately. "I'm his nephew."

If he hoped this would gain him some sympathy, he couldn't tell whether it had. "May I have a name, please."

"He was my uncle—" At once David's mind was as blank as the screen of the dozing computer. He was about to shove himself out of the chair and find some way of disguising the reason for the pause while he looked up the name in the news report – perhaps he could feign a coughing fit, though wouldn't she also overhear him at the keyboard? – when he managed to make his mind work. "He was my uncle, obviously," he wished at once he hadn't bothered saying. "Uncle Donny. Uncle Don."

"I was asking for your name, sir."

"Oh, mine." Once again David felt as if his mind had fallen into the same mode as the computer, except that it was close to freezing with panic. He'd no sooner thought of a name than he let it out. "Luke," he said, which at least was nothing like his, not even by a letter. "Luke Sugden."

Silence met this, and he was afraid he'd somehow given himself away. Would a nephew have the dead man's surname? Apparently the woman was recording the information, because she said "And your address."

"Look, do you really need all this? I only want to ask a question. I haven't got much time." With a surge of what he supposed a writer might call inspiration David said "I'm just trying to put my mother's mind at rest. She's been worrying about what happened to her brother."

"I'm afraid we're required to take these details."

"Nineteen—" That was the number of his own house, and he made a wild bid to head off any further carelessness. "Nineteen Newless Way," he said.

"Nineteen nineteen Newless Way. And the postcode, please."

"We never use it. My mother doesn't believe in them. I honestly couldn't tell you." Was this how a writer might improvise? David felt more like a character at the mercy of his creator. "We're in Newcastle," he said, the most remote place he could bring to mind.

"Newcastle." He thought the lack of the accent had betrayed him until she said "Newcastle upon Tyne."

"That's the one. Now if I could just—"

"And may I take a phone number?"

"Take any you like and stick it wherever it fits." Though David refrained from saying that, his answer felt not much less out of control. "One two," he said, "two one, three, one one, two five…"

Were those too many digits or still too few? He'd tried to give the woman time to hint when she thought he should have finished. Now that he'd reached the end of the name he was transforming into numbers he heard himself asking "Is that all?"

"That should cover it, Mr Sugden. Can you tell me what your enquiry is?"

"As I say, it's my mother's really," David said, which felt like denying who he was. "She's convinced there might have been some kind of foul play."

"What kind?"

He would far rather not have put that into words. And hadn't the woman's voice sharpened, leaving politeness behind? "She believes he may have been assaulted," David said.

"What leads her to think that?"

"Look, I can't speak for her, can I?" He was close to giggling wildly at the thought that nobody else could. Before the woman had a chance to point out that he was doing exactly that, David tried saying "She's just got it into her head."

"You're saying she has no basis for it."

"I wouldn't quite say that." If he said too little the woman might wonder why he'd called at all or suspect him of withholding information. "It just doesn't sound like my uncle," he tried protesting. "We've never known him to have any trouble with his heart."

How likely was that, given Sugden's corpulence? Even if the woman didn't know his medical history, wouldn't she be able to guess from his appearance? David had to hold his breath until she said "Where does your mother think the assault took place?"

"She's got the idea it was in the lift."

The last word was barely out when David felt he'd strayed into a trap. He was struggling to think how to explain his answer when the woman said "Does she have some reason to believe someone had targeted him?"

"No, nobody. I mean, no reason. He'd no enemies we knew of, none at all." Yet again David felt he was denying too much. "And why she thought the lift," he said in haste, "because you've got cameras on the platform, haven't you. Or have you got them in the lift as well?"

"We don't give out data from the cameras unless we're seeking help from the public."

"You mean there is one in the lift." A pause brought no answer, and so David said "You're saying there's no need in my uncle's case. I mean, you're not looking for help." The silence that met this was at best inexplicit, and he had to say "Does that mean nothing showed up on the camera?"

He couldn't tell if he sounded too eager. Surely the woman would put that down to his concern for his relative, it didn't matter which one, but she said "You're still asking for data, Mr Sugden."

"Only for my mother. Just to give her closure." Even the fashionable jargon didn't seem to move the woman – and then David had an inspiration that felt reckless. "Now she's here," he complained.

"Perhaps we'd better have a word with her."

"I don't mean here. Not right here, not yet. I mean she's coming, coming up the road. She wouldn't have wanted me to make this call."

"Why not, Mr Sugden?"

"She doesn't like to trouble anyone." David felt he was reaching the end of his words, but he managed to add "Unless you tell me if there was someone in the lift with him she'll just carry on being troubled herself." This time the silence was so prolonged that he was afraid the woman was waiting to hear if not speak to his mother. He was opening his mouth, though he'd no idea what he was about to say, when the woman said "You may tell her that your uncle died of natural causes."

David hoped the breath he let out wasn't too audible a gasp. "You're saying the camera shows he was on his own when it happened."

"That's correct, Mr Sugden. Please don't ask for you or your mother to be shown the footage."

"Of course I won't. I trust you. You've put a mind at rest. You've been very understanding," David said and hoped she hadn't understood more than he wanted as, having thanked her, he ended the call and sank back in the chair.

How relieved was he entitled to feel? There was still the problem of the blog, and he could see no explanation other than that he was somehow writing it himself. What tricks might his brain have been playing on him? Could he have heard about Sudgen's death and Dent's fall outside his house and then caricatured them online without knowing? Might the very act of writing have erased the memories both of the events he'd learned about and of the writing itself? The idea made his mind feel as unfamiliar and dangerous as it had the night he'd ended up in the moonlit field, but what else could make sense of the situation? There was no point in telling himself that he didn't recognise the voice of the blog – that he didn't think he had ever used some of those words. Perhaps this would at least mean nobody would associate the blog with him.

He was close to feeling tentatively reassured when a thought occurred to him. As he touched the keyboard of the laptop the *Better Out Than In* page rose from the darkness of the dormant screen, and he felt as if it had been lying in wait for him. He dismissed it and typed words in the search box, and then he held his breath. It came out along with a groan as he read the news item he'd discovered. While he'd never heard of Robert Thoroughgood, he couldn't pretend he didn't know who the man had been. Witnesses said he must have lost control of his mobility scooter, because he'd sped helplessly into the road in front of a van.

CHAPTER FIFTEEN

As David stepped down from the bus a wind brought a takeaway carton clattering towards him. No doubt the squeaky bivalve came from one of the food outlets that faced Stephanie's apartment across the dual carriageway – Cod Almighty or Nice With Rice or Fab Kebab or Curry In A Hurry that had started life as 24 Hour Chapatti People, though the carton was the wrong shape for Picka Pukka Pizza – but it reminded him of far too much. He found he was glad not to see anyone to blame for littering as he crossed the road.

The front of the apartment overlooked Newsham Park. Skateboarders and equally unlit cyclists were racing about the paths in the dark beneath the trees. As David reached Stephanie's gate he heard a scream, and faltered until it turned into girlish mirth in a park shelter. He hurried along the stone jigsaw of a path between rhododendrons restless as a swarm of beetles and let himself into the house.

The table in the entrance hall was strewn with multicoloured leaflets and the glum buff envelopes of bills, none of them addressed to Stephanie. On the ground floor the mournful strains of a string quartet were audible beyond the door identified by a rakish number 1, but the upper floors were silent. The wide stairs yielded the occasional carpeted creak as David tramped up to the third floor, which was faintly redolent of spices, an aroma that grew more pronounced when he unlocked Stephanie's door. "It's only me," he called as if he could be someone else.

He was on the edge of calling out once more when he heard movement in the kitchen at the far end of the hall, beyond the walls covered with framed postcards. Whenever David saw them he was touched by the precision with which she arranged these souvenirs of every holiday she'd taken with her parents. In a moment the door opened, giving him a view of knives ranked by size on a rack on the russet tiles of the wall. He couldn't help finding their gleams ominous, together with the oddly tentative progress of the door, until Stephanie appeared with a glass of wine in each hand and a bottle of Chablis under one arm. "Are we celebrating?" David said.

They met halfway along the hall, between a cartoon postcard of an almost spherical bather poking his stomach out of the sea above an ambiguous caption and a card of a Turkish lagoon. Stephanie gave him a quick kiss and a glass. "I just thought we might like a drink," she told him, "but let's celebrate if you're saying we should."

The living-room boasted even more books than she kept in the kitchen. As her armchair gave a delicate leathery sigh David sat on a chair that didn't quite face hers. "I don't suppose I am."

"We don't know who they're getting rid of."

This seemed both too pointed and too vague, and David's chair amplified his uneasy restlessness. "Who?"

"That's what I'm asking. We don't, do we?"

"I'm not sure what you're talking about," David said and was still more disconcerted to realise that he should have grasped it. "Work, you mean. You're thinking of Andrea."

"That's who, the snotty ex. Ex marks the snot."

"More like Rex does. He's the new man. Maybe not such a new kind, the way he seems to treat her. Still, I get the feeling that's what she may like."

Stephanie took quite a drink from her glass. "Are you wishing you'd had the chance?"

"I'm not wishing for anything I haven't got."

"No complaints at all? Now's the time to bring them up."

"You shouldn't even wonder if there could be."

"Don't make me out to be too ideal, David. Nobody can live up to that all the time. They shouldn't be expected to. So to get back to Andrea…"

"She's still deciding as far as any of us know. We haven't even heard when she thinks she'll have to."

"She couldn't just be saying it to keep you all on your toes."

"Lying about it, you mean?" His flare of rage went out as he said "I wouldn't be able to tell. I don't feel I know her since she was promoted. Maybe that means I never really did."

"I think there's more inside us all than anyone else knows, except I hope that isn't true for us."

Everything he'd said so far had felt like a postponement, but now it seemed more like a barrier he had to struggle over. "I don't know," he said and tried again. "I don't know if you've had a chance to look at that blog I was telling you about."

"Do you mind if we don't talk about that just now?"

"Why?" Even this felt more like a hurdle than a question. "What have you found on it?" he had to ask.

"I haven't looked." She topped up his glass as an excuse for replenishing her own. "To tell you the truth, I'd forgotten about it," she said. "I've had other things on my mind."

At once David felt he should have had, and guilty too. "You mean Mick's."

"He thinks we should be open seven days from lunchtime. He's been talking about opening for breakfast too."

"He can't expect you to cope with all that by yourself, can he?"

"He's started hiring short-term help for me so he doesn't have to pay them too much, and to be truthful they aren't very good. He's insisting on serving meals when I'm not happy with them."

"Tell him it's your kitchen and your reputation."

"He says they're mostly his and he can live with them."

"Then let him and you find somewhere that appreciates you."

"I've been looking around, believe me. There's nothing at the moment that seems like a good move." Stephanie restrained herself to a sip of wine before saying "We're about to lose a waiter. Mick's taking over some of his service. I can't say I'm particularly looking forward to shutting down every night."

It took David some seconds to understand. "Being on your

own with him, you mean," he said, and when Stephanie stayed quiet "What's he been up to?"

"Nothing I can't deal with, David. It's just uncomfortable, that's all."

"Would you like me to have a word with him?"

"Oh, David." With an affectionate laugh that he tried not to find patronising she said "I wasn't trying to make you play the avenger. That isn't what I want you for."

"You're making me feel helpless."

"You mustn't. I'm not, so you aren't. I'm lucky I've found you." She took a sip that seemed designed to demonstrate she didn't need more of a drink. "I feel better for talking, so you've helped," she said. "Now what did you want to tell me about your blog?"

"It isn't mine. That's all." The opportunity to talk about it had grown so remote that he felt as if the words had been snatched from him. He stood the glass beside his chair and went to her. "Are we ready for bed?" he murmured and took her glass to plant it on the carpet. As she rose to her feet he put an arm around her shoulders and squeezed them hard enough to be trying to crush his thoughts. He'd said enough for now – for longer than that. He needn't feel secretive just because she couldn't see his face.

CHAPTER SIXTEEN

No, I don't need a menu. I'll just sit here in the darkest corner and watch. Anyway, I can read the menu on the table that's closest to my lurking orphan chair. I expect the format's meant to tell people how fresh the food is, because the card looks like a slate covered with childish writing you can wipe off – in fact, an idle diner has turned MARINATED OLIVES into MA I ATE LIVES. I'm guessing the misspelled list is the work of the manager, since he mispronounces items every timehe insists on talking his customers through them. He's a pneumatic sweaty object in a dinner suit that leaves him looking like a bouncer in disguise, and he greets newcomers with horrible jollity and seems determined to take as many orders as he can, a performance his staff have to try to make amends for. He's playing the sommelier as well, and when he uncorks some wine for a pair of women he asks "Who's the man?" He lectures a fellow on how to taste wine – "Just sip it like a girl" – and does his best to shame another diner into not ordering his steak well done – "Everything's well done here, no, it's better." If anyone leaves food on their plate he interrogates them about it while straining to seem chummy, which makes him sound like a father talking down to a child, maybe even one with learning difficulties, that new excuse for bad behaviour. Everyone has some of those, and it's my job to help them learn, but they always catch on too late.

Not that the diners don't deserve Mr Prick. Some of them might be trying to act worse than him. One man picks fish-bones out of his open mouth and drops them next to his plate, and another doesn't just blow his nose over his food but pokes his handkerchief up each nostril and screws it around with his little finger – I'm surprised he doesn't use the tablecloth. A woman scowls at her meal and digs it over with a fork like a customs officer searching for illegal substances, and a granny sucks her wrinkled whitish lips in as if she's fending off her soup before she even tastes it, a routine that makes her mouth look like the hole she must be sitting on. The worse his clientele behave, the more obsequious the manager grows. "You're the customer," he keeps telling them, but the question isn't who deserves him most – it's who deserves me.

The competition's hotting up. Two men who've been stroking each other's hands throughout their appetisers have leaned their heads together, not for a kiss but to complain. The high rapid muted racket puts me in mind of headphone leakage, a noise that always makes me want to squeeze the phones until they're squashed deep into the wearer's ears. When their muttering fails to attract Mr Prick they add shrill tuts and increasingly unrestrained groans that sound less like gripes than evidence of some kind of mutual pleasure. Perhaps the idea offends the manly manager, because he makes it plain he's dealing with someone else's bill and then spends time ushering the escapees to the door, where he shakes the man's hand and pecks the woman's fleeing cheek before he says "Don't forget us. Come back soonest" for the entire restaurant to hear. At last he saunters over to the gay couple, that's to say the glum duo. "Can I do something for you gentlemen?" he says not much more quietly than he saw the leavers off.

The taller and floppier of the pair flaps a hand at his mate's plate. "You assured us this wouldn't be contaminated."

The manager peers at the pasta and less happily at him. "Nothing's that way here that I've heard of," he says like at the very least a challenge.

"You guaranteed it was gluten free."

"Who's saying different?"

"My spouse is."

"Sensitive sort, is he? Can't he speak for himself?"

"He most certainly can. You tell him."

"Grateful, I'm sure. I will." The sufferer is squat and wide enough to take anything his partner can offer him. "I have a pain," he informs the manager.

"Looks like you're dining with him. Aren't you going to ask them who's the man?"

No doubt Prick can't hear my suggestion, but he does say "Maybe you brought it with you. Where've you got it?"

"Here." Faddyfat rubs his outthrust stomach and winces like a mime. "In my tummy," he says as well.

"No call for that," the manager warns Wristy as he extends a limp soothing hand. "How long have you been ailing?"

"As soon as he swallowed your first mouthful," Wristy declares.

The manager looks close to responding with more than a retort until Faddyfat says "I know what's wrong with me."

"You're not the only one, and you can't have got it here." With enough of a pause to have changed the subject Prick says "My chef makes the pasta and she knows what to do about your kind."

While Wristy looks eager to take this as an insult Faddyfat says "I knew what it was the moment I put it in my mouth."

Prick makes it obvious that he's suppressing an answer before he strides to the kitchen entrance. "Can you get out here? There's a couple want a word."

"Give me a minute and I'll be with you."

"That's women for you. Never ready when they're needed." When this meets no appreciation the manager stares at Wristy's plate. "Are you another one like him?"

"Whatever can he mean?" Wristy asks his partner. "I couldn't begin to imagine."

"Another one that doesn't like flour. Because if you're not," Prick says, "you could try swapping. I reckon you don't mind what's been in each other's mouth."

There's a silence that the other diners add to, but it's broken by the chef. "Here I am. Who wants me?"

I wonder what she thinks she looks like with Prick's name printed on the apron across her breasts. Her eyebrows are raised as if her hopes are high, but she doesn't know how much of a smile to put on. Prick indicates the couple with a thumb that glistens from having wiped his forehead. "They're telling me that's not pure."

Chefanny turns to the pasta protester. "You're the gentleman who's gluten intolerant, yes?"

Faddyfat sticks out his belly to caress it. "I know when it feels wrong."

"Go on, tell him you bet he does."

I don't suppose Prick hears my suggestion, and the chef says "I've told everyone I work with in the kitchen about keeping ingredients separate."

The manager doesn't so much swing towards her as lurch. He's going for a tackle, even if it's only verbal. "You saying you didn't make it yourself?"

"Bartek did. He has before. I've been satisfied with him."

"He better hadn't be getting his own back. Weren't you keeping an eye on him?"

"Not all the time. I was sure he knew what he was doing."

"Maybe I'm sure as well."

How long have they all been arguing about an ingredient? It feels as if they're using up the last of the air in the restaurant, burning it up like the candles on the tables that are occupied. I have to restrain myself from flying out of my corner and stopping at least one of them from needing any more air. Now it's Wristy's turn to waste some. "Since you've admitted liability, what would you like to offer us?"

"What are you, a lawyer?" When the man lets him think so Prick says "What would I like? I've already said you can swap."

"Can't we give them more than that?" Chefanny protests.

"Want to spend my profits, do you? We'll be having a talk in the changing room."

Faddyfat greets this with a comical squeal to which Wristy adds a hoot, and the manager turns on them. "Expecting to come back for a comp?"

"No," Wristy says. "We just aren't expecting to pay for this meal."

"Maybe you'd like a chat with the police."

"We wouldn't mind at all," Faddyfat assures him. "Fond of men in uniform, is it?"

"Fonder than you can afford to be," Wristy says and takes his partner's hand as they rise to their feet. "You've said a few things they might be interested to hear."

"What do you think you look like?" Prick swings round in search of some agreement from the other diners, but he doesn't find it or me. "You lot won't be happy," he tells the couple, "till you've pinched half our words and stopped us saying the rest."

Faddyfat offers Chefanny a sad look. "Commiserations if you have to put up with this sort of thing."

"All girls together, eh?" As if he's scored with that the manager says "Go on, take yourselves off and do whatever you do. We used to have a couple like you on the team, and they were no use to the rest of us either. Too interested in everybody else's balls and not the ball."

"Oh," Wristy says with a good deal of surprise, "were you a player?"

That's their exit line, and the manager follows them to the door. He looks eager to speed them on their way with a pair of hefty kicks, if he's capable of those any more, but contents himself with waving one hand while he rests the back of the other on his hip. He shuts the door with an expressive slam and turns to his customers. "Maybe now we can say what we like."

"We'd like the bill," says Nostrilpoker.

"I'll get it. You be seeing to the kitchen," Prick tells the chef and fetches the bill from behind the bar. "Enjoy your evening?" he barely asks.

"We didn't care for the floor show."

"Too much of a song and dance, eh? They pranced about all right."

The silence feels choked until Nostrilpoker says "We didn't care for how you spoke to them."

"I can speak how I like in my own bloody place. Anyone think different?"

I see Prick thinking that nobody does or else they don't dare to argue with him. Nostrilpoker pays the bill and is holding the door open for his wife when he says "We'd have left a tip except it's you. God help your staff."

"Good fucking riddance to you and all," the manager shouts after them and is stomping back to the bar when the fellow who strewed the tablecloth with bones says "We'll have our bill too, please."

"Happy to oblige." Though he doesn't look it, he tries to improve his demeanour as he brings the bill. "Have you had a good evening with us?" he apparently believes he's entitled to ask.

"We appreciated the food. You might want to learn how to treat the public."

"I treat them how they ask for and I'll carry on. You could learn a few manners yourself."

Bonedropper's mouth sprawls open almost too loosely to speak. "What do you mean by that?"

"Dumping your crap on my table like you did. You're lucky I don't send you the laundry bill."

"No, I'm Lucky and someone's going to know."

Even if they weren't confronting each other I don't suppose they'd hear me. Once Bonedropper and his wife have marched out, the remaining diners call for their bills, and nobody else has much to say despite being challenged by the manager. Soon he's alone in the dining area, or at least he thinks so. As he locks the door he shouts "That's all the rubbish chucked out. No tips for anyone tonight."

The chef is silent long enough to be having several thoughts before she calls "Shall we try and make sure there are some tomorrow?"

"Wait now, here's a tip. I'll give you one." When she comes to the kitchen entrance he says "You stick to what you're good at and let me fucking do the same."

She doesn't move except for looking sad. "I'm sorry if you think I made things worse. Maybe it's time I—"

"For fuck's sake don't stand there like the wife. I've had her doing that too often lately, like she can't bear to be near. Sit down and have a drink."

"I'd like to finish in the kitchen and head off if you don't mind."

"Well, I do. It's enough going to bed at night with one woman in a mood. If you've got something to say, spit it out but sit down first."

She leaves the kitchen none too eagerly and pulls out a chair from a table that wasn't occupied tonight. I didn't expect her to comply, but it shows that everyone deserves what comes to them. Maybe she thinks she's safest by the window, though the back street isn't much better than deserted. "What's your pleasure?" says Prick.

"I won't have anything to drink, thanks. I'm best keeping a clear head."

"Your head's just fine," he says and tramps like a sulky schoolboy to the bar, where he pours himself a vintage whisky and throws the glassful back. When he's refilled the glass to the brim he slurps it on the way to joining Chefanny. "Here's to us," he says, elevating the glass as he lands on the chair nearest hers.

The chef lifts a loosely cupped hand that I'd say was expressing its emptiness. "Why did you think Bartek might be getting his own back?"

"We had words about his pay and he wasn't over chuffed. He'll have to take a bit less or his family back home will."

"Just Bartek?"

"Not just fucking Bartek. Even me, I may have to take a cut. The ould woman's going to be moaning when she can't afford her sparklies." He peers over the glass he downs and says "I don't know about your money yet. We'll have to see how we get on."

"By getting on you mean…"

"Don't give me that crap. You're not stupid and I'm not. I reckon you're not satisfied any more than I am."

"We're talking about the restaurant."

"Now you're teasing, right? I don't mind a bit of that to start with." He gropes for her hand, but she moves it out of reach and plants it on her knee. "You need a bit more in your life like me," Prick insists. "That feller of yours can't be giving you enough. Seemed like he wanted to hide behind his mam and dad the night his lot was here."

"I don't know where you could have got that idea. Now if you'll excuse me—"

"Struck me he let them do all the talking for him. Maybe he wants somebody to do other stuff for him as well."

Chefanny stands up, keeping the table between them. "He's all I want, so could I ask you to remember that? Now I'd appreciate it if you'd let me finish what you pay me for."

"Don't talk to me like that, love. You know you're not saying what you're thinking." Prick staggers to his feet and makes a grab for her, colliding with his table and clattering the whisky glass. "Can't leave you alone," he calls after her in a kind of sly dogged triumph. "Tables still need clearing."

She reappears at speed from the kitchen with a tray and clears one. She's hardly vanished with the tray before she comes back to load it again. The manager slumps on his chair and fumbles for his glass, watching her as if she's a show he's determined to enjoy. She removes the tablecloths and returns with fresh ones, which she flaps not unlike a bullfighter challenging a bull. She still has to set out utensils and glasses, and by now the manager looks almost as bored as I am. When she eventually stays in the kitchen he begins to nod as if he's agreeing with his own dull thoughts, but when she ventures forth in her overcoat he lurches to meet her. "Let's not leave it like this," he mumbles as he stumbles. "Sorry if you thought I showed you up in front of anyone. Give us a hug at least if I'm forgiven."

Is she hearing how he must plead with his wife? "We'll sort it out tomorrow," she says, but perhaps she would feel undignified if not worse for dodging around him and making a dash for the street. She suffers a profuse sloppy hug and even pats his back, but when a hand wanders to her breast she lifts it by the cuff between finger and thumb and lets it drop to his crotch as she steps well away. "That really is enough," she says. "Try and sleep it off."

While she doesn't quite run to the door, she doesn't hide her eagerness to go. The lock must be stiff, because she adds her other hand to the one that's trying to twist the latch. "I'll do it for you," the manager slurs – his words are as indistinct as his intentions – and moves towards her in a crouch that looks like the start of a tackle. Then the door swings wide and the chef darts onto the street, turning to say firmly "I'll see you tomorrow."

"There'll be other fucking nights," Prick vows to his reflection in the door he's locked behind her. "You'll come round. You'd better," he says with a grin that's pretending he's satisfied as he blunders across

the restaurant to stare at the crowd of photographs on the walls –
pictures of football teams, each of them including less of him than
there is now. A couple of photographs are strewn with signatures that
wish him well. He executes a little clumsy footwork that I imagine
he'd call dribbling and then wags his thumbs at the teams. "Still got
it," he mutters. "They can't take the ball off me."

He desists once he starts panting and holds the back of a chair
while he wipes his forehead. He rubs the hand with the less sweaty one
and peers around the restaurant for anything still to be done. His gaze
drifts across the kitchen entrance and then veers unsteadily back to
it. At first he can't be sure he's seeing me, even when he takes a heavy
step towards me. He narrows his eyes, which tugs his brows lower
and seems to shrink the rest of his face. "Who the fuck are you?" he
gasps and tries to sound more threatening. "What do you think you're
doing there?"

"Just call me Lucky. And I've been watching you live up to your
name, Mr Prick."

He jerks his lowered head forward as if it's meeting a football. "I
asked you what you're doing in my place."

"Let's say I'm here on somebody's behalf. I'm the man who sorts
things out for them."

"Who're you doing that for?" he says while his lips grope for a
sneer. "Doesn't sound like much of a man, and you don't look like
much of one either."

"I'll be happy for you to find out how much I am."

"I won't be wasting my time." His mouth has settled on a disgusted
grimace. As he makes for the phone behind the bar he says "You can
tell it to the law."

"I wouldn't call them till you've seen the state of the place. Maybe
it's against one of those laws you don't like."

"I'll tell you what's against a lot of laws, chum. You are." His gaze
wanders around the restaurant before he blusters "What's wrong
with it? Nothing except you."

"The kitchen. You don't go in there too often, do you? I think you'll
find somebody's left something on."

"She's been getting her own back and all, has she?" the manager snarls and swerves towards the kitchen. "Fuck her, and you bet I will."

"Don't blame your chef. She left everything in order. Well, you won't be telling anybody otherwise."

If he hears me he doesn't take time to understand. He staggers through the doorway and glares down the room, where the grill has been on for quite a while – long enough for the metal network to turn red with the halo of gas jets. "Waste my fucking money, will she?" he cries and tramps rather less than straight to the grill.

He slips on the olive oil that I've spilled on the floor. He barely misses clutching at the grill, catching hold of the metal edge on either side instead. "What's she trying to do," he nearly screams, "trash the place?"

"I've told you once it wasn't her. How often do you need to hear?" As he makes to swing around, having realised how close I am behind him, I say "Lucky Newless at your service. Take a closer look."

I don't mean at me. I take one myself by springing up, using his head for leverage. My view isn't as close as his, since I've planted his face on the grill. When I weary of watching his hands drum without much rhythm on the metal that flanks it – that's while they aren't flailing the air – I step back. His muffled cries don't sound like a man at all. They grow louder and shriller as he rears up, waving his hands on either side of his face as if he thinks they can cool it down. It puts me in mind of a pie decorated with a pastry lattice, not least because the grill has crossed both his eyes out. That must be why he flounders straight towards me, unless his condition has somehow deluded him into fancying I'll help.

This time he does lose his footing on the oil. Before he hits the floor like a side of beef flung on a slab he encounters the knife I've been poising for him to find. It penetrates his neck, and his fall drives it deeper, then sends it skittering across the linoleum. His hands continue jerking for a while – I'm amused to see one close convulsively around the handle of the knife and then the blade – as his shrieks peter out and the oil on the floor is invaded by red as if someone's mixing a dressing or a marinade. At last his hands give up their feeble antics and he's just one more piece of meat in his restaurant. "Now you know what goes on in the kitchen," I say and leave him.

CHAPTER SEVENTEEN

"I've got something for us all to think about," Andrea said. "A new slogan for the shop."

David wondered if his colleagues shared his thought that since she was including everyone, nobody was scheduled to be fired. He'd begun to relax when she said more sharply "Who wants to start while we've no customers?"

He stared at his computer screen as if this might help him concentrate on the task, only to be troubled by a sense of the blog lurking somewhere behind the travel details on the screen. He hadn't looked at it since he'd read about the man on the mobility scooter, and he managed to put it out of his mind as he heard Helen say "See more by sea."

"That's too much like telling people not to fly. We don't want to put the public off anything we sell."

"We could have one about flying as well." Having tilted her head to indicate she was thinking, Helen added "Don't fight for a flight."

"If it needs explaining that means it doesn't work."

Helen tipped her head the other way, and Emily relieved the silence by saying "Trust our travel."

"That's more like it," Andrea said without conveying how much, and Emily's cheeks grew pinker. "What have the men got for us?"

Bill prefaced his suggestion with a laugh. "Broaden yourself abroad."

"There's a time and place for jokes, and we don't need too many here."

"I didn't think it was just a joke." His smile turned wistful as he said "I meant you should broaden your mind."

"I think it's perfectly adequate, thank you." Before Bill could tell her he wasn't referring to hers Andrea said "Well, David?"

For a distracted moment he thought she was seeking his opinion of her mind, and then Emily said "Go on, David. Show us all how."

He felt cornered, just as he had at All Write. No less desperately than he'd produced the title at the writers' group he said "Fly fast and far."

"That's good, isn't it, Andrea?" Emily said. "I'd go for that."

"I think it's the best we've had," Helen seemed pleased to establish. "It's got my vote as well," Bill said.

"I wasn't asking for one," Andrea told him. "Would anybody like to hear mine?"

"Of course we would," David said.

Perhaps she thought his encouragement was inappropriate, unless her silence was designed to build anticipation. "Let yourself go," she said.

"That's good too," Emily wanted her to know. "Better than mine," David tried saying.

The general murmur might have been expressing consideration or disagreement, and Andrea contributed a shrill cough. "I'll submit them all if it keeps everyone happy," she said. "Speaking of head office, David, I've had their verdict."

Not just the word made him feel accused. "What did they say?"

"They'll be obtaining a permit to give us free use of the streets." She paused as if she expected him to rejoice before she added "On balance they're supporting you, since the council won't be taking any action."

"You mean he was right to keep on handing out our offers," Bill said. "I said exactly what I meant." Andrea emphasised it with another piercing cough. "And while we're on the subject of promotions, let's see a few of everyone's holiday photos on the wall. The sunnier the better, and make sure you're in them."

She hadn't finished speaking when David heard another voice related to the business. *I go Fru-go-go, I go Fru-go-go...* The chant was in his pocket – the official ringtone Andrea had convinced the staff it was advisable to download. He gave her an apologetic grimace as he took out the phone. "It's Stephanie," he said. "She wouldn't call if it wasn't important. She knows I'm at work."

"Take it then, but be quick."

He was making to do so when Bill said "There's a thought."

"Hold on, Steph." David wished he didn't have to delay hearing from her so as to ask "What is?"

"Just thinking about advertising us. Maybe she could make some foreign dishes to hand out to our passing trade."

David suspected this was a bid to placate Andrea, who said "Ask her, David."

"Steph, I'm here. What's the matter?"

"This is going to sound strange." As he made to urge her to go on she said "I wondered if you knew if there's a locksmith round here."

"A locksmith." In some confusion David said to his colleagues "A locksmith round here."

"I know where there's one." When he held out a hand to get the information from her Andrea said "You haven't done what I asked yet."

His bemusement seemed to leave him no words of his own. "What you asked…"

"Shall I speak to her myself?" As her point caught up with him Andrea said "Dishes for a promotion."

"Just quickly, Steph, we wondered if you'd like to come up with a few dishes we could use to advertise some of the countries we're offering."

"Bring them over from the restaurant, you mean? I'll ask Mick when I see him. He should have opened up by now, but he isn't here and we can't get in."

"Has someone called him?"

"Of course I did. He isn't answering. His wife will have a spare key, but she's in Tenerife." Much like an apology Stephanie said "I don't know if she booked through you."

"That doesn't matter now." As Andrea's face made it plain that she wanted to know what he meant, David said "The restaurant's locked up and nobody's got a key."

"There's a locksmith opposite the bombed church."

"Andrea says there's a locksmith at the top of your road." With an urgency he couldn't explain to himself David said "Will you let me know when everything's sorted out?"

"I'll call you. I'm going up the hill right now."

He had an acute sense that despite being just a few hundred yards away she was somehow out of reach. As he pocketed the phone he told Andrea "She'll have to ask her manager about the food."

"Maybe I should just speak direct to him."

"They don't know what's happened to him," David said and was overtaken by a terrible suspicion. "I'm sure he must be all right," he blurted, which came nowhere near convincing him.

Would it help to look at the Lucky blog? Before he could make for the staffroom the phones rang in chorus on the counter. He had an irrational notion that the call might be related to his fears, and grabbed the extension next to his computer, only to find that the caller was a woman hoping for an upgrade on a Caribbean cruise. It took him almost half an hour of keying options and listening to yet another pledge of the importance of his call to bring him a live voice. At least there had been a cancellation on the voyage, and he was able to book a better cabin. Once he'd left the message on the customer's phone he told Andrea "I'd like to take my break."

The smell of coffee that always lingered in the staffroom seemed unusually acrid, and caught in his dry throat as he shut the door. When he sat on an unyielding chair and laid his mobile on the table, the internet icon seemed to grow restless with the pulse in his eyes. His finger was as loath to touch the screen as it had been eager to jab the keys at the counter. It was hovering over the phone when its closeness wakened the connection as though something was impatient to be seen. Now he had no excuse not to bring up the blog, and there was a new phrase at the top of the stack in the sidebar. No, I don't need, it said.

He'd barely tapped the words when the entry took over the miniature screen. As he read the rest of the opening sentence, not just his finger but his entire body froze. No, I don't need a menu. It could be a coincidence, he tried to think – but his gaze was straying down the page, and a black swarm of words seemed to rise to meet it. "No," he found himself repeating and then simply thinking, as if the first word of the entry had lodged in his head to taunt him.

As he read on he felt he was growing hollow, no more than a vulnerable shell. When he reached the end, the page seemed to trap his gaze and his mind. He couldn't look away, and he was afraid to think. While he was desperate to speak to Stephanie, he was just as scared to hear. The blogger's full name was in the open now, and he felt as if it was mocking him. Nobody could know it except David – at least, only Stephanie did, and he had to dismiss the deranged idea that she could be in any way responsible for the blog. He didn't know how long he'd stared at the screen – long enough that a stain of decay appeared to spread around every word – when he heard the door open behind him. He twisted around in a convulsion of guilt to see Emily watching him. "Andrea's wondering what's happened to you," she said.

"Nothing. Nothing's happened. I'm the same." As Emily made for the percolator he switched off his mobile for fear that she might glimpse the blog. "I lost track, that's all," he said and dodged out of the room.

He was escaping her scrutiny, but there was more at the counter. Before he could try to hide himself in work Helen said "Are you feeling ill, David?"

"Not had any bad news, have you, old son?" Bill said as if he hoped he could extend his grin.

"No news at all, and nothing's wrong with me," David said.

"That isn't how you looked," Helen said and tilted her head as he confirmed her concern by lurching almost out of the chair.

The contents of his pocket had jerked like an extra set of nerves. As he snatched out the phone, nearly dropping it from haste, it began to chant. *I go Fru-* He cut off the ringtone and pleaded "Yes, Steph."

"Gosh, you sound worried. Is everything all right?"

For a parched moment he couldn't speak. "If it is with you," he was able to wish.

"Everything's fine here. I was just calling to say."

"It's all right with me, then," David said and risked asking "Still no sign of Mick?"

"Not a sound. You can thank Andrea for me if you like. The locksmith's here and he's opening the door."

David felt as if he was striving to hold the situation together – to keep it no worse than mundane – by telling Andrea "Steph says thank you for the locksmith."

Her frown at the phone call relented a little. "Has she had time to think up any dishes for us?"

At least he would be keeping Stephanie in touch with him. "Steph…"

"Hold on, he's giving me a receipt. Goodbye and thanks again." Having veered away, her voice came back. "All fixed, David," she said. "I'm going in now."

She was ending the call. Almost too fast for clarity he said "Andrea was wondering if you'd thought about our promotion."

"Her problems matter more than anybody else's, you mean. Did she hear that? I don't really care if she did." More gently Stephanie said "I'll do it if it helps you, David. Just let me hang my coat up and I'll think."

She was heading for the kitchen. David didn't know if he was holding his breath or simply unable to breathe. He sucked in a gasp's worth of air as he heard her say "Oh. Oh gosh."

"What's wrong?" Her tone wasn't letting him know how serious the problem was. "What is it, Steph?" he begged.

"Bartek. He's here."

"That's your assistant. You're saying he's arrived. Is that what you're saying?"

"I'm talking to him," Stephanie said, and her voice receded. "Can you come here, Bartek? I don't want to put the light on till you do."

"Why not?" Even more nervously David said "Where are you now?" Perhaps she didn't hear him, unless she hadn't time to answer. In the distance he heard her say "He's been here all the time, Bartek. Mick, can you hear us? Oh, good."

For an instant David was able to believe she'd meant that, and then he grasped that whatever she could see had stopped her halfway through a dismayed phrase. Her phone must have been close to the light-switch, since the click sounded ominously loud. It was followed by far too prolonged a silence before Stephanie said "Don't touch him. Call an ambulance."

David heard a faraway response in which he couldn't distinguish a word. "I'll do it myself," Stephanie said less patiently than he'd ever known her to speak, and then her voice returned to him. "I've got to ring off, David. We need the medics, and maybe I should call the police as well."

"Before you go," David said and forced himself to continue, "can't you tell me what's wrong?"

"Mick." As David's mouth grew drier still she said "I don't know if we should touch him, but there's a lot of blood." The sight or the idea seemed to catch up with her, because it took her an audible effort to add "I'll call you when I can."

David was holding a voiceless phone, and all his workmates were watching him. He had to take an unsteady breath to help himself grasp that they were wondering why he'd sounded anxious. "Her manager," he said, struggling to confine himself to what he was supposed to know. "He's been injured or it may be worse than that. They can't tell yet," he said and glanced at Andrea. He was looking for disappointment, he realised – for her to betray that she was more concerned with her life than with anybody else's. He couldn't see any evidence of that, but until he looked away he was possessed by loathing. It was so intense that it terrified him almost as much as the Newless blog, not least because it was just as impossible to understand.

CHAPTER EIGHTEEN

As soon as Andrea told him to take his lunch David retreated to the staffroom and called Stephanie. She answered readily enough – her voice did, asking whoever he was to leave a message. When he tried phoning the restaurant, it was Mick who greeted him. The manager told him the opening hours and exhorted him to leave at least his name and number, at which point David made haste to end the call. He couldn't bear to know as little as he did, although might more knowledge prove to be even more unbearable? He was pacing the room like a trapped beast, and there seemed to be nowhere else to go except over to Mediterranean Mick's.

The glow from a sky like a wad of fog muffled all the colours of the streets and of everybody in them. The yellow and white of the police van with two of its wheels on the pavement outside Mick's looked as deadened as the lights on its roof. When David crossed the narrow street he did his best to feel defiant – he had every excuse to be there; he was with Stephanie, after all – but by the time he reached the window he'd decided he was just a passer-by with no reason to be questioned by the police. Though all the lights were on inside the restaurant the place was deserted, which he took to mean that the police were in the kitchen – the scene of the crime. Was the body still in there? Might they be examining the disfigured face, the gashed throat, or finding fingerprints on the knife? As he glimpsed a blurred shadow on its way to emerging from the kitchen he dodged out of sight, impelled by a sense of guilt too confused to deal with or even define. He could only try to lose himself in the crowds until he had to go back to work.

At least he needn't hide his state. His colleagues would expect him to be concerned for Stephanie, after all. Even Andrea made the effort to meet him with a relatively sympathetic look. He had customers to distract him, though the automated messages he had to listen to on their behalf and the lifeless interludes of waiting to be answered let all his hectic thoughts swarm back. Once he deleted an entire booking he'd just taken, and as he took the customer's details again he found he didn't care whether Andrea had noticed his incompetence. Apparently she hadn't, and when she locked up for the night she said "Tell Stephanie not to worry too much about what we need till she's recovered if she has to."

David let her and the rest of the staff leave him behind on the way downhill, but he'd taken just a few steps when he was aware of being watched. At first he didn't see who was waiting on a bench in the middle of the pedestrian pavement that occupied the road. "How long have you been there?" he said, close to a rebuke.

"Not too long," Stephanie said, pinching her coat collar shut with the hand she wasn't holding out to him. "I didn't want to come in when Andrea might have objected. I can do without that just now."

"Sorry," David said, which referred to a good deal and was wholly inadequate. "How are you feeling?"

As she squeezed his hand and then held on she said "A bit shaken still."

"So, Mick." When this proved insufficient David had to say "He's…"

"Yes," Stephanie said as if they were enacting the kind of derivative script he would have produced as a writer. "I had to touch him after all to see if there was a pulse. He felt like meat that's just defrosted." Plainly she needed to say this, along with "Maybe I thought that because there was a knife."

David wasn't eager for any more details. "Sorry," he said.

"You don't have to keep saying that. Nothing's any fault of yours."

He felt his mouth open before he knew what would escape. "Will you have talked to the police?"

"Do you mind if we walk? I think I've sat here long enough."

Perhaps she didn't want the woman who'd just found space on the bench to overhear, but the delay worked on his nerves. He and Stephanie were wandering downhill by the time she said "Why do you ask?"

"I just—" Rather than admit his reasons David said "I was hoping they didn't make you feel worse."

"They did their best not to. They've their job to do like us."

"What did they want to know?"

"Just the circumstances. In case they had any bearing, I suppose."

The details felt too imminent again, however desperate he was to learn them. "Would you like a drink somewhere?" David said.

"Not yet. I might soon. Shall we just go home?"

He wasn't sure whose home she meant until she led the way through the crowds to the bus stop, where he couldn't keep quiet any longer. "You were saying the circumstances," he murmured.

"I don't think I did."

"You were saying the police wanted to hear about them."

"I mean I don't think I told them to you."

He mustn't lose patience when she'd had to deal with finding Mick, but he urged "Well, do it now."

She might have if a bus hadn't swung around the corner to cruise uphill to the stop. David followed her to the nearest empty seat on the single-decker, in the front section where the seats crouched low – the stalls, he thought a writer might have called them, with the circle elevated behind. As the bus left the stop he felt as if his nervousness was tugging his lips apart. "What happened before, before you found him?"

"You know, David."

He was afraid he did, but how could she realise? Had she read the Newless blog? He didn't know if that would come as a relief or aggravate his panic. "How do I?" he demanded.

"David, what's the matter with you? You took my calls."

"Not the lock." He nearly laughed but was nervous of how

it might sound. "Before that," he said and managed to add "Say last night."

"Why are you thinking of that?"

"Because, because I thought the police might have asked about it."

"A few things did happen." As the bus reached the next stop she said "Arguments with customers, for one thing."

Stephanie fell silent while passengers crowded onto the bus. "Who?" David had to prompt her. "Who was arguing?"

"Mick with some of them."

By now the aisle was packed, and a fleshy man made bulkier by a quilted coat grabbed the metal pole in front of David. "Pull your knee in, mate."

Pressing his knees together made David feel they were helping him force out a question. "What was the argument about?"

"He took a dislike to a couple." Not much louder than the muffled rumble of the wheels Stephanie said "They weren't men enough for his taste."

"That was all there was to it," David yearned to believe.

"I wish it had been. No, I wouldn't have wanted that either." Almost too quietly for him to catch Stephanie said "One of them had a gluten problem and we must have served him a taste. Bartek swears he didn't mean to let it anywhere near. I know it wasn't me."

With less hope than ever David said "Was that all?"

"Mick blamed both of us. Well, the kitchen's my responsibility."

"Then he should have paid you what you're worth." This didn't save David from having to add "I meant was that all with the customers."

"It wasn't quite."

The bus sped past a queue it had no room for, and the man in the aisle lurched against David. "Watch the elbow, pal."

David hauled the arm across his body and clasped Stephanie's hand with that one too. "What else?"

"Some of the other diners didn't like the way he spoke to

those and told him so, and then he started lecturing somebody about his table manners."

David was almost as reluctant to continue as to be alone with his thoughts. "You said the arguments were one thing."

"Did I?" Stephanie was silent while the bus swung uphill out of town, and then she said "It really doesn't matter any more, but he was drinking after we locked up and he tried to get too friendly. Don't worry, he didn't take much fending off."

"Did you tell the police?"

"What reason would I have? I don't think I would have told them even if he'd been alive."

"I meant in case they could possibly have thought you—"

The bus came to an abrupt halt – a passenger had belatedly rung the bell – and the man in the aisle bumped into David's shoulder. "Can't you shove up, lad?"

"Where would you like him to go?" Stephanie retorted. "He's given you more room than you deserve. He can't project himself somewhere else."

"You've got a fierce one there, lad," the man said, not entirely in admiration. "Watch out she doesn't turn on you as well. Trust me, I know what it's like."

"Maybe you don't know enough." David hardly knew what he was saying. "Maybe you need to be taught."

The man transferred his unfavourable gaze to him. "Want to get off?"

"I think you should."

The man's lips writhed as if he was about to spit. "Good job for you my stop's next."

"I'm sure it's a good job for someone."

The man kept staring at him but steadied himself with the pole so as not to touch David as the bus slowed for the stop. Once he'd sidled clumsily along the aisle and dropped his bulk off the bus Stephanie murmured "Well, that was unexpected. I'm not saying you were wrong."

"You wouldn't have thought I'd face up to him, you mean."

"Of course I would, David. Maybe just not quite like that."

"I was only following your lead." This wasn't what he needed to say, and before he could falter he said "Would you have wanted—"

"I certainly wouldn't have liked you to have a fight with him."

"Then you wouldn't have liked—" David was faltering after all. "You wouldn't have wanted what happened last night," he said, but even this wasn't enough. With an effort he added "To Mick."

When she turned to gaze at him he had to meet her troubled eyes. "David, how can you possibly ask?"

"I don't mean what actually happened. Maybe something not so bad." He was well in retreat now and, worse, forgetting how it must have been for her. "I'm sorry. I'm sorry," he protested. "I'm reminding you. You had to see what did."

"I had to identify him."

"Steph, forgive me. I didn't realise." David felt still guiltier for asking "Was it bad?"

"I hope I never have to do anything like it again."

"He wasn't too disfigured, though." This sounded like underestimation, and David hastened to explain "For you to identify, I mean."

"Disfigured."

She was gazing at him because he'd betrayed he knew more than he ought to. He did his best to sound both convinced and convincing as he said "Didn't you say something like that? I'm sure you did."

"I don't know what you think you heard, David. You're talking about his face."

"I'm sorry." He saw that his apologies had begun to weary her, and said "Yes."

"You needn't worry about that. It wasn't."

Once he realised his mouth was open he had to find it some speech. "Wasn't…"

"Disfigured. He looked as if he couldn't believe what was happening, but nothing else was wrong with it."

David was beyond grasping how this made him feel. "So what do they think happened," he tried asking, "the police?"

"That he got so drunk he did it all to himself. They don't seem to think he meant to."

David was ashamed of interrogating her, but he had to know. "Did what?"

"He smashed a bottle of olive oil. I think he could have done that in a rage. I shouldn't say that really, should I? It's not as if we're ever going to find out." Remorse silenced her, and David was on the edge of prompting her when she said "He slipped on it, and he must have slipped trying to get up, because you could see he'd fallen twice. And he'd knocked over a knife block, and he was so drunk he tried to use one to help him up. Only that slipped on the work surface, you could just see the mark, and it went in him."

David had no idea how to respond. Too much that he'd begun to accept, however reluctantly and nervously, seemed not to be the case after all. When she said "Don't let's miss our stop" he had an impression of starting awake. The pavement underfoot felt less present than his thoughts, and he had to concentrate on waiting for traffic lights to let him usher Stephanie across the dual carriageway, unless she was ushering him. As they reached the far side it occurred to him to ask "What's going to happen to the restaurant?"

"Mick's wife is on her way home and she'll decide. Shall we have a little walk in the park?"

At least Stephanie hadn't lost her job, then. David wished he could use that as an excuse to feel relieved, but relief was keeping its distance while he was unable to grasp how the Newless rant related to the events at Mick's. If only there was someone he could question – and then he realised what he had to do. "Let's walk," he said, though besides a postponement this was a way of hiding his thoughts, and recaptured Stephanie's hand to lead her into the park.

CHAPTER NINETEEN

As he crossed the road David willed Mrs Robbins not to be involved with rubbish for once. She wasn't in her front room, which resembled a sample of a show house. Three straight-backed armchairs wore lace caps that put him in mind of maids, and an intensely polished table crouched between the chairs, displaying a magazine about the week ahead on television. The flat screen of the television looked as scrubbed as a blank slate, and the oval mirror above the hearthless mantel gleamed so much that it reduced David's watchful reflection to a silhouette. When he rang the doorbell it responded with all the quarters of Big Ben but fell short of the hour. It was running through a repetition when the door inched wide to reveal Mrs Robbins clutching a precarious stack of crumpled paperbacks against her flattened breasts. "Mr Botham," she said, more a statement than a question. "Do you read books?"

"I've read a few things in my time."

"You won't have read these."

If this was any kind of query it was masquerading as an assertion, and disapproval was involved as well. David had to lean towards her squashed bosom in order to make out the titles on the wrinkled spines. *Call the Revenger, The Revenger Again, Vengeance for the Revenger, The Revenger Never Forgets…* "They aren't really my style," he said.

"Then there's just one place for them."

"You could donate them to one of the charity shops," David said, though he didn't understand why he was anxious to prevent her from behaving as she so often did. "I could take them in the car if you like."

"There's already too much of this sort of stuff in the world. It's a pity whoever wrote them didn't keep them to himself." She dumped the books on a stair in the hall and rubbed her hands clean. "I'm clearing out the boy's room," she said. "It's long past time somebody did."

"He'll be your son."

"That's right, he'll always be, and you don't stop being a parent either. You're responsible for what you create whether you like it or not." David couldn't tell if this was a complaint or a declaration of principle, unless it was both. "Anyway," Mrs Robbins said, "that's our business and nobody else's. What is it, Mr Botham?"

From her tone he might have imagined she was requiring him to parrot the comment about her business. "I wondered if you'd found out about Mr Dent," David said.

"He's still in hospital."

"Did you happen to hear where? You said you'd let me know."

"I was waiting for you to come over, Mr Botham. That's what neighbours do occasionally, you might know. I assumed you'd lost interest."

He mustn't waste time arguing. "So where is he?"

"You'll be paying him a visit, will you?" She waited for confirmation before she said "He's at Arrowe Park."

"I'll go right now," David said and then thought to ask "Do we know his first name?"

"I've no idea what you know, Mr Botham. I think you might if you're so concerned about him."

"I don't know who else I could ask."

"Then you should make yourself more of a member of the community. Nobody knows much about you at all."

"That's because there isn't much to know." As he wished there were less David said "So you'll know his name."

"As a matter of fact we aren't on those terms, Mr Botham. There's a sight too much familiarity these days."

David felt as if she was determined to portray someone she hadn't been just a few moments ago — as if the personalities hadn't even been introduced to each other. "Do you know if he has many visitors?" he said.

"I'm sure you'll be allowed if you say you're a friend." Before

David could determine how scornful this was meant to be — surely she had no reason to suspect he was the opposite, or why he needed to be alone with Dent — Mrs Robbins said "Please wish him a speedy recovery."

As David returned to his house he heard a series of dull thuds at his back — the fall of books onto bags of garbage — and the slam of the plastic lid. "Living up to your name again," he muttered and had to remind himself that she wasn't doing so at all.

His mobile showed him that the intensive care unit at the hospital was open for visitors in half an hour. Mrs Robbins watched him from her window as he swung the car onto the road. How guilty should he feel? At least Stephanie seemed to have recovered from the shock of finding Mick, and now she was at the restaurant with Mick's widow. He hoped the day would resolve that situation and his own as well.

In five minutes he was on the motorway. He'd scarcely joined it when he was brought almost to a halt by a lumbering mass of traffic. The matrix signs were warning of a queue ahead and set to thirty miles an hour. When at last he rounded a long curve and saw the way ahead, there seemed to be no reason for the queue except for the signs themselves. As he regained speed he encountered a car still crawling along the middle lane, however many drivers urged its venerable occupant to move over. David pulled out to overtake, only to find a Jaguar racing up behind him at not much if any less than a hundred miles an hour. He had to swerve in front of the elderly hindrance, who rewarded him with a blinding glare of headlights and a prolonged squawk of the horn. As he returned to the inner lane he saw a car swell up in the mirror, overtaking on the inside and treating him to another dazzle of lights and a blare of the horn. "Idiot. Idiot. Idiot," he heard himself repeating like some kind of charm well after he'd left the motorway for the road to the hospital.

The post at the entrance to the car park teased him with a glimpse of a paper tongue before putting out the ticket once again for him to snatch. Seconds later the post raised its grudging metal arm to let him through. At least half a dozen cars were cruising between the ranks of vehicles in search of a space. More than ten minutes later David saw a car emerging from a space behind him. He was indicating to reverse into it when a battered Datsun veered in. "That's the way to do it, son," he heard the driver declare.

David thought he was being mocked until the man let out his son, a small but equally thickset boy aiming to match his father's baldness. The driver stalked over to David, jerking his head up and twitching his eyes narrow. "What you waiting for? Got a problem?"

"None you'd want to know about," David couldn't resist saying. "You're quite a role model."

"What the fuck you talking like that for? You a teacher?"

"You wouldn't like the lesson," David said, but only to himself. He was ashamed of worsening the man's behaviour in front of his son, however loyally pugnacious the boy looked. He drove out of the car park and eventually found a space nearly half a mile away on the main road.

Despite the chill of the grey afternoon, his body prickled with exertion as he tramped back to the hospital. Beyond the automatic doors, which stood back for a man levering himself along on crutches with a wincing grin at every step, the lobby felt as oppressive as fever. By the time David reached the intensive care unit his mouth was almost too dry to let him swallow, while his armpits felt full of hot ash. "Can I see Mr Dent?" he croaked at a nurse behind a desk.

She blinked several times on the way to looking up from a computer. "Mr..."

"Dent." Perhaps she was asking for the first name, unless David's voice was so parched that she hadn't understood. "He fell off a ladder," he said as distinctly as the threat of a desiccated cough would let him.

"Are you a relative?"

"No, I'm just..."

The notion of claiming he was a friend left David almost too guilty to speak, but the nurse gave him an encouraging smile. "You're just?"

"That's what I am." He hadn't meant to say that; he could have fancied someone else had. "Just a neighbour," he said.

"I expect he'll be glad to see someone. Third bed down on the left. Don't expect too much, will you? And I'm afraid you haven't got very long."

At first David couldn't see Dent for the visitors around the intervening beds. The man was lying on his back with his head only slightly elevated by a pillow. A chunky bandage capped his scalp, and a padded pink ruff encircled his neck. Tubes led to plastic bags from one bruised arm that lay on the sheet and from underneath the covering, and wires connected him to monitors. David had the notion that the whole of the man had been rendered remote, and couldn't help wondering how that would feel. There was no telling from Dent's face, both sides of which drooped inertly towards the pillow. His moist reddened eyes were gazing upwards, apparently unaware of his visitor, even when David advanced from the foot of the bed to stand beside the pillow. "Mr Dent?" he said.

The slack brow wrinkled feebly and then winced as if the movement had roused a bruise. Dent's eyes shifted in their sockets, dislodging a trickle from the left one, but came nowhere near focusing on David. "Can you hear me, Mr Dent?" David said a little louder.

"Who?" While this was barely audible, it appeared to exhaust Dent's breath. Perhaps it wasn't the entire question, since he made a visible effort to speak as his head lolled sideways to help his watery gaze find the visitor. "Who's that?" he gasped.

"It's David Botham. I live round the corner from you."

Dent's forehead stirred again, tugging at the hem of the bandage. "Do I know you?" he said too faintly for his tone to be anything like clear.

David was thrown by how reassured he felt not to be recognised. "As I say, we're neighbours. We've spoken now and then."

"Don't remember. Don't remember much," Dent mumbled mostly to himself.

Perhaps the lack of recognition wasn't so heartening after all. "You used to help me get out of my drive," David risked saying.

"Did I? Good neighbour then."

This sounded too indistinct for a memory, more like an idea no sooner found than lost again. "I live across from Mrs Robbins. The lady who's forever at her bins," David said. "Mrs Robbins. She hopes you'll be better soon, and I do."

"Bins."

It might have been all of her name that Dent had the breath to articulate. "So how are you feeling?" David said.

"Not all here." Dent's mouth worked to shape more words and possibly a rueful grimace. "Like the rest of me's somewhere else."

"They're taking care of you, though."

For a moment Dent seemed to recall something, and then his brows relaxed, having failed to grasp it. "Doing their best," he said.

David couldn't put off the question any longer; it was why he was there. "Do you mind if I ask what happened to you?"

"Fell." Dent's head lolled another inch in his direction, and a thread of drool escaped onto the pillow. He was regaining more awareness, dabbing at the general area of his mouth with the hand that wasn't hindered by a tube. "Fell off a ladder," he said. "Should have got someone else."

"You'll know another time, won't you?" David couldn't help emphasising the situation since it absolved him, even if it hardly explained the Newless blog. "So long as you're getting better," he said.

"Wait." The skin beneath Dent's eyes twitched, perhaps to help them focus. "There was," he breathed.

David couldn't tell or more accurately hoped he didn't know why his mouth had grown parched again. "Was what?"

"Someone else," Dent said and stared so hard at David that his eyes bulged. "What did you say your name was?"

"It's David Botham."

"No." Dent's head moved weakly from side to side on the pillow but kept its gaze on David. "No, that's not right," he said. "Have you got a brother?"

"Not even a sister." This went nowhere near assuaging David's panic. "I'm the only one," he said, which felt just as ineffectual.

"Someone else close, then. Somebody that's got your face."

"Who'd want it?" This didn't work either. "There's nobody," David almost pleaded. "There's only me."

"Have you come to see me before?"

"Here in the hospital, you mean?" Too late David realised he oughtn't to make that distinction. "I'm sorry," he said and had to swallow before going on. "I've never been anywhere near you."

"Then I must have dreamed it when they had me under."

David swallowed again, but his voice came out thin. "What did you dream?"

"Nothing you'd ever do. You wouldn't be here now if you were like that. I'd be embarrassed to tell you, Mr Botham."

"Was it—" As David's voice threatened to let him down he succeeded in saying "Was it about the ladder?"

"What else do you think would be on my mind?" All the same, Dent's gaze wavered as if he wasn't altogether happy with the sight of David's face. "I think I'd like to rest now," he said. "Thank you for coming and thank your neighbour for me."

David turned away and trudged almost blindly out of the ward, feeling as if his senses were somewhere else. He'd learned more than he would have liked to know, and it left him riddled with helpless bewilderment. Whatever expression he was displaying, the nurse at the desk blinked rapidly at it until he changed it into an automatic smile that made him feel even more concealed inside himself. He was heading for the exit – perhaps the chill out there might tone down his feverishness, if that wasn't just a symptom of his thoughts – when he heard a voice behind him. "Don't you ever fucking show me up again like that, you little fucking shit. I taught you how to fucking behave."

David hunched up his shoulders as though they could keep him from turning his head, but the man called after him "There's the fucking teacher. Got anything to say to me?"

"Don't let the boy see." If this was addressed to the father, David's voice was too low for him to hear. He didn't know where his words might have ended up, which dismayed him so much that despite the man's jeers he almost ran out of the hospital.

CHAPTER TWENTY

"I'm sorry I'm not better company, David. I'm feeling guilty, that's all."

"You're the last person who should feel that, Steph."

"It's just that I feel as if I could have wished what happened to Mick."

"I'm certain you'd never have done anything of the kind. And if anyone had a reason to wish he'd sort himself out, you had."

"I think his wife might have had more of one. She doesn't seem too unhappy now he's gone."

"Then you've even less of a reason to feel bad."

They were in the dining-room of Stephanie's apartment. Under the paralysed tears of a chandelier the table had pulled in its midriff to accommodate just twice as many people as were dining. The hint of a chill kept surging through the window, outside which the park waved its trees. The walls bore menus that had amused Stephanie so much she'd had them framed, from a restaurant that offered Hot and Spicy Rabbi, a specialist in dishes from another Chinese region that apparently included Human Ribs, a French restaurant that promised Bee Bourgignon, which had prompted David to suggest that was why bees were disappearing... He didn't feel like finding any jokes now, but raised his glass of Rioja towards the casserole on the table. "And there's a reason why you should feel good."

It was one of her signature dishes, a Portuguese pork and bean stew to which she added herbs he'd never been able to guess. Having several signatures could suggest she had a hidden personality, an idea David supposed might occur to a writer, which meant it didn't appeal to him. As he dunked a chunk of her sourdough in his bowl she said "I hope Mrs Mick shares your enthusiasm."

"I'm sure she'll see your customers do when she opens up again. Does she really call herself Mrs Mick?"

"No, that's what I just did." Too late David saw that Stephanie had been trying to lighten the mood. "Her name's Rhoda Magee," she said. "We'll be staying closed until at least after the funeral. I'll have time to think up dishes for your stunt if you still want me to."

After dinner David cleared the table while Stephanie emptied the dishwasher. Once it was loaded she replenished David's glass and hers. "I may as well start thinking of your dishes," she said.

"You won't need me, will you?" His mind was elsewhere, and he needed to be. "I'll just walk off my dinner," he said. "So good I ate too much."

He gave her a quick kiss and then struggled into his fat unwieldy coat as he hurried along the hall. A piano on the ground floor accompanied his descent with a jolly variation on a sombre tune, which was interrupted by an electronic stutter as he let himself out of the house. He didn't look back until he was beneath the trees at the edge of the park. Although Stephanie's windows were curtained, he put more trees between him and the house before taking out his mobile. He thumbed the key to call a number in his contacts list and turned his back to the wind, which brought him a rumble of thunder – no, the sound of roller skates in the depths of the park. The trees overhead were growing frantic with the wind by the time his father said "Alan Botham."

"Hi, dad. It's David."

"David. It couldn't be anyone else."

"Why couldn't it?"

"Calling me that. There certainly couldn't be now." David's father sent away a hint of wistfulness by adding "Have you called to say you're coming to see us?"

"We will soon. I'll talk to Steph."

"Have a word with her now if you like."

"She isn't here just at the moment." In a bid to approach why he'd called David said "How are you both? How's work?"

"There are pressures. I'm sure you have them in your own job and Stephanie's. How is she getting on with that fellow at the restaurant?"

"She isn't any more." David was nervous of continuing until he thought to say "She said he had an accident. A fatal one."

"Well, I'm sorry to hear that, as I would be about anyone. How will it affect her?"

"We aren't sure yet. She's working on some recipes right now and she didn't want me in the way." However far this deviated from the truth, David hadn't time to care. "Speaking of accidents," he said, "I understand mother's client who we were talking about had one."

"Which client would that have been?"

"The one who attacked the policeman. The girl at work who knows about him said—"

"Let me apologise, David. I should have asked how life has been for you since your previous lady took the reins where you work."

"I can still do my job, that's what matters." David's effort to recall a name felt like drawing on someone else's memory. "Moorcroft, that's what he was called," he declared. "What happened to him?"

"As you say, he had an accident. I'm not sure what else you'd want to know."

"How bad was it?"

"How bad would you like it to have been? No, that's not fair to you. Blame the pressures I was mentioning. We know you're not that sort at all."

David felt unworthy of the observation. Before he could persist his father said "Sounds violent, I must say. Where exactly have you gone?"

"What do you mean, violent?" David had wandered down a side path in a vain attempt to avoid the gusts that were roaming the park. "What is?" he demanded.

"Whatever's there with you. Is it the wind?"

"That's what you'll be hearing. Anyway, what can you tell me about Moorcroft? My friend at work would like to know."

"You can assure her that he isn't likely to be a threat to anyone for quite some time."

"I will," David said and was afraid that his father might think this was all he wanted to know. "So what did happen to him?"

His father let out a sigh that contained a generous helping of patience. "He fell down an escalator not far from where you work."

"How did he, do we know?"

"From the top to the bottom." David couldn't tell how sardonic this was intended to be until his father said "It was quite a fall."

"No," David said and had to work on taking a breath, since the wind snatched half of it. "I meant what made him."

"Carelessness, if you believe someone who saw what he did."

"Who else is there to believe?"

"Well, precisely." As David parted his lips in frustration his father said "Not Mr Moorcroft, certainly."

"Why, what did he say?"

"Does it matter?" David was on the edge of admitting that it might when his father said "He insisted somebody was waiting at the top for him."

"Anybody," David said and was tempted to let the wind steal his words, "anybody in particular?"

"You really ought to ask Susan. He had her number on him when she was in town at the time. She stayed with him till the ambulance came, but she says he was making even less sense than usual."

"As you say, perhaps I'd better—"

"She thought at first he was saying he'd been lucky."

Perhaps it was just the chill wind that set David's teeth clacking. He managed to control his jaws so as to ask "What was he saying instead?"

"Something about someone else who was, as far as Susan could make out. And then he said – what was it, now? Do you really need me to wrack my brains like this, David?"

"I needn't trouble you with it if I can speak to mother."

"Just wait a moment." The pause was more than long enough for David's father to have handed her the phone, but the next voice that spoke was still his. "I remember now," he said. "She thought he must have been talking about himself this time. As far as she could make out he said someone had been clueless."

A shiver travelled through David's body before finding his mouth. Though it jerked most of the breath out of him he succeeded in asking "Could I have a word with her?"

"Not just now, David."

He felt childish for demanding "Why not?"

"She's lying down upstairs. As I said, there are pressures in this job.

She's under quite a few at present. Well, one in particular."

"I'm sorry," David said, not least in case she was worried about Moorcroft. "Can you say what it is?"

"Another difficult client. I do believe some of them are getting more so, unless it's our age creeping up on us." David's father seemed suddenly grateful to talk. "This one makes Mr Moorcroft seem as straightforward as you are, David."

David almost laughed, though it wouldn't have involved mirth. "Who is he? What's his problem?"

"We shouldn't give out names, you know. Still, if we can confide in anyone it's you. We know you won't be doing anything about it." Perhaps he took David's silence for confirmation, because he said "The name's Luther Payne and he lives up to the last part, believe me."

David felt as if he meant to emulate his parents by asking "Does he have any excuse?"

"Susan thinks so. His father's a headmaster and his mother runs the Blackomplishment arts festival. And she put on that exhibition of female Dadaists last year, the Mama show." As David wondered what kind of an excuse any of this was his father said "His parents stayed together till he went to university, and Susan thinks he blames himself for splitting them by growing up. It's her theory that he's trying to reverse that, being adolescent ten years after he should have been. She thinks he was too anxious to conform back then, too eager to impress them."

Trees bowed towards David as if they were intent on the conversation, and the wind brought a rumble of wheels out of the dark. "So what's he doing now?" David said.

"Taking every street drug as soon as it's invented. I very much doubt he knows what he's doing to himself any more. He hasn't had a job since he dropped out of university without finishing his degree. His parents seem to be competing to subsidise him whenever his benefits don't meet his needs."

"Then they should take all the responsibility for him, shouldn't they?"

"That's what I've told Susan, but she feels it's hers since he's her case. The real trouble is he's fixated on her and she blames herself for it. The way I see it, he's rebelling against her as if she's his mother. It's part of acting out his adolescence."

"You still aren't saying what he does."

"Maybe I've already said too much." In a moment David's father resigned himself to adding "He rings her up whenever he's at his worst on whatever he's taken, and half the time that's in the middle of the night. He knows she can't switch her phone off. I won't tell you the language he subjects her to or what he says about her. And when the drug's worn off he calls her again, so full of apologies it's embarrassing. They say that kind of drug isn't addictive, but it seems to me he's addicted to the personality it lets loose."

"Can't she have him stopped from calling?"

"She won't, David. The police know about it, but she'd have to bring a complaint. She won't even let me talk to him when he calls, because she thinks it would undermine their relationship she's built up. She won't admit how much all this is wearing her down."

David could hear it was having the same effect on his father. "Isn't there anything you can do?"

"I wish—" More audibly his father said "No, I mustn't say that. I shouldn't even think it."

"You can say anything to me, dad. You said so."

"She's made it clear I mustn't intervene. If I try she'll want nothing to do with me, and I don't believe she's exaggerating. Between ourselves and nobody else, David, I rather wish it could have been Payne on that escalator."

The admission dismayed David as much as anything he'd heard, and yet he felt as if another part of his mind had a secret response. "Look after her, dad," he urged. "Situations change, don't they? Maybe this one will."

"I'll do my best, and you do the same with your lady."

"I'll speak to her about visiting," David said and was reminded of Dent in hospital. He pocketed the mobile and was turning purposefully towards the dark when a skater hurtled at him, missing him by inches before racing up a slope and down the far side. "Fucking retard," he shouted, not necessarily at David. "Some stupid cunt standing on the path."

"I still am. I don't need to move." This felt more like a threat than anything David had ever previously said, but he didn't want to waste it on the skater. "Luther Payne," he murmured, "I know you can find him," and strode fast out of the dark.

CHAPTER TWENTY-ONE

"Why are you listening to that, David?"

He'd hoped the radio was on too low to waken Stephanie. He managed to find an innocent smile before he faced her. "Just for something," he said, "something to do while I'm making us coffee."

"Why the local station? You don't have it on normally."

"Maybe I'm not normal, then."

"I don't know anyone who's more so."

He could tell she was still puzzled, and he'd no sooner made up an explanation than he let it out. "That's why. Listen to the language."

The news bulletin had begun. The guvvament was gunner bring in a bill to help struggaling families, and a minister would be interviewed in the next ow-er. A mum accused of neglecting her chiyuld had been released on police bayil. Fiyer crews were dealing with a blaze at an oyil refinery. A leading athalete would be retiyering from sport next yee-ar. The overnight rayin was moving north to leave a cleyar but cold day for the region... That was the end of the news, and David switched it off before he realised how this might betray why he'd had the radio on. "I didn't know words bothered you so much," Stephanie said. "Maybe you're shaping up to be a writer after all. I'll have to watch my language."

"It's me that ought to. I need to stop my words getting away from me."

The gurgle of the percolator gave him an excuse to turn his back. Once he'd handed Stephanie a mug of coffee he took his to the bathroom. A version of himself came to meet him, though it didn't seem eager to look him in the eye. The shower felt harsh on his skin and yet remote, so that he found it hard to judge what temperature he could bear. He saw off most of a bowl of muesli topped with yoghurt to prevent Stephanie from wondering why he hadn't more of an appetite, which seemed to be somewhere else as well. "You aren't coming downtown with me, are you?" he said.

"Not unless you want me to talk Ms Randall through my dishes."

"You know where I am if you need me," David said and felt as though he was trying to reassure himself.

As he left the house the inert sunless morning fitted its chill to his hands like frozen gloves, to his face like an icy mask, but that wasn't why he shivered. What had he done last night? Had whatever he'd brought about happened yet? Had he made Newless more real? His doubts and fears had caught up with him while he'd lain in bed, afraid to stir in case Stephanie wasn't as asleep as she'd seemed. Could he take back the wish that he'd hardly even put into words? Wouldn't that be like wishing the worst for his mother instead? How could he be more concerned for her than for somebody he would never meet and, by the sound of it, wouldn't care to? How fearful did he need to be when Mick's fate had been so unlike the deranged account on the blog? But he didn't know what he'd set loose or might be responsible for, and the longer he waited to hear, the more nervously uncertain he was growing. Even if it wasn't on the news, his mother might have heard by now. He'd reached the bus stop, and he moved away from the queue to make a call. Surely it wasn't too early, and he only had to tell his mother that his father had left him anxious on her behalf.

She was waiting to answer, or at least her voice was – her detached voice. "Just seeing how you were," he had to say. "Give me a ring if there's any reason." A bus was approaching the stop, where several people had taken his place in the queue, and his sudden rage took him off guard until he controlled himself. He had to stand in the aisle and cling to a chilly pole as the bus lurched and swerved and abruptly halted, often for no reason he could see. The woman seated closest to him had a lapful of bags and a collapsed umbrella that kept poking his thigh. "That's all right," he heard himself keep saying, and wondered what Newless would have said.

People were already hawking magazines and distributing leaflets in the streets. They reminded him of his first encounter with Kinnear and his altercation with the man on the mobility scooter, but he had an uneasy notion that he should remember something else. Perhaps he preferred not to, because he made for work fast enough to leave the thought behind.

Andrea was filing brochures in the racks while Helen counted out foreign money customers had ordered. Bill and Emily were fixing holiday photographs to the wall behind the counter. David had forgotten that idea of Andrea's, and he could have thought her glance was convicting him of having let the firm down. When he returned from the staffroom, however, she said "I've had the list for the promotion."

"From Steph, you mean. Did she tell you about her manager?"

"All I've had from her are her ideas for food."

David found he had been hoping not to need to say "He died."

"Dear me." After a pause possibly intended to denote respect Andrea said "How will that affect the restaurant?"

"She doesn't know yet. If we'll be advertising it I expect that'll help."

"I'll need to speak to head office about that," Andrea said, having loosed a pointed cough. "They may not want to be associated with a business that's in trouble."

"Maybe Steph won't want to be involved if we don't push her and the restaurant."

"I hope she won't let us down after she undertook to help. It wouldn't reflect too well on you either, David."

He sensed how all his colleagues were pretending to be unaware of Andrea. It felt like a denial of animosity, so oppressive that it seemed to steal his breath. At least some customers had arrived to end the discussion, and he tried to concentrate on dealing with them. When he was able to retreat to the staffroom he checked the Newless blog, but the last posting was the one he'd previously read. Once again he felt there was something he ought to remember – and then he thought of the street preacher and Norville from the council. Might their inclusion in the blog imply they were in danger? He couldn't say when he had so little sense of how it worked.

The question and everything it revived in his mind brought him close to panic. As soon as Andrea sent him for lunch he grabbed his coat and hurried downhill, feeling watched. A childish sketch of a man blazed red to halt him at the foot of the hill, and he could hardly wait for its sibling to shine green before he dashed across the road. He was disconcerted to be able to recognise a voice somewhere ahead. It led him straight to the preacher, who was surrounded by a few spectators in the midst of the uninterested crowd. "Every one of us is a sinner," the man was assuring all those within earshot, "and the worst is he who says he has not sinned."

As David ventured closer the evangelist's discontented gaze found him. "Every one of us has sinned in thought, word and deed," he said like a greeting, and David felt provoked to argue, even if not aloud. He'd had none of the thoughts on the Newless blog, and he'd never used some of the words it did. He certainly hadn't committed any of the deeds it gloated over; in fact, he was here to forestall another of their kind. He took a step forward and held out a hand to the preacher. "Excuse me…"

"Only the Almighty may do that, my friend. Confess your sins to Him and pray for forgiveness."

The preacher had signified the sacred pronoun with a wheeze, and David struggled not to wonder how that might sound to someone else. "Could I have a word?"

"You may have God's. His is the only word that matters in this world or the next."

David advanced another step in the hope this would make him seem less like a heckler. "Don't think I'm being rude, but can you stop that for a moment? I need to talk to you."

"It is God we need to talk to, you and I and everybody on this earth. I am nothing but the way He spreads His word."

"Oh, for—" David barely managed to cut the phrase short. "When do you stop?" he said, which wasn't too deft either. "I mean, when do you take a break?"

"God takes no breaks, my friend, and none of us should from devoting our lives to His word."

"Look, just listen to me for your own sake. Try and hear what I'm actually saying. I—"

"The only word we need hear for our own sake is God's."

"Don't you know how unbearable you're being?" This seemed to reach the preacher – he pressed his thin lips paler, multiplying wrinkles on his greyish face – and David took the cue. "I wanted to tell you I think you've annoyed someone," he said, "and they could be dangerous."

"Anyone who is annoyed by God's word should examine their conscience."

"I don't know if he's got one." David's head was throbbing with frustration. "I'm telling you to watch out for him," he said.

"We should all watch out, my friend. Watch out for the traps God's adversary sets for us." The preacher had regained his poise and dealt himself some more as well. "How shall I know him?" he said as if he scarcely cared.

The question almost robbed David of words. "You will if you see him," he tried saying, "only then it might be too late."

"I think your friend is afraid to show his face."

"He's no friend of mine, and as for being afraid—"

"Then why has he sent you to speak for him?"

"He's done nothing of the kind. I'm trying to warn you, that's all."

"Don't waste your concern for me. Save it for your brother."

"He's not my brother," David said wildly, "any more than he's my friend. We aren't related at all."

"We are all brothers in the Lord. We are all children of God."

With a stare that might have been searching inside David for his soul the evangelist said "Why are you so anxious to deny him?"

"I'm not denying anything. I'm telling you the truth. I don't even know him. I only know about him."

"I think you know more than you care to admit, my friend. May I advise you on how to proceed?"

"I don't see how you can when you don't know the situation."

"Perhaps I see clearer than you, and God sees more clearly than any of us." Not unlike a farewell the preacher said "Do your best to take His word to whoever you have in mind, and perhaps it will be the salvation of you both."

David felt as if he had collided with an obstacle so unyielding that it left him numb with dullness. Even the spectators had lost interest and moved on. Or was one loitering nearby? When David glanced around he couldn't see any. "I wouldn't know where to find him," he was desperate to make plain. "I can't be responsible for him."

The preacher looked saddened but determined. "We are each of us responsible for our brethren."

"Then you can be responsible for him," David cried, "and you'll be responsible for whatever happens to you as well." He was afraid that the longer the man argued, the worse he might be bringing down upon himself. "I've done my best to warn you," he said, "don't throw that back at me," and dodged into the crowd without giving the evangelist time to respond.

Was there any point in trying to warn Norville when he'd found so little that he could say to the preacher? If he didn't try he would feel even more helpless. As he headed for the arcade where he'd encountered the official he heard the evangelist proclaim that the word was everywhere. Both sides of the arcade were lined with shops, and there was no sign of a council office. Beyond an avenue of plastic torsos raised on stalks in a boutique and dressed in items that came nowhere near covering them, a security guard as broad as several of the torsos was talking to a girl behind the till. He might know Norville, and David was making for him when an alarm began to bleep like the countdown of a bomb in a film. "That wasn't me, was it?" he called as it fell silent at his back.

The guard had turned his shaven head on its ruddy corrugated neck. "If it wasn't you it must have been the other feller."

Presumably this was a joke, since David saw nobody else near the entrance. "I've got nothing on me and this is who I am," he said, wagging his badge.

"We'll believe you," the guard said but peered at it. "Makes me think of my lad's nursery. Helps them remember who they are."

David wondered why the mention of a nursery should trouble him. As he concluded that it must remind him of when Lucky was conceived, the guard remarked "Like I said, the other feller must have set off the alarm."

David's suddenly dry mouth felt capable of closing up his throat. "Who?"

"Don't ask me. Nobody we're watching out for. I thought he was with you at first till he sloped off."

David swallowed in order to say "What did he look like?"

"Tell you the truth, I wish you hadn't asked me that." The guard fingered his pate as if he was feeling for his thoughts. "I should've got more of a look however fast he ran off," he said. "Maybe he didn't want me finding what he had on him."

With some relief but uneasily as well David said "So you can't say what he looked like at all."

"I might have mixed him up with you if I wasn't careful."

David found he didn't want to enquire any further, but he had to say "I'm trying to find someone who's involved with security round here. His name's Norville, and I was wondering—"

"He comes past here most days. Hang around and I expect you'll catch him."

"I have to be back at work soon. Can't you tell me where to find him?"

"Somewhere across town is my guess. Give the council a bell and they ought to hook you up." As David's resolve began to falter the guard said "Want me to pass on a message if I see him?"

"Somebody may be, may be after him."

"That'll be you, will it?"

"Not me at all. Nobody like me." With a sense of abandoning caution David said "A lot more like whoever set off your alarm."

"Him again, eh?" The guard gazed at David for an uncomfortable few seconds before saying "And what's this feller who's like him want with Larry Norville?"

"I think he may mean him some harm."

At once David was afraid he'd admitted too much. "Better say what else you know," the guard said.

"That's all I do. Just tell Mr Norville to be on his guard for anyone who looks suspicious."

"Hang on," the guard said and moved towards him. "You're not telling me you know that much and don't know any more."

"If you don't believe me I can't help it," David said, backing past the shiny half-clothed torsos. "Just make sure you tell him when you see him. It's your responsibility to tell him."

"Hang on," the guard repeated and tramped faster towards David, whose innards clenched as he retreated through the security arch. The alarm stayed dormant, but this didn't stay reassuring for long. When he looked back from the corner of the arcade he saw the guard watching him from outside the boutique. As David headed back to work he thought of calling Norville, and took out his phone to see there was still no message from his mother. He cared more about saving her than Norville or the preacher – and then he wondered if he could achieve all that simultaneously. For once he felt inspired enough to be a writer. "It's Payne you want," he murmured too low to be heard by anyone he could see in the crowded street. "Just Payne. Nobody but him."

CHAPTER TWENTY-TWO

"It's done, David."

He was nervous of learning what Andrea meant – what was in the official envelope that she pushed towards him under the currency window. "Is that for me?"

"It's for you to take, and I've left it open in case you have anything to say about it. I think it's appropriate for you to be involved."

It was addressed to Stephanie. Andrea had printed out the email with comments of her own. To Stephanie's six dishes she'd added half a dozen from other countries Frugogo offered. The food should be served from cartons, not plates. Bread for dips had to be hot. All the meat dishes needed vegetarian and vegan alternatives, and there must be no ingredients to which any member of the public could be allergic. "I'll leave it to Steph," David said.

"Whatever you think is advisable. I just thought you might like to speak up for once."

David took a breath that was meant to keep his words in, but it turned into several. "I expect you're trying to do the best job, and I can tell you Steph is. But she can do her talking for herself, and I don't want anyone to do it for me either."

"Well said, Dave," Bill muttered without looking at him, and David was aware that Emily and Helen were silently applauding. The counter hid their hands from Andrea, who said "I suppose I asked for that, but please don't make a habit of it."

David sensed that his colleagues thought this unfair and quite possibly aimed at them as well. He sealed the printout in the envelope and stowed it under the counter. Why was he feeling watched? When he glanced at Andrea she was busy on the computer. Surely nobody was spying on him through the window, where the faint outlines of words on the posters for holiday offers might almost have been striving to convey secrets in reverse: OWT ROF MOOR, DEDULCNI THGILF, GNIRETAC FLES, YCNAPUCCO ELBUOD... He logged on his terminal and was frowning at a tour operator's standard response to a complaint about a cruise – highest standards maintained, frequent hygiene checks, infection brought on board by passengers – when a movement at the window caught his attention. Eyes were peering at him over a poster that appeared to lend them an obscure caption, ENOG YLRAEN. Then the small man marched into the shop and up to the counter, where he leaned his large face at David as if his considerable eyebrows were weighing it down. "I'm told you have a message for me."

"Mr Norville, you didn't need—"

"Excuse me?" Andrea coughed and tapped just as shrilly on the currency window. "Are you the Mr Norville from the council?"

"I am, yes," Norville said and straightened up as if his identity required it. "And you will be..."

"Andrea Randall." Having locked the inner door behind her, she hurried to extend a hand. "I'm sorry if we weren't as professional as you have every right to expect, Mr Norville," she said. "We ought to have checked whether any permit was required."

Norville gave her hand two terse shakes. "I believe the matter has been settled to everybody's satisfaction."

"It was kind of you to let us have the permit and the one for our gastronomic promotion."

"I wasn't personally responsible, Ms Randall."

"You've been very kind all the same," Andrea said and indicated David with a frown. "Now I believe you wanted a word."

"Can we talk in private, Mr Norville? Andrea, if I could take him—"

"I haven't much time, Mr Botham."

"If it's anything to do with us," Andrea said, "I'd better hear it too."

"It hasn't, I promise you, so can't I just—"

"I've no idea what it has to do with," Norville said. "I'm told somebody is supposed to be threatening me, according to Mr Botham."

"You need to explain that, David," Andrea said, adding a cough like an exclamation mark.

"Someone," he told Norville and wished he could leave it at that. "Someone didn't like how you spoke to me in the street."

"I'm sorry if they objected to my doing the job I'm paid to do. Who might this person be?"

"I couldn't tell you. I've never seen them before."

"In that case what did they look like?"

"I can't tell you that either." David felt his tale was escaping his control. "Like someone you wouldn't notice if you passed them in the street," he said. "I'm sorry, I'm no good at describing people. I'm not a writer."

"They'd be on your security cameras, wouldn't they, Mr Norville?" Andrea said.

As David kept his doubts to himself Norville said "I don't know if they sound significant enough for anyone to bother. May I assume we're talking about a man?"

"A man, yes, and I think you should be bothered." David didn't know how much he might be about to reveal as he said "He was saying, you'll have to forgive me, he was saying he didn't like people like you, and he'd let a few of them know he didn't."

"Did he indeed." As Andrea's stare added weight to the comment Norville said "And what are we supposed to think happened to them?"

"I can't say." Fearing this sounded too much like an admission, David said "But I honestly got the feeling he was serious."

"Thank you, Mr Botham," Norville said as he might have addressed a subordinate. "I may have it looked into. We can do without people like that at large on our streets."

He strode in his small way to the door and opened it, only to hesitate. For a moment David thought he'd encountered someone coming in, but nobody seemed to be near. "Well, David," Andrea said and gave him time to wonder why. "I'd like to know what made you think that had nothing to do with us."

"Because it hadn't, and not with me either."

"It sounds as if this person was taking our side, but we don't want that kind of support. How many people will know what he said?"

"Not many," David said and realised he had no idea who might read Newless. "Maybe just me," he said and did his best to hope.

"So long as anyone who heard him won't associate him with us."

"He's never said anything that would," David assured her and then couldn't breathe for hearing the trick his words had played on him. "I mean," he managed to say, "he didn't and nobody could think so."

Her frown rose and then pinched her forehead again. "I must say it doesn't seem much like you, David."

"He isn't. Nothing like at all."

"No, I mean I'm surprised you got in touch with Mr Norville. What you said happened doesn't seem much of a reason."

"You didn't see him," David was forced to protest, "the person I was talking about."

"It sounds as if you hardly did. What was it about him that bothered you so much?"

"The words he used. The way I could tell he sees everyone." David felt too close to the truth to risk continuing along that route. "Anyway, it's like you said," he tried saying. "We don't want to be mixed up with anyone like him."

Her lingering frown used to mean that she expected him to tell her more and would return to the subject under discussion until he did. It kept hold of her brow as she went back to the currency desk. Perhaps that was why he kept feeling watched, even while he was dealing with customers. The impression was so distracting that when he left work he almost forgot to retrieve the envelope from the drawer in the counter.

On the bus he was joined by a woman who took up most of the

seat and overlapped on him as well. She wasn't so much clutching as squashing a shapeless canvas bag that sagged onto David's thigh. Despite all this she kept mumbling "Give us a bit of room." At least no skaters were to be heard in the park, though why should that concern him? As he climbed the stairs to Stephanie's apartment he heard muted voices singing a requiem. He couldn't help feeling anxious to shut it out, and the slam of the door brought Stephanie into the hall. "Has something come for me?" she said.

"I hope that's not what I seem like."

Her question had thrown him so badly that his response had no time to resemble a joke. He stayed nervous until she pointed at the envelope in his hand. "Didn't you pick that up downstairs?"

"No, it's from Andrea. I hope you like the messenger at least."

Stephanie halted between a Venetian sunset and a postcard of a rotund family scoffing at elephants whose shapes they shared. "Whatever she's saying, I don't know if I'll be able to provide," she said. "Rhoda's closed the restaurant till she sees her accountant. She isn't sure it's making enough to be worth her while."

She led the way into the living-room and held out her hand for the envelope as she sat on the edge of a chair. "Had you better look around for somewhere else?" David said.

"What do you think I've been doing all day?" Her response was sharp enough to stop him short of taking her hand. "I'm sorry, David," she said at once. "None of this is your fault. I can't imagine who could be less to blame."

She opened the envelope and greeted the contents with small noises increasingly like laughs chopped thin. "Well, this is ambitious. What facilities is she offering? The usual staffroom items?"

"Just a microwave and a hob."

"I can't do half of this anywhere like that, and quite a lot of it I can't transport from here. Do you want to see what she's expecting?"

"I already have, and I—"

Stephanie's hand drooped along with the page she was holding out. "You're saying you opened it."

"She left it open for me to say what I thought, but I said you should be the judge."

"I wonder what she thinks she's playing at. I'd say she needs an eye kept on her. I'll be putting my thoughts in an email. Don't worry," Stephanie said as if she'd sensed the unease he was trying to conceal. "I'll let you see before I send it. I won't be giving her any excuse to let you go."

That wasn't why David was nervous. He simply didn't like to think of someone watching Andrea, let alone imagine their motives. "I'll let you sort your thoughts out, then," he said. "I'll give my parents a call."

Just now the menus in the dining-room failed to amuse him with their words that had got out of control. He eased the door shut — no need for Stephanie to know he didn't mean to let her overhear — and took out his phone as he sat at the table. The bell in his ear seemed acutely shrill, as if the sound had been stretched thin as a nerve. He was close to willing it to stop by the time his father said "Alan Botham."

He sounded guarded if not wary. "How's the situation?" David said. "David." This might have been the answer until his father said "I'm glad it's you."

"I'd have called sooner but I didn't want to disturb you, either of you.

I thought you would have called me if there was a reason."

"I understand. You needn't blame yourself. I'm happy to hear from you now."

"It's the least I could do." None of this brought David any closer to the news he was anxious to hear. "So," he made himself say, "the situation. Has it changed at all?"

"It has, David."

David swallowed, but his mouth stayed dry. "For the better, I hope."

"You might like to think so."

"I'd more than like." David sat forward to brace himself for whatever he was about to hear, and between his elbows on the polished table an embryonic version of his face loomed up at him.

"Just to be certain," he said, "we're talking about Payne."

"There's been plenty of that for Susan."

Perhaps this was the best joke his father could manage just now, or could it be a misunderstanding? "Luther Payne," David said.

"That's the name of the reason."

"I'm sorry," David said despite having yet to learn what he might be responsible for.

"You're not alone."

"And mother isn't when you're there," David said in a bid to render the phrase less ominous. "So how are you saying the situation has changed?"

"Mr Payne has. I don't know if I'd say it was any improvement."

"Just as long as it is for my mother."

"That's what I'm doubting. She's no better for it. In fact I'm not sure she won't end up even worse."

"It won't last, will it?" David's surge of guilt was close to panic. "You'll help her get over it," he pleaded, "and we can."

"I don't see how." With a hint of exasperation that David didn't understand his father said "What are we talking about?"

"Whatever's happened to Payne."

"Nothing's happened to him."

David's mouth was parched again, but it was too soon to know why. "I thought you said he'd changed."

"He's done that all right. He's more insistent than ever."

David managed to restrain himself before too many words escaped. "But how…"

"He's taken to calling her in the daytime. He didn't call last night, but of course she didn't know he mightn't, and so she got no sleep to speak of. And there's no guarantee he won't revert to calling at all hours. Between ourselves, David, she's so exhausted that I'm worried she'll have an accident while she's driving."

David felt as if one brand of guilt had made space for a worse one — the sense of having failed his mother. Beyond that he was too confused to think, which was why he said "At least you're answering the phone now."

"It's her mobile he calls, but she'd probably have answered this one as well, except she fell asleep in her chair not five minutes ago."

"Let her sleep, then." David was so distracted he lowered his voice. "Will you let me know if anything changes?" he said. "I know we don't pray, but if we did I would."

"I'm afraid it doesn't work," his father said, adding a sound too short to incorporate mirth. "I've been giving it a try myself."

David said goodbye along with an attempt at optimism, and then he stared at the phone lying inert on the rudimentary image of his face, covering its indistinct mouth. How could his wish on his mother's behalf not have worked? If it was taking its time, why should that be? The delay was bringing back his doubts – if he'd been right to make the wish and how it could be carried out, not just the method but whether he could honestly believe anything of the kind would take place. Might the hindrance be that he'd never met Payne? After all, he'd encountered most of the people he was afraid to bring to mind. He was wondering if he could somehow contrive to meet his mother's tormentor – he was disturbed to find himself trying to think of a way – when Stephanie came into the room. "I've finished if you want to read it," she said. "How's everyone? Oh dear, as bad as that?"

"One of her cases is ruining her sleep. Not just her sleep, by the sound of it her life. I wouldn't usually wish anyone dead, but—"

"Don't say that, David. I know you don't mean it, but don't say it either."

David had been on the brink of the admission he was both desperate and afraid to make. "Don't be so sure I didn't mean it, Steph."

"Then I'd rather not hear if you don't mind. I've had enough death for a while."

"I'm sorry. I should have realised I was reminding you of Mick."

"Not just him."

David's throat seemed to shrink, and his voice came out pinched. "Who else?"

"Well, I didn't actually see." As he groped to clasp her hand if not grip it Stephanie said "It wasn't long after you went out this morning. I was in the shower when I heard something happen on the road, and when I looked the traffic was backed up all along it. I should have known it couldn't really have been you, but I didn't even think to phone." Her wince made him relax his grasp on her hand before she said "I went down and someone told me it was a skater. He must have been one of the boys we see in the park. The lady who saw it said he lost control somehow and went straight in front of a bus."

CHAPTER TWENTY-THREE

I can see him between the words. He's behind the counter, next to the girl whose small face looks scrubbed raw or at any rate too pink and the woman who keeps tilting her head as if she's tipping her chatter out of the bin of her mind. Beside her is the character who might be after a clown's job, given the grin that he can't seem to keep off his face. Beyond all of them is the woman with a big face squeezed to a point at the chin. She's behind a window that her customers have to stoop to speak through, which makes me think of visiting a prison or going to confession, not that I'll ever do either. When our hero stops clacking his keyboard and the door to the staff quarters shuts behind him I go into the shop.

Nobody notices me at the racks of holiday brochures. I don't know when I fell into the habit of trying to be unobtrusive, even though nobody sees me unless I want them to. I leaf through a brochure full of slim young items as glossy as the pages, posed on beaches or in front of mountains or by swimming pools as if they're waiting for a guide to help them get acquainted with the locations – to kick them into the water and shove their heads all the way down to the tiles, or drag their artificially enthusiastic faces and their throats over the sharpest rocks, or grind their mouths and noses into the sand for as long as they continue to twitch; a foot on the back of each head ought to do the trick. All this is lending me some energy, but the man who's left at the counter reminds me I'm here to observe. "Are you letting us into the secret yet?" he says.

He sounds as if he's leaving himself the option to pass this off as a joke. The woman at the money desk responds with a cough like the yip of the kind of little dog you'd like to trample on and snap its back. "I didn't know we had any secrets here."

"Who's going, I meant." More than ever like a joke if it needs to be one, Smirkmug says "Or did he just go?"

"You mustn't say that," young Blushpuss protests but adds a giggle like her simper rendered audible, not to say even more insufferable. "You wouldn't want him hearing."

"Nobody's listening but us," Cockhead says and cants her cranium. "We ought to talk while we can."

"Speak up, then," Yaphack says through the money window. "What would anybody like me to take into consideration?"

Apparently none of them is eager to go first. I'm about to answer, though nobody would hear, when Blushpuss risks asking "What would you like us to say?"

"I don't want anyone to think I'm unsympathetic to your preferences. The rest of us will have to work together, so I think it would be only fair if you all tell me who you'd choose to go."

"We're having a vote on it, you mean?" says Smirkmug. "You may see it that way if you wish."

"Then there's someone we aren't giving one," Smirkmug points out, though he hasn't stopped sounding amused.

"Of course he'll have it if he needs it. Perhaps he won't when he comes back."

I don't know if the silence means they're grasping Yaphack's implication or reluctant to commit themselves, and she sharpens her voice with a cough. "Has nobody anything to contribute?"

"Maybe he's got enough trouble in his life just now," Smirkmug says.

"May I ask what you're saying is trouble?"

"Mightn't his girlfriend be out of a job?" Presumably Smirkmug sees it's not enough just to let Yaphack know he wasn't talking about her, because he's in a hurry to add "He'll be worried and that's why he wasn't much use with your food idea."

"That's right, he was no use. Any other thoughts for me?"

As I wonder how many of them realise Smirkmug was simply pretending not to make our hero's chances worse, Cockhead says "Do you think she's why he's being argumentative?"

"With whom?"

"With you." In case ingratiating herself with Yaphack doesn't secure her job Cockhead says "And with people in the street when he was meant to be giving out your offers. You don't want him talking to customers like that."

Yaphack nods as if someone's yanked her chin down and then stares at Blushpuss. "We haven't heard from you yet."

"You don't mind working with him, do you?" Having let Yaphack take this how she likes, Blushpuss affects to find an issue too small to make a difference. "He hasn't put up any photos yet," she says. "He'll have a lot on his mind."

"He's not the only one, but some of us don't let it affect our work. Anything else any of you want me to take into account?"

Has Yaphack decided it's her choice after all, or does she want them to believe it wasn't theirs? "I think we've said enough," says Smirkmug.

"Is there anybody else I need to hear from?" When there's silence apart from a trumpet fumbling for a tune down the hill Yaphack says "Then that's settled, is it?"

"We don't have to vote," Smirkmug pretends to ask.

"I don't want to," Blushpuss says not at all as though she isn't voting, but can't stop her face from turning pinker.

"I'd miss either of you two," Cockhead makes sure Yaphack hears as well, "if someone has to move on."

"That's mutual, ladies," Smirkmug says and puts on a show of including Yaphack.

"You know I would, both of you." Blushpuss doesn't pause too long before adding "But I'd miss him too."

She doesn't know I saw her glance at Yaphack first to check that her opinion comes too late to make a difference. Perhaps she even thinks she's innocent; I'm sure she would insist she was. She'd be more than surprised if I grabbed her by the hair and knocked out her teeth on the edge of the counter. That would see off her artificial smile and bring some more red to her face, and mightn't her colleagues think she was doing it to herself? It amuses me to conjure up the frantic antics she'd perform, but I don't suppose I should risk drawing the attention of an audience. I stay by the racks, where I imagine the staff may have the vague impression of a customer they don't need to acknowledge. "Somebody's going to have to be missed," Yaphack says. "Please keep all this to yourselves. I'll need to speak to head office before I make the announcement."

Suppose I make it when our hero reappears? How would that work? For a moment that feels like losing all my substance I'm confused almost beyond words. What would happen if I wait for him to come out of the staffroom – if I try to speak to him? The prospect seems to paralyse me, and I feel in danger of growing no more perceptible to myself than I am to the hypocrites lined up behind the counter like targets in a fairground. Loathing them lets me feel present again, but I'm at a loss where to go until I see someone heading for the shop. I ought to know him.

CHAPTER TWENTY-FOUR

As he makes to open the door I put a name to him. He's about to cross the threshold when I block his way, and he steps back. "Look where you're going, chum," he says with no chumminess at all.

"I am."

"I want to get in there," he complains and then pokes his large sharp face at me like an animal peering out of its lair. "Hang on, though. You're not—"

"What aren't I? Or are you saying who?"

"For a second there I thought you were someone else."

I've shut the door and am standing with my back to it. "You mean somebody who works here."

"That's him," he says and peers harder at me. "You're not related, are you?"

"You could say that."

"Thought so." He shoves a hand out so abruptly that I can't tell whether he's offering a handshake or trying to clear me out of his way. "Met him at All Write," he says. "Maybe you've heard about me."

"All your fame has preceded you, definitely."

"Anyway, I'm here for him," he says, nodding at the door like a threat to butt me if I don't move.

"And me. He's not available just now."

Scrawlrat squints between two of the posters on the window. "How do you mean, not available?"

"Not here. I don't see him, do you?"

He doesn't, but I can't tell how much longer this will last, and I wonder what the staff inside are seeing through the window – just the customer they've lost? If he looks as if he's talking to himself, presumably they'll assume he's on a phone, unless they have a vague sense of a companion with him, too generalised an impression to deserve a second glance. Everybody is too brainless to notice more than that, and their stupidity is multiplied when they're a crowd, like the one that's all around us. "Anything I can pass on?" I say to Scrawlrat.

"Don't say that, chum, if you don't mind."

"Forgive me," I say without remotely meaning it, "what's the problem?"

"My old nan used to talk about passing on and she hasn't long done it herself."

"I expect you'll be visiting her soon, will you? I can see you must feel close." I arrange a sympathetic expression on my face, mostly to hide my amusement. "How would you like me to put it, then?" I say. "You give me the words. You're the writer."

"Give us a hint what you're on about, chum."

For somebody who calls himself a writer he seems to have too much trouble with language. "I'm asking what message you'd like me to pass on to him."

Have I antagonised Scrawlrat by using the phrase he was whining about? I'm preparing to feign remorse – it amuses me to try – when he says "Tell him I warned him."

"I didn't catch you."

When I gesture at the trumpeter, who may fancy his racket is jazz, Scrawlrat trudges grudgingly uphill. He can't be seen by anybody in the shop now. "I said," he complains, "I warned him."

"I should know what about, should I?"

"He told us a title he'd thought up when he came to All Write. I said he should watch out nobody stole it, and somebody did."

"You don't think it could have been him all the time."

"I can't believe he'd be the kind to write that stuff. There's some things you shouldn't ever say."

"That doesn't sound like a writer." Before Scrawlrat has time to feel insulted I say "So is that your message?"

"I came to tell him it's got worse, the blog. I've been keeping an eye on it since I told him."

"And what do you think you've been seeing?"

Scrawlrat stares at me. I'd be delighted to learn he's figured out more than I thought, but he says "It's got no ideas of its own for a start. It just pinches from the news."

"Originality's the name of the game, is it?"

"I don't like anyone that steals ideas. They're all we've got, us writers. They're our lives."

"You want to do away with whatever you dislike, do you? I know how you feel." I give him a look innocent enough for Blushpuss as I say "You couldn't be mistaken about the blog."

"How am I going to be that?"

"If it was there first."

I'd enjoy provoking his suspicions, but he only says "Tell you what, chum, you've got a weird mind."

"Aren't writers meant to have those?"

"Not that weird. You'd know what I mean if you saw the blog."

"By all means show me what's on your mind."

No doubt he takes my smile to underline the invitation, though in fact I'm fancying how it might feel to scoop out the contents of his skull through whichever orifice I could find or make. "My phone's at home charging," he complains. "Got yours?"

"I've never needed one. I'm electronic enough. You can show me on a computer."

"That's at home as well."

Scrawlrat's stare looks like the end of his words, but I say "Don't you think I should see what you want me to tell him about?"

The stare seems to begrudge Scrawlrat's answer. "You'd have to walk."

"I've learned to do that pretty well, you'll find."

"Funny with it, eh?" Scrawlrat says but doesn't laugh, and trudges uphill without looking back.

I could let him wonder where I've gone and surprise him with my reappearance, except there are questions I'd like to pursue. Once I'm alongside him he glances sideways as if at first he's not entirely certain what he's seeing. "So what do you think ought to be done?" I ask him.

"How do you mean, chum?"

"I'm asking what you think he ought to do."

Scrawlrat turns right opposite a church that has doffed its roof to God – it's as grey and empty as the sky – and heads towards Chinatown. "He'd better let folk know he's not mixed up with that thing online."

"How do you suggest he does that?"

"Come and tell them at All Write. They're the ones that heard his title."

"You aren't capable of telling them on his behalf."

"Len says we should all have our own voice. What's up with your brother?

Can't he talk for himself?"

For a moment I can't talk either, and I don't know why. It's too soon to do without words; there's more I mean to learn. "What are you saying he ought to deny?"

"All that stuff on the blog. It even went on about Mick Magee last week."

"Should I know the name?"

"Mick Magee." When repeating it brings him no acknowledgement Scrawlrat says "Don't you know your footie?"

"I'm interested in other games."

"Not much of a Scouser if you don't care about football." This seems to be the worst he can say about me. "He died the other night and that blog made out he suffered even more than he would have," he says in the same offended tone. "You'd think whoever it is had some sort of grudge."

"Would I? Do you think he might have had some reason?"

"No reason about it, chum. More like he's mad."

A Chinese family dodges past me on the pavement, and I wonder if they'd be unable to see me in any detail even if they weren't all busy chattering. "Angry, do you mean?" I suggest to Scrawlrat.

"Sick in the head. He even goes for people that are as mad as him. Some other head case fell down an escalator, and this twat seems to want to think he made him. Same as someone that collapsed in a loo at the pictures, and another one died in a lift at the station. Don't tell me he's got that many grudges. He'd need to have them against the whole world."

"What do you think is behind it, then?"

"Weren't you listening? I told you, he's got maggots upstairs. If you ask me the net's responsible for half his kind. Lets you say anything you like even if it's not worth saying and nobody with any sense would want to know."

I'm amused by how much this enrages me and by storing up my rage behind a smile. "So am I to believe you're a writer yourself?"

"Better had, chum. I am."

"Will I find you on the rack?"

"There's some shops stock me. Len at We're Still Left does for one. The big places, all they want is the big names their publishers pay to make big."

"Let's hope something adds to your fame quite soon." I indicate a porcelain Oriental cat that nods and nods in the window of the shop we're passing. "Perhaps that means your luck is on the way," I suggest. "Tell me something you're proud of."

His frown looks as if it's straining to squeeze a thought out of his brain. "I'm proud of quite a lot, chum."

"Give me a title, then."

"*Get Your Fortune Told Here.* That's my latest. Heard of it?"

"I don't think I've ever heard anything quite like it before. What might it be about?"

"A feller that's not happy in his job. He goes to a woman at a fair and she tells him three things that's going to happen to him."

"I expect you'd like to be able to see your future too. So what does she tell him?"

"There's somebody at work whose job he wants. She says he'll get it, and then he gets a text saying he has."

"Well, that's uncanny. Whatever else?"

"She says he'll get the supervisor's job on top of that, and when he goes to work that's what they give him."

"Someone isn't satisfied, though."

Scrawlrat scowls as if I've stolen his inspiration. "He tells his wife and she says he's worth better."

"Because the clairvoyant has promised that he'll have the boss's job."

"I said that, didn't I?" Scrawlrat searches my face, if he isn't searching for it, before admitting "Any road, she did."

"And what does the wife do about that?"

"Has the boss round for dinner and then she gets her feller to batter him to death on his way home. Only he makes it look like a druggie did it, and he kills them as well so they can't talk."

"That won't be the end of it, though."

"One of the fellers whose job he got starts to suspect, so he has to kill him. Then the wife goes mad with all the murdering, and then—" Scrawlrat glowers and says "You won't want to buy it if I tell you any more."

We're in sight of the arch at the entrance to Chinatown. Under the dull sky its multicoloured scales look dusty, and beyond it a tenement block faces a few restaurants. "Shall I tell you the rest?" I ask him.

"Think you can?" This sounds close to a challenge to a fight. "Go on, then," Scrawlrat says. "Give us a laugh."

"Our hero goes back to ask what's in store for him now. And the clairvoyant tells him he's completely safe unless, oh, let's say unless the trees in the park in front of his house start to walk about. Which is fine till the police start watching the house and using bushes for cover. They don't just hide behind them, they bring some and use them to creep up on the house. And she could tell him he's safe from anyone who's been born like a human. You'd feel safe if you thought that, wouldn't you? Only—"

I'm about to give him yet another hint when Scrawlrat says "How'd you know all that? You must have read my book."

"Perhaps it was a lucky guess. I could just be lucky. Perhaps that's my name."

"That's the sick bastard's name on that blog." For someone who thinks he's a writer Scrawlrat is dispiritingly deficient in imagination, and he confirms it by demanding "Is that what you're on about? Did you know about it all along?"

"You surely can't believe you're the only one who knows."

He grimaces as he strives to make me out, and then he glances around the deserted street in front of the tenements. "Are you trying to pretend you're him?"

"Now why do you imagine anyone would do that? Don't you think they would be afraid he'd come to find them?"

"If you're trying to put the wind up me, chum, you've no chance," Scrawlrat says and squeezes his eyes thin. "Hang about, though. Have you got his other name?"

"Does Newless sound familiar?"

"Sounds like something somebody made up when they couldn't come up with anything better. What's it meant to mean?"

"I really couldn't tell you if I cared to." I'm infuriated by the question, even if that's how I relish feeling. "Maybe I was new," I tell him, "but I'm the longest way from less."

Perhaps Scrawlrat sees I've stopped being playful, because he retreats towards the tenement block. "Stay away from me, whatever your name is," he says, raising his voice. "Come any closer and I'll be calling the law."

The empty concrete balconies send back his flattened shout. It seems to provoke an outburst of Chinese in one of the locked restaurants, but I can tell this sounds useless to him. As he hurries up the enclosed steps to the fourth floor of the tenements his echoes clatter after him. He may well imagine that's me, but there's no need. His keys are clanking in his hand before he's halfway up the steps. He jabs a key into the lock on a nondescript door, rattling the plastic number that dangles from a solitary screw. The single digit shakes again as if it's betraying the nervousness he tries to hide by slamming the door behind him.

The front room of his flat looks out on the balcony through a window smeared and spotted with old rain – at least, it peers through the unevenly skewed slats of a cheap venetian blind. Yesterday's clothes sprawl on a sagging couch, or perhaps they aren't even so recent an outfit. Beyond an open door to a perfunctory hall a kitchen bin gapes, unable to swallow a takeaway carton. Scrawlrat tramps to a table that squats in front of the couch. A laptop lies low on the table, next to a mug stained with dregs of coffee, which has printed circles like a disintegrating Olympic emblem on the dull wood. He plugs the laptop into the wall and sits in a chair, having cleared it of a book with his name and a borrowed photograph on the shiny cover. So much for his dislike of stealing material – apparently images at large online don't count – and I wonder if he reads anyone besides himself. Yes, he reads me, and I watch him plant the computer on his knees and bring my thoughts onscreen. Might it be diverting to watch him read about himself? The notion that he might see these very thoughts makes me feel as if I could be in two places at once. It's a disconcerting sensation, too much like losing substance, and so I step forward to show myself.

I come as such a shock that his entire body jerks as if he's been electrocuted, and the laptop crashes to the floor. "You," he cries, or perhaps it's the start of an insult until he finds his vocabulary doesn't run to any words sufficiently vicious. "Look what you've made me do."

Apparently the threat of damage to his creations on the computer distracts him from the larger situation. "It won't affect me," I assure him. "No great loss."

By now his position has caught up with him, and he blusters "How did you get in?"

"More easily than you. I was waiting by the time you did."

"I said what I'd do if you didn't stay clear," he declares and grabs his phone from the charger beside the chair. He must be clinging to his banal notion of the world – that all he has to do is call the police. His bravado doesn't convince either of us, and I only have to take another rapid step towards him to make him jerk from head to foot again, flinging the phone out of his slack hand. "Help," he cries as if the police may yet hear him and be capable of rescuing him. "He's got in."

His words aren't worth hearing – his range of language seems to be shrinking by the moment – but it amuses me to say "You'll be pleased to hear you've inspired me. Shall I tell you how?"

As I stoop to his computer he lurches at it, out of the chair. I wouldn't have counted on his being so predictable, but no doubt his kind are. I watch him grab the laptop to protect his tales, only to realise that it's still plugged in. I let him seize the plug and then close my hand around his, crushing the fingers and more than doubling his grip. "What are you—" he screams as the plastic splinters before shattering in his grasp. Now he's holding the metal prongs that he has tugged partly out of the socket, and even his resulting performance is trite – a mass of uncontrollable convulsive jerks that don't improve much on the ones I kept startling from him. I lean my face around his to watch him grimace and dribble and stretch his eyes wide as though he's straining to make out the contents of mine. "Nothing to see," I inform him, and soon there isn't in his, though not before I have to watch so many spasms they grow tedious. Once he slumps to the threadbare carpet and lies still, if not even sooner, I forget about him. He wasn't much more than a distraction. Someone else earned my attention before him.

CHAPTER TWENTY-FIVE

A convulsion that seemed to shake not just his entire body but the house around him wakened David. It felt like sensing someone too close to him in the dark. He had to find Stephanie next to him across the chilly mattress and put his arm around her before he could blink his eyes open. Nobody was visible beyond her in the room, which grudgingly began to gather dimness on its outlines, but was anyone behind him? He raised his unsteady head and twisted it around, having let go of Stephanie so as not to rouse her. The rest of the room appeared to be deserted too. Perhaps he had been wakened by nothing but a dream, which had already retreated into the depths of his mind. It wasn't why he slipped out of bed and sneaked out of the room.

He'd lain awake for hours, battling a compulsion to check his phone, before he'd drifted into an uneasy sleep. The urge hadn't even been rational. The phone had been switched on and within reach, but it had already been too late to expect a message from either of his parents – at least, unless his mother's state had grown much worse. As he crept downstairs he consulted the phone, but it was devoid of messages. Nevertheless he felt the situation had changed, and he made for the computer.

The cramped glow between the curtains let him cross the front room without switching on the light. As he switched on the laptop he found himself putting a wish if not a prayer almost into words. When he went online he saw that the computer was listing the Newless blog as a favourite place. It was the opposite, but he called it up at once and saw that a new fragment had been added to the list of opening sentences: I can see him... He was hoping he knew who that meant as he brought the entry onscreen.

He'd read just a few sentences when he began to feel he needed to remember how to breathe. "You bastard," he muttered, and "You shit" as well, but he grew mute and dry-mouthed less than halfway through the entry on the blog. Once he'd finished reading he stared at the screen until the last words on it began to flicker and crawl. The sun had started to hint at its presence behind Mrs Robbins' house by the time he heard Stephanie's footsteps overhead.

As he fumbled to shut the computer down she came to the top of the stairs. "Where are you, David?"

"Making us coffee," he called and saw the Newless blog hide in the dark of the screen.

"You don't sound as if you're there."

"I'm saying I'll make it now," David said from the hall and willed her not to wonder why he'd been in the front room.

"Let me. I've got more time than you while I'm off work."

He thought he'd satisfied her curiosity until they met on the stairs, where she said "You weren't calling your mother so early, were you?"

"I might have been thinking of it, but you're right. Best to let her catch up on her sleep if she can."

In the bathroom his reflection eyed him like a conspirator, and he felt like one who'd been kept in ignorance of far too much of the plot. The thin jabs of water from the shower made his mind feel separated from his body; he could hardly even judge the temperature on his skin. As he towelled his face roughly, hoping to rub it more awake, he saw his face keep peering over the towel in the mirror. It reminded him of a childish game played by somebody unable to grow up, and it seemed to parody his secretiveness as well.

Downstairs Stephanie met him with a mug of coffee and a remark she had plainly been waiting to make. "You're still worried about her, then. I knew there was something in the night."

"I tried not to disturb you."

"I know when something's wrong. I'll only wonder what it is

if you try to hide it." As David parted his lips despite having no idea what he might say, Stephanie protested "Is that all you want for breakfast?"

He'd hardly even been aware of taking an apple from the bowl, but he began to chop it up in a dish. "I don't want to be late for work," he said, only to wonder how he might behave there.

"I'll make us a good dinner while I'm waiting to hear from someone." Even this troubled his nerves. "Who?"

"Your boss or mine."

He doused the slivers of apple in yoghurt, from which they protruded like ribs. Surely only a writer would have found the resemblance significant, but it didn't help David to crunch the tart segments and swallow the flavourless fluid. As an excuse for leaving half of the concoction he said "I'd better go."

Stephanie waved at him from the front door as he climbed into his car. She shut the door when he reached the road, and at once, like a reflection that had grown unsynchronised, the front door opposite theirs swung open. Before David had time to accelerate, Mrs Robbins trotted to the pavement. "Mr Botham," she called.

He was tempted to floor the accelerator, but he halted by the kerb on her side of the road and watched her put on bulk in the mirror. As he lowered the passenger window he thought it best to say "I'm just off to work."

"Yes, I saw you being seen off, Mr Botham."

"Nobody's objecting, are they?"

"I'm sure nobody would dare."

For just an instant he wondered if she was afraid to antagonise him, since she was standing back some feet from the car. No doubt this let her look at him without having to stoop. "So what can I do for you?" David said.

"I thought you might have been to see me."

"I haven't." He was almost too unnerved to ask "What made you think I had?"

Her stare looked as if it was stressing the distance between them. "I said I thought you might."

"Why?" As he heard how offensive this sounded he grasped the answer to his own question. "Sorry, I meant—"

"If you visited Mr Dent as you said you would."

"I did go. He thanked you for asking after him."

"You talked to him, then. Someone who went yesterday said he didn't seem to know she was there."

"He certainly talked to me," David said without wanting to remember.

"He recognised you, did he? You must mean something special to him."

"I'm sure I don't," David said, which only made him feel more desperate. "Why would I?"

"I couldn't say, Mr Botham, but it sounds as if you must for him to know you. The lady who was there was told his brain is permanently damaged, and it's likely to get worse."

"I'm sorry. Sorry to hear it," David said at, he feared, unnecessary length.

"It's a great shame, but I suppose we'd have to say he did bring it on himself." As David tried not to think about that Mrs Robbins said "Do give him my best wishes when you see him."

"I don't think I will be." Her disappointed look drove him to add "Seeing him, I mean."

"You're the one he knows. He seems to count you as more of a friend than anybody else round here."

"Only because of his brain," David said and almost followed this with too much of the truth. "You ought to see if he remembers you. Now if you'll excuse me, I really need to be at work."

Soon enough she dwindled in the mirror and shrank around the corner that took him past Dent's house, but the guilt she'd bestowed on David travelled with him. "Brain damage," he heard himself muttering. "Happy with that? Think you've done enough?" That silenced him, but not for long. "Why don't you do what you're asked to?" he mumbled as he drove into the station car park. "You know who I mean. Payne's the name."

All of this felt too much like a denial, a ruse to avoid confronting what the Newless blog revealed about his workmates. Or was that as distorted a version of the truth as the account of his encounter with the evangelist and Norville had been, if not — as he surely hoped — more warped? On the station platform dead leaves like scraps of the past skittered around the feet of dozens of waiting commuters. A train was due in eight minutes, but as the digit on the matrix sign lost a number of segments he heard a tinny chant repeating the Frugogo slogan. When he pulled out the phone he saw that the call was from his mother.

At once he was nervous of being overheard. He hurried to the far end of the platform, which was deserted apart from a few sodden leaves that were struggling to crawl about beyond the station canopy. "I'm here," he said urgently. "Yes, it's me."

"I wasn't expecting anyone else." His mother sounded not far from amused, close enough to let him hope. "Well, you could have been one other person."

"Who?" Not quite in time to head off his disquiet David realised "Steph, you mean."

"I don't need to mean anyone but her, do I?"

"You know you don't." The exchange was working on David's nerves. "How are things?" he said, the most he seemed able to risk.

"They're fine so long as you both are."

"They are," David said, bracing himself for whatever he was about to hear. "So you—"

"I did say if you are. You shouldn't try to fool your mother, David."

"I'm not. There's nothing the matter with us."

"David," she said as she used to in his childhood. "You ought to have realised your father and I would find out what happened."

David was nervous of learning "What do you think has?"

"It was in the paper, David." Not much less like a reproof she said "I only wish we'd seen it sooner."

"Seen what?"

"Oh, David. Stephanie." As this brought him to the edge of panic his mother said "Finding her manager however she did."

"I didn't know she'd been in the paper. We didn't want to give you and dad any more to worry about, that's all."

"Can we stop yet?"

Even this bewildered David, not least by delaying the questions he needed to ask. "Can we stop what?"

"David." She sounded weary now. "Can your father and I stop wondering how Stephanie is," she said, "and her job."

His mother's voice had grown so flat he might almost have imagined she didn't want to know. "We're waiting to hear what will happen with the restaurant," David said. "But I've told you, we're both fine."

"If you say so, David. We've had enough death and damage."

"Why," he said and had to swallow, "who else?"

"Nobody. That's just what I'm saying. But I know you've been wishing there were."

For a moment David's mouth felt parched of words. "How do you know?"

"Because Alan said you felt the same as him. I understand why, but you mustn't. You don't know what it does."

"Maybe you don't and I do," David said, surely too low for his mother to hear. "We're talking about that client of yours," he needed to establish. "Luther Payne."

"Alan told you his name, did he? He shouldn't have, not even you."

"Nobody knows it from me." Of course this wasn't true, and could she tell? She'd fallen silent, and the only sound was a thin metallic whine that sounded as chill as the wind. It was creeping up on David – the reverberation of a train along the track – and he took an effortful breath. "What," he said, "what's happened to him?"

"Nothing has. Lord forgive me, I can hear how much you wish it had."

David felt worse than let down – hollow and deluded and inadequate. "Why forgive you?"

"Because I've got you and Alan worrying about me when it's my clients who matter."

"And you do. Dad told me how you've been losing your sleep."

"The doctor's given me something for that. But I won't blame Luther, and you mustn't either. Thinking you're wishing him ill doesn't help me at all."

"It sounds as if you're blaming me instead."

"Of course I'm not, you or your father. I just want you to realise how dreadful I'd feel if something bad happened to Luther and that was the way he stopped troubling me. Maybe you've forgotten I lost a client like that recently. Helping Luther take control of his life, that's how I want to finish with him."

The train was approaching with an elongated squeal of brakes. "Will you promise not to let it bother you any more?" David's mother said. "Otherwise I'll feel as if you don't think I'm professional enough to deal with him, and that's bound to keep me awake."

David had a sense of abandoning some responsibility as he said "If that's what you honestly want."

"I give you my word it is, David. I've lost quite enough in my life without feeling I've wished someone else away just for my own convenience."

David barely heard the last few words over the mouthless screech of brakes. All at once he had another question, but he couldn't ask it in the midst of the crowd that was piling into the nearest carriage. "I'll promise," he said as he found a seat, because he mustn't wish anything that might aggravate her condition. Even if he fell short of sharing her compassion, he could put Payne out of his mind. He had enough people to think of.

Who was the worst? Perhaps it was Andrea, who had waited until David was out of the way so as to encourage the others to decide they could do without him. Or perhaps in a sense they were even worse, and Emily most of all for pretending to sympathise with him. No, he mustn't give in to thinking like that; when had the blog ever told the truth? The trouble was that however exaggerated it might be, its ravings were versions of actual events. And how did that relate to Frank Cubbins, the man from All

Write? He was certainly persistent, and if he had indeed kept on reading the blog… Surely it contained nothing he would associate with David.

Those were only David's most coherent thoughts. He was distracted not just by spillage from his seatmate's headphones but by a sense of being watched. He couldn't see anyone doing so, and whenever he looked for the culprit he simply grew more aware of the underground darkness into which the train was bearing him. The impression of a watcher followed him off the train and up the escalators into the street, where the crowds under the introverted pallid sky might have been helping an observer to stay unseen. Even once he'd shut the door of the agency behind him David felt spied upon, but now Andrea was gazing at him across the counter. "You haven't brought anything, then," she said.

"I thought Steph emailed you."

"She has and I've told her what I think." After a pause that he could easily have taken as some kind of accusation Andrea said "The arrangements won't be satisfactory as they stand."

David would have responded more immediately if he hadn't been aware how Bill and Helen weren't looking at him. Neither was Emily, who wasn't with them behind the counter, nor at the currency desk. "And what does Steph say about that?" he retorted.

"She hasn't yet. I'm giving her the chance."

This angered him as much as his workmates' pretence of not listening. He wasn't far from saying so, but he only said "So what were you expecting me to bring?"

"The same as everybody else." With a pause that he suspected was meant to seem official Andrea said "Your photographs."

"I'll try and remember tonight. I've quite a lot else on my mind," David said and made for the staffroom. It was deserted, and the corridor between it and the shop was hollow with silence.

David dragged at his cuff, catching a nail on the segmented metal strap of his watch. He was only just in time for work, and Emily was always several minutes earlier. He fumbled to unzip his coat and felt as if he was struggling with a captor as he flung it off.

The scrawny hanger clanged against the walls of his locker in the corridor before he managed to capture it and hang up the coat. He slammed the lid of the upright man-sized box and hurried out to the counter. "Where's Emily?" he said, to get it over with.

Bill and Helen glanced up, but it was Andrea who said "She won't be with us."

All three of them were looking at him now. Even if he saw no condemnation in their eyes, he felt arrested by it, afraid to open his mouth again for fear of contradicting himself. He felt his tongue poke his lips apart and lick them before he could say "Why, what…"

His three judges seemed to be waiting for him to own up to more than that. Eventually Helen took some sort of pity on him. "Somebody else was here with us," she said, "and we didn't notice."

"Maybe she didn't," Bill said.

Andrea gave her head a curt shake, which didn't help David ask "Who?"

The word was scarcely audible, which might have been one reason why Andrea looked impatient. "She's found she's going to have a baby," she said not entirely unlike a complaint. "She'll be the one I'm letting go."

CHAPTER TWENTY-SIX

As soon as Andrea went for her break David made to ask the question. He waited until he heard the staffroom door shut and her cough beyond it, reassuring him that she wouldn't be back for at least a quarter of an hour. When he cleared his throat Helen leaned her head in his direction while Bill responded with the slightest heightening of his vague smile. David did his best not to let these traits distract him, however acutely aware of them the Newless blog had left him. "What were you—" he began just as somebody entered the shop.

He was an unhurried shambling man with a wide flat face and a profusion of windblown greyish hair, some of which spilled over the half of his coat collar he'd turned up. He gazed at the racks of brochures and then quite as indecisively at the staff behind the counter, and then emitted a sniff sharp enough for a question. "Can I help?" David said in the hope of dealing swiftly with him.

The man wandered none too directly over to him and sprawled in the chair opposite him. "Wife wants somewhere Italian," he complained. "Don't ask me why."

"I think I'll have to if we're going to fix you up."

"You tell me." The man paused long enough to seem to mean exactly that, and then he uttered another sniff. "She can get lots of it here," he said. "Prosecco and pasta and blahdiblahdiblah."

"Have you thought about Pompeii?" David said pretty well at random.

"Seen pictures," the man said with a fierce dismissive sniff. "Looked like a lot of walking and not much to see."

"You can take the same train from Naples to Herculaneum, and that's smaller."

"Even less to see, then. Anyway," the man said, which sounded like a farewell until he added "What else have you got?"

"I think your wife might like Rome."

"That's the colossal thingyo, isn't it? Where the lions ate all the Christians. We saw it in a show with Nero in. Don't need to see what's left of it now."

In some desperation, not least at how time was trundling onwards, David said "What about Pisa?"

"That's where the tower's tipped over. Don't see the point of it myself. Anyway," the man said but, despite a pause that he filled with a sniff, not as a goodbye. "She likes galleries as well. Pictures and sculptures and blahdiblahdiblah."

David felt his toes clench. "Rome has those, and Venice does."

"That's all the water, isn't it? Not my style. I get sick watching shows with the sea in," the man said, adding a sniff sufficiently liquid to represent sickness.

David's toenails had begun to scrape the insides of his shoes. "How about Florence, then?"

"That's the Romeo and Juliet place. Wherefore art thou Romeo and blahdi—"

"You'll be reminded of Shakespeare all over Italy." David managed to unclench his toes, having felt the nails start to bend away from them. "The world's his stage," he said like the writer he wasn't, only to recall Frank Cubbins' novel on the Newless blog.

"He's just old stuff even she's not got much time for. Anyway," the man said but didn't move. "She's into churches too. Not for all the blahdiblahdiblah and thingyo, just walking around for a look. Maybe she'd like Spain."

David lurched to his feet, wincing as his nails twinged. "Would you like some brochures to show her?"

"Might be a good plan at that. Should have said in the first place." Surely he was blaming himself, not David. He took the Spanish Splendours brochure David handed him, and Eternal Italy too. When David retreated behind the counter the man stayed at the racks, and David felt another minute shrinking. Eventually the man selected a Mediterranean Magnificence brochure and mumbled "Anyway" before ambling to the door. David wasn't sure if he should take the fellow's parting sniff as a comment on the service, and he hadn't time to wonder. "Well," Helen said, tilting her head in the direction of the door and raising an eyebrow towards it. "I won't mind if we've seen the last of him."

"He did seem a bit of a joke," Bill said without varying his smile.

"I'm glad I'm not the only one he bothered," David said as he glanced at his watch. He should have about five minutes, and he made haste to ask "Just while I think, what was someone saying about me yesterday?" While Bill and Helen didn't look at each other, he was sure they wanted to. Each seemed to be waiting for the other one to speak, but at last Helen said "Who was that, David?"

"Whoever was. Somebody here."

"When are we meant to be talking about?" Bill said. "When I wasn't here."

"You don't think we'd talk about you behind your back," Helen said more like an accuser than someone accused.

"She didn't put it like that." Having grown desperate enough to say that, David could only add "Emily said."

Surely they wouldn't check. He couldn't think of any other way to make them own up. At the end of another silence that felt like mute communication Helen glanced towards the staff quarters. "We were saying we thought Andrea wasn't being fair."

"What about?"

Bill twisted his smile wry. "About you, old chap."

"What was she saying?"

"Why, you know, David." When her gaze failed to convince him that he did Helen said "Making you take messages to your girlfriend. We wondered if she's jealous."

"Andrea, that is," Bill said, "but you mustn't let on we were saying."

"Weren't you all discussing who would have to leave?"

David saw guilt flickering in Helen's eyes as Bill said "It's not our fault you weren't here."

"Maybe it was Andrea's, but didn't you go along with it?"

"It wasn't like that, David." Defensively enough to sound resentful Helen said "We didn't realise it would mean that much to you."

"You didn't."

"She was going to tell you." Bill appeared to think this was some form of reassurance. "She just didn't get the chance."

"So you all left it to her even though you knew what was supposed to happen."

"I don't understand why you're so peeved," Helen objected. "You know about it now."

"I wonder when I would have if she hadn't had to change her mind."

Both of them looked bewildered, which infected David too. "Who did?" Bill said with an uncertain grin.

"Who else have we been talking about? The boss."

"Andrea?" Bill said while his grin grew surer of itself. "We meant Emily, old chap."

"We thought you were miffed because she didn't tell you her good news herself," Helen said, but then she gazed harder at David. "What were you really thinking? That we'd all decided you ought to be the one to go?"

"I thought maybe somebody did," David said and felt compelled to add "I'm sorry."

"I'm sorrier," Bill said as his grin sagged, though it seemed unable to desert him. "I didn't know you had that kind of opinion of us."

"I certainly don't think we've given you any reason," Helen said.

"I'm really sorry. I don't know what I can have been thinking of," David said and saw it fail to reach them. "I'm not saying it's an excuse, but I've got too much on my mind. We don't know whether Steph still has her job, and my mother isn't well because of how one of her cases is behaving."

However Helen might have responded, she looked away from him as they heard Andrea cough outside the staffroom. He was angered to see his colleagues turn to their work like schoolchildren who'd heard a teacher approaching, and even angrier to find himself trying to appear busy at his computer terminal. He was unhappy to have antagonised Bill and Helen but more concerned with the Newless blog. If it had so completely misrepresented the discussion about David, what did that tell him? Might Frank Cubbins be unharmed? The rest of the morning – the fifteen-minute waits for phones to be answered except by a machine, the intermittent stream of customers – felt like a series of cumbersome hindrances. He didn't have time to resent Andrea's briskness when she said "Will you go for lunch now, David."

The hanger clanged like an ominous bell as he grabbed his coat from the locker. He shoved his fists through the cumbersome sleeves on his way past the counter, not looking at Helen and Bill, since he couldn't decide on an expression to present to them. When he reached the street the chill that fitted itself to his face felt capable of turning his features into a mask. He clamped his lips together so as not to mutter to himself while he tried to think what to say to Cubbins – how much, or how little? "You've been reading someone's thoughts, have you? So long as you don't think you can read mine"…"You can see it isn't true. You wouldn't be here if it was"…"Did you have something to say to me, Mr Cubbins?"…"I believe you were looking for me"… Surely David needn't even prompt the man. He'd wait for Cubbins to speak first, he decided as he came in sight of the Chinatown arch.

At first he was thrown by how unstable the tall scaly gateway looked, and then he realised it was flickering with light. He might have imagined someone was using up fireworks left over from last month's new year celebrations, except that the flares were silent. Apprehensiveness let more of the March chill find him as he ventured to the arch. The flashing lights belonged to an ambulance parked outside a tenement block.

Two ambulance attendants were manoeuvring a stretcher laden

with a sheeted body down the enclosed steps from the fourth floor. David almost dodged out of sight and fled, but why couldn't he pass for a carelessly interested spectator? As he wavered, wondering how close he dared to go, a woman emerged from a flat on the second level and encountered the attendants on the steps. She spoke to them at length before hurrying ahead of them, and when she made for the arch David accosted her. "What's happened?" he said as casually as he could.

Had his tone offended her? By the time she spoke he'd begun to wonder if he should risk betraying an interest. "Someone's died," she said.

"Oh dear, I'm sorry." Surely most people would say something of the sort – it needn't betray any involvement – and he tried asking "A neighbour of yours?"

"Two floors up. We didn't know him that well."

"That's sad, isn't it, when people die and nobody remembers them."

In attempting to prompt her David seemed to have provoked her to retort "I didn't say we won't remember."

"I'm sure you will." With an effort that he strove to hide David said "What do you know about him, then?"

He almost neglected to add the last word and wasn't sure of its effect once he had. "He was supposed to be some kind of a writer," she said.

David found he'd been hoping not to hear anything of the kind, and couldn't tell how indifferent he managed to sound as he said "How did, do you know how he—"

"Electrocuted himself, they said, trying to plug in his computer. We're always having trouble with the electrics, us as well."

"You want to get that seen to before..." David scarcely knew whether he was trying to advise her or simply clutching at an explanation of the death that he would prefer to believe. The rationalisation trailed off, abandoning him with doubts and worse than doubts, and he was searching for a way to end the conversation when his mobile did it for him.

I go Fru-go-go, I go Fru-go-go... The attendants had shut their burden in the ambulance and were watching David through the arch. He flourished the phone and gave them an apologetic grimace, only to realise how closely the ringtone might be identifying him. "Excuse me," he told the woman, and was leaving Chinatown behind when a glance at the phone showed him his father's number.

He was seized by a feeling so violent that he couldn't have put it into words. He didn't even know how much of it was panic. He took such a breath that he was barely in time to head off his own answering message. "Yes, dad? Hello?"

"Ah, you are there after all. Hello, David." After too prolonged a pause for David's taste his father said "How's life treating you both?"

At least this didn't sound like the threat of any news, though David wasn't sure how he felt about that either. "We're getting along," he said. "Getting on with it, I mean."

"What's the latest on Stephanie's situation?"

"We're waiting to hear what will happen at Mick's."

"I'm sure none of us would have wished him to end up that way, but since he did I don't think it's wrong to hope she benefits from developments." As David held back a response his father said "Along those lines, perhaps you can stop thinking about Susan."

David halted opposite the roofless church, outside which several men were communing with a bottle of wine on the steps. "Why do you want me to do that?" he felt incautious for demanding.

"I just thought you might like to have a bit less on your mind."

"And you're saying that because..." Perhaps his father was waiting for him to finish, since David had to ask "Why are you saying?"

"Susan's client who was giving her so much trouble is no longer with us."

David trudged away from the remains of the church, whether in a bid to leave behind some of his thoughts or so that none of the crowd around him would have time to overhear much. "He's moved, you mean?"

"He's made his last move. Gone for good."

David had begun to feel watched, perhaps only because passers-by kept glancing at whatever expression had escaped onto his face. "What happened to him?"

"Apparently an overdose of the latest substance."

"I suppose we might have expected that sooner or later." David wondered if he could yield to relief, though not before he learned "How's mother coping?"

"She doesn't seem to feel as guilty as I was afraid she might. I believe she's starting to appreciate that it's given her more time to devote to her other clients. I hope you won't think any the less of her, but the issue that seems to be bothering her most is just an odd coincidence."

David couldn't have said why his mouth had grown parched. "Which one is that?"

"You may recall what I told you her other client said after he fell on the escalator. The drug Payne took, the medics understood him to be saying it was called Lucky, unless that was the name of whoever supplied it to him. The police are looking into both."

For an indeterminate length of time David was aware only of his own mind, and then he saw that he'd strayed back to the Frugogo agency. "Well, that's…" he said as he hurried past almost swiftly enough to outdistance his thoughts. "That's certainly a coincidence."

"That's all it can be, of course."

"Of course." David hardly heard the echo he'd become; he was remembering the question he'd failed to ask his mother as he boarded the train. "While we're talking," he blurted, "I know this may not be the best time to bring it up, but it's been on my mind. Did I nearly have a brother once?"

The silence felt like being scrutinised, and not only by his father. He was peering at the crowd without managing to identify a watcher when his father said "What made you think that, David?"

"I don't know if I remember. I've got the idea that you and

mother may have talked about it when you thought I was too young to understand."

"We wouldn't have done anything like that if we'd thought you could hear. I was asking what made you think of it now."

"The last time I spoke to mother..." At least he didn't have to mention the Newless blog. "She talked about wishing somebody away," David said. "It nearly reminded me, but I didn't want to bother her while she was upset. So was I ever going to have a brother?"

He heard his father take a breath and let it loose. "We don't know what we would have had."

"What don't you know?"

"It was before Susan had you, David. You were wanted, trust me. Wanted twice as much because of what we'd agreed we had to do the other time. That wasn't planned, that's to say they weren't. You very assuredly were."

"But you're saying you got rid of whoever they would have been."

"If you want to put it that way I'm afraid so. We'd just bought our first house and furnished it, and we couldn't afford for Susan to take so much time off work. You'll remember she took years off for you till you were in school. Don't raise any of this with her, will you? It preyed on her mind for quite some time."

David was attempting to reassure himself by saying "Even though it wasn't developed enough for anyone to tell its sex."

"We could have found that out. We just didn't want to. I'm afraid we put the intervention off longer than we really ought to have, and that upset Susan even more. Between ourselves, I blame myself for not insisting."

David could have felt that someone else was using him to ask "Did you ever start thinking of names?"

"Heaven forbid. It was lucky we didn't. We'd have felt even worse." His father sighed and said "At least you can learn by our example. Never create a life unless you're sure you want it to live."

"That's good advice," David said, only to feel it came too late for him. He had to promise not to mention their discussion to his mother before his father was willing to end the call. He stumbled to a halt at the bottom of the hill while he tried to sort out at least some of his thoughts. Everything around him – the swarms of people, the dogged routine of the traffic lights, an amplified voice announcing bargains from inside a shop, a trumpet poking none too tunefully at a tune – seemed to merge into a vast distraction, but he couldn't use that as an excuse for neglecting to confirm what he was afraid he knew.

As soon as he brought up the Newless blog on his phone he saw there was a new addition to the list of first lines. He touched it with a fingertip that left an apprehensive mark on the screen, and once the entry appeared he didn't have to read much. Still after drugs to show you things you've never seen before? I'll show you something not many people have seen, and they aren't around to tell you about it. Maybe you'll think it isn't real, but won't you be surprised. It's me… When the phone shook in his hand David thought he'd started trembling, but someone was calling the mobile. As he raised it to his face he saw Stephanie's number.

CHAPTER TWENTY-SEVEN

Once he'd taken his place between Bill and Helen at the counter David said "The restaurant won't be opening again. Steph's lost her job."

Helen tilted her head as if she hoped to catch some words he'd left unspoken. "I'm sorry for her, then."

Bill seemed more forgiving, or at any rate his pained grin did. "No wonder you were bothered about jobs."

"Even so," Helen said and then to some extent relented. "She'll find somewhere else with her reputation, won't she? And helping out with our promotion will advertise her as well."

"It might." David felt desperate to focus on whatever he could still regard as normal in his life. Andrea was busy with a queue at the currency desk, but the last of her customers wasn't out of the shop when David asked her "Have you heard from Steph?"

"Yes."

"Today, I mean."

"Yes."

Though her tone scarcely invited a response, he wasn't to be put off saying "Will you be—"

"She'll have my decision in good time."

Surely his persistence wouldn't affect it – surely he wouldn't cause yet another result he'd never intended. He would have made a wish on Stephanie's behalf if he'd known how. Of everything he'd learned today he was most concerned about her situation, perhaps because it was the easiest to think about, the most mundane. Besides, what could he do with the rest of the information he'd gained? If he'd turned out to have a brother in some unnatural sense, it didn't make him feel that the other was related to him in any meaningful way; in fact it seemed to prove how separate they were. He'd once conjured up a wicked childhood playmate that he'd revived as a surrogate teenage rebel, and even if his imaginary companion had managed to return in some form, the other appeared hardly to have grown up. His thoughts weren't David's, and David had so little control over him that he surely needn't feel responsible. The way Luther Payne's fate – the only intervention David could recall wishing for – had been deferred seemed to show how independent the culprit was. Could the delay have been meant to demonstrate as much? That seemed almost unreasonably reassuring, since it meant that none of the deaths was David's fault. He couldn't direct events for good or ill, and he found he was able to put them out of his mind and concentrate on work.

On his way to Stephanie's that night he saw nobody who looked familiar. Suppose searching for someone he preferred not to name could attract the other? He didn't think he felt watched, and it seemed better not to search the crowd on the bus or in the streets for a face he might realise he knew. As he let himself into Stephanie's building a flimsy obstruction hindered him – some mail behind the door. He had time to hope it had brought her some good news, but the crumpled papers were menus from takeaways on the main road, the Eager Vegan and Plato Potato, the Greek vegetarian. A premature song about summer fell away below him on the stairs, and when he unlocked the apartment door several Indian aromas met him. "You've been busy," he called, having almost said "I'm home."

Stephanie came out of the kitchen, wiping her hands on a cloth she stowed in a pocket of her apron that said STEF THE CHEF. At the time he had been pleased that she'd liked it so much, but now having had it customised for her seemed like a feeble bid to play the writer. "I said when you went out I'd try and make it special," she said.

"You're that all by yourself."

"No more than you are, David."

He didn't need to hear a surreptitious inadvertent meaning in her words. He followed her into the kitchen, where several steel casseroles were spicing the air. "Shall I pop a bottle?" he said.

As he slid a Merlot out of the rack Stephanie said "We aren't celebrating, are we?"

"We can if you like. Andrea's made her decision."

"She's sent you with it, has she? I wouldn't call that too professional."

"Who we're doing without, I mean. Emily's pregnant, so it's her."

"David, I'm a bitch." Stephanie touched his arm as he levered the cork free. "Thinking of nobody except myself," she said, "when it could have been your job."

"You're nothing of the kind. If anybody is we both know who. She hasn't been in touch, then."

"I expect she'll find the time for me when she gets around to it," Stephanie said and raised the glass he handed her. "Here's to your hidden benefactor."

David's glass stopped short of clinking against hers. "Who do you mean?"

"Emily's baby. Who else could I mean?"

He opened his mouth, only to feel as though his words had been snatched out of reach. "There's more, isn't there?" Stephanie said. "You seem as if your mind's somewhere else."

"Well, it's not. It's here with you." David downed a mouthful as an aid to saying "I did speak to my father. The case that was wearing my mother down, he's dead of an overdose. At least now she can concentrate on the clients she's got left."

"That has to be good, hasn't it?" When David could only nod Stephanie said "Was that all?"

For an unhelpful moment David was reminded how Andrea would interrogate him on matters he'd found too trivial for words. "All what?"

Stephanie gave him a look that declared her patience. "All that you have on your mind, David."

"My father—" David took a breath that had to emerge as a response. "He said I could have had a brother."

"David." Stephanie planted her glass on the table so as to take his hand in both of hers. "Why is he telling you that now?"

"Because I asked. I told him I thought I remembered him and mother talking about it when I was very young."

"Emily's reminded you." Before David could deny this Stephanie said "Was he born?"

"They couldn't afford it, Steph."

"I don't think I could ever have a termination. It would be like denying I'd made a life." She let go of his hand and retrieved her glass. "He must have developed quite a bit," she said, "for them to know he was a boy."

"I said my father said he could have been." David felt as if too many of his words had been not just stolen from him but borne out of reach by the thief. "And I thought he was," he managed to pronounce. "I'll tell you what else I think. He was my imaginary playmate."

"Oh, David, that's so—" Stephanie clasped his hand again. "You heard Susan and Alan talking about him," she said, "and you tried to wish him alive."

"No." David felt as if Stephanie was helping the thief of his words prevent him from uttering the truth. "I told my father I heard them, but—"

He wasn't sure which interruption came first: the jaunty scrap of Mozart her mobile emitted or the failure of his voice. Stephanie let go of him to retrieve the phone from its perch on the spice rack, where presumably coincidence rather than her sense of order had placed it between jars of mint and nutmeg. "I don't know who this is," she said, having frowned at the screen.

Surely nobody was calling to keep David quiet, but he experienced a twinge of panic. "Better find out."

"I'm about to. Hello?"

She didn't mean the last word as a rebuke to him, David told himself. It was a usage he loathed. She listened and widened her eyes without letting an expression into them as she said "I'll just put this down, Andrea. I'll be able to hear you, but I'm in the middle of making dinner."

She amplified the sound in time for David to hear Andrea say "For yourself and David, you mean."

"Who else do you think I could have?"

"You might have had our promotion in mind."

"I wouldn't call that dinner," Stephanie said and gave the largest casserole a stir. "Depending when you need me, I may have more time."

"Yes, David told me your restaurant has shut down. Since you put your number in your email I thought it best to call."

"He's keeping you informed about me, is he? I suppose he must have used to tell you everything." Before David could answer this, not that he felt invited to, Stephanie said "Since I'm between jobs except for yours I'll do all I can."

Andrea sent her a cough sharp enough for the tone of an incoming message. "Unfortunately that isn't my decision."

"Whose is it, then?"

"I assure you it's very much mine." Andrea gave this some moments to gather authority and said "I was saying I'm afraid I haven't been able to decide in your favour."

As Stephanie parted her lips without shaping a word David demanded "Why not?"

"Oh, are you actually there, David? I did wonder when you've been so quiet about it. Anyway, I was speaking to Stephanie." Andrea indicated with a cough that she'd finished talking to him and said "Part of my scheme was mutual advertising, and sadly you're in no position to offer that any longer."

"You'd be advertising Steph," David protested. "You'd be helping her."

"I have to show head office something I believe in so they will. I'm very much afraid we can't afford to be a charity these days."

As David thought she was by no means sufficiently afraid, Stephanie said "When are you planning your promotion? Perhaps

I'll be with another restaurant by then."

"That won't matter, I'm afraid. I've already made alternative arrangements. Rex, no doubt David will tell you who he is if you've any need to know, Rex has put me in touch with one of the businesses he handles advertising for. I really should have gone to him in the first place."

David saw Stephanie restrain herself on his behalf as she said "It's been an education working with you, Andrea."

"I wouldn't have said that was work," Andrea retorted, and then Stephanie ended the call.

"Rex is my replacement. They deserve each other." As Stephanie took quite a long drink David said "As you say, what a bitch, and a cunt as well."

"I don't use that word, David, and I didn't think you did." Stephanie abandoned her disapproval to say "At least she's given me more time to find a job."

"You oughtn't to need much. Everyone with restaurants should know how good you are."

"We'd better see how good that is," Stephanie said and headed for the cooker.

"I'll be back in a minute to help." David hurried to the bathroom, where he watched his face grow furious in the mirror. "You haven't fixed it for Steph yet," he muttered fiercely. "Do whatever you have to do."

CHAPTER TWENTY-EIGHT

He wasn't late for work, David reminded himself. Bill and Helen were earlier, that was all. They weren't in a competition, or even if his colleagues thought they were, he didn't need to join in. Stephanie's job was the problem, not his. Bill's grin as he came to let David in was meant as a welcome rather than hinting at triumph. David didn't need to impress Andrea with his commitment to the company, at least not by turning up earlier still. Besides, she was nowhere to be seen.

He didn't know why that made him feel guilty. How could her absence help Stephanie? Surely he needn't be afraid to learn why she wasn't there — and then he realised that she had to be; otherwise Bill and Helen wouldn't have been able to get in. As Bill twisted the latch David saw the door to the staff quarters swing open beyond him. It was indeed Andrea who appeared, but she didn't shut the door at once. Having followed her, Emily did.

David felt as if the chill of the day had seized him by the guts. The noises of the street — the crowd's murmur blurred beyond words, the wheezing wail of an accordion, a shout too distant to be comprehensible — seemed to recede from him, isolating him at the core of himself. He was close to fleeing, not least because he didn't understand why the sight of Emily should disturb him so much. He'd only managed to shiver from head to foot by the time Bill opened the door. "What's up, old chap?"

Nodding at Emily felt like butting an insubstantial opponent, though David had never butted anyone in his life. "Just wasn't expecting to see…"

"Not much to see at the present. Oh, the girl herself, you mean."

As David ventured into the shop Andrea asked him "What weren't you expecting?"

"I thought Emily had left us."

"She still has her notice to work off." Andrea wasn't alone in gazing at him. "Don't worry, she hasn't taken your job."

"I didn't think she had," David said, which failed to explain why Emily's presence troubled him. "I wasn't trying to get rid of you, Emily."

"I wouldn't ever have thought you were."

"While we're on the subject," Helen said, "maybe you wouldn't mind telling David we weren't trying to get rid of him."

"I should think we weren't. Who said we were?"

"I'm rather afraid David said you did."

"That isn't what I said at all." David hardly knew what his panic was making him say. "Anyway," he declared, "I was mistaken."

"Just so long as you know you were," Helen said.

Emily looked puzzled, and David could only pray with no audience in mind that she wouldn't seek an explanation. In the corridor behind the scenes the hanger jangled against the back of the locker, and the thin shrill sound might have been giving voice to his nerves. Surely now that he knew why he'd found Emily's presence threatening he ought to be able to stop feeling anxious, or was there another reason to be apprehensive? Suppose the Newless blog had told more of the truth than he wanted to recognise about his workmates, whatever they said to his face? It hadn't been too inaccurate about Cubbins and Payne, after all. Just the same, he didn't think this was the source of his foreboding, which distracted him so much that he almost forgot to retrieve the envelope from one capacious pocket. When he returned to the shop he couldn't tell whether the others had been discussing him. He took the photographs out of the envelope and flourished them at Andrea. "See, I remembered," he said and immediately felt there was something else that it was crucial to recall.

She watched him fasten the first of the photographs to the wall behind the counter. "I didn't realise you'd been to Switzerland."

"You know I was at Steph's last night. I didn't want to let you down again, so I borrowed these."

"I've no idea where you were, David, and no interest. Are you in any of the photographs?"

"We haven't been away together yet. She isn't in them either."

"The idea is to show where we've been. That means letting people see us there, not hiding. You can help in another way instead."

She stared at the Swiss image until he returned it to the envelope, and then he had to ask "What way?"

"Rex will be here to advise about the promotion, but you can represent us on the street. I'm sure we can expect you to do better out there than last time."

Was she really obliging him to work with her boyfriend? The silence of his colleagues felt close to palpable, the unspoken growing solid. He couldn't separate it from a sense of being spied upon, but whenever he glanced towards the street he was unable to locate a watcher. He was trying to concentrate on working at his terminal, though even this put him in mind of the Newless blog, when Bill said "Here's the man himself."

Rex was backing uphill outside the window, holding up his hands to ward off a threat. David's head began to throb as if the sight had set off an alarm inside his skull, and then he was confused to see Rex beckon the menace. He let out a breath when he saw that Rex was guiding a van. The Indian driver looked impatient with the guidance. As the van inched up the pedestrianised slope, words on its side came into view. It belonged to ALI AND ALEXI'S GLOBAL GRUB, apparently the WORLD'S BEST SITDOWN MEDITERRANEAN EUROPEAN ASIAN BUFFET RESTAURANT. David might have laughed on Stephanie's behalf, though not with much amusement, but managed to restrain himself even when Bill read out the slogan on the van. "More tastes than we've got a name for. Sounds a bit kinky to me."

Andrea stared at him before informing him "Rex created that and he's had no complaints."

There was silence while Bill struggled to rescind his grin. As the driver set about unloading the van and Rex bustled bulkily around him, still stockier for a quilted overcoat, David turned back to his computer. He was aware that Rex was helping the driver erect a pair of trestle tables outside the window – miming the action, at any rate. Hot plates came next, and as the driver loaded them with foods Rex trotted into the shop. "Who'll be outside with me?"

"I'm told I am."

"David, isn't it?" Rex said, glancing at the badge as if to make sure. "Better pin that on your coat so people know who you're meant to be."

The jangle of the hanger seemed to resound inside David's skull. He zipped up his jacket and poked the pin through the hole in the tag of the zipper, where the badge dealt his chest a peremptory tap with every step he took. It felt like an attempt to remind him what he still needed to remember. As he tramped back to the counter Rex said "Here's some slogans for you to say out there. Taste the world and a world of tastes."

"They don't really sell our business, do they?"

"If you've any better ideas I'm sure Andy will listen."

David waited for her to object to the name, but her only response was a curt cough. "How about..." he said, which simply revived how he'd felt when Darius Hall had badgered him for a title. As soon as a phrase fell together in his brain he said "Taste our holidays."

"I think that's better," Emily said and folded her hands over her rounded midriff.

"It'd bring me in," Bill said, and Helen added a nod. "Say what you're comfortable with," Andrea said.

"Pipe up if you prefer his, Andy," Rex said. "You know I'm not bothered by competition. It's my meat and my bread and butter."

David couldn't help wondering what Newless would think of all this – the petty hostilities, the unadmitted alliances, the grotesque pinched triviality of the entire confrontation. Presumably Andrea meant to terminate it as well as exhibit her authority by saying "I think it's time for you to go to work, David."

Rex held the door open just long enough to make David hurry to it. The driver set out stacks of paper plates inscribed with the name of the eatery and embraced Rex before driving uphill. Passers-by were glancing at the tables, and David swung his upturned hand towards the food. "Taste our holidays."

"You want to speak up a bit more," Rex advised him not nearly quietly enough.

"Taste our holidays." Raising his voice gained David a nod of approval that he tried not to find condescending. At least he'd enticed several customers, who loaded plates with a dinner's worth of food. "We can send you where those come from," he said.

"They do good nosh at Ali's," a diner assured him.

"No, I mean the countries," David said, but she and her fellow gluttons were on their way downhill. "Taste our holidays," he called and saw Rex shake his head along with an equally imperative finger. "What's wrong now?"

"Take it to your public. Just let them have a taste that'll leave them hungry for the rest you've got for them."

David had a sense that someone was watching with more than ordinary interest – that Rex's behaviour was attracting a kind of attention Rex wouldn't like. "Here," Rex said too much in the manner of a summons, and spent time artfully arranging items on the quarters of a paper plate – seekh kebabs, dim sum, chorizo in wine, Greek village sausages that only the name tag in front of the hot plate distinguished from frankfurters. "You need to make a veggie selection," he said.

David put together a plateful of onion bhajis and halloumi cheese, along with patatas bravas and Chinese spring onion pancakes. He was making to offer it to the public when Rex said "You've got two hands, haven't you? Give the people the whole package."

"And what will you be doing?"

"I'm just here to optimise the campaign. It's your identity that counts."

"Which one is that?" David said and was uneasy that he had.

"You're the man with the badge," Rex said and scrutinised David's face. "Say if you want me to take over. Better ask Andy first, though."

"I had the impression she'll do as you tell her."

"Yes, but we're talking about you, Davey. You had your chance, and it sounds like you never found your inner man."

At least taking the second plate let David turn away from the pale smug pudgy face under its calculatedly unkempt shock of red hair, and from his impulse to punch it softer still. He found he was searching the crowd in the street, and was unnerved to feel he might be inviting someone, but could see nobody who lived up to his nervousness. As he held up the flimsy plates, the edges of which had begun to flutter in the wind, he felt like a figure wielding a pair of scales – a caricature of justice. "Taste our holidays," he called and saw someone veer towards him.

He might have welcomed the approach if he hadn't recognised the sharp face taut with purpose, the greying hair that trailed various lengths over the tweed collar. "Still shouting in the street?" Len Kinnear said.

"I seem to whenever you're about." David's panic was back, and gave him little chance to think. "Taste our holidays," he said somewhere between calling out and quoting.

"Hope you didn't spend much time thinking that up."

"Not too much, but why are you saying that?"

"You're wasting yourself. Do a day job if you've got to pay the rent but keep your words out of it. They're for telling the truth with."

"I wonder how you think David could do his job without them," Rex said.

"You're the chef, are you?" Kinnear hardly seemed to want to know. "I'm a partner in Merseyside Publicity Solutions." Not much less haughtily Rex added "But I'd be proud to be the chef."

"I'm guessing he's a client of yours." Before Rex could do more than protrude his lips Kinnear said "All I'm saying is you should hear David when he gets mad. You'd think he was a different man."

"Just not a better one," David said.

"Don't deny yourself, mate. David Botham," Kinnear said as if David needed to be reminded who he was. "I'll be looking for your name. You've got too much inside you not to let it out."

David felt the plates he was holding quiver in the wind. Now he could have imagined he was a silent comedian poised to hurl the plates in Kinnear's face – anything to shut him up, except that hardly would. "You don't know me at all," he protested.

"I know a writer when I see them. I've met a few that tried to say they weren't. It's like being mad. If you say you're not that means you are." As David struggled against feeling trapped by the notion Kinnear said "What was that title of yours again?"

"It wasn't mine." In case this didn't fend the danger off David said "I don't remember."

"Well, it was a good one. Anyone that comes up with a title like that, they're a writer. If I think of it I'll let you know."

"Don't try," David called after him and was afraid he'd said too much. Might Kinnear wonder why he was anxious to prevent him from remembering the title? Suppose he recollected it and looked it up online? If he read the entry about Frank Cubbins he was bound to blame it on David – the entry and perhaps more than that. David was watching him recede uphill – he was willing Kinnear to decide the title wasn't worth the effort, any more than David was – when he glimpsed someone following the bookseller.

He'd barely distinguished the figure when it vanished, only to reappear for a moment further uphill. It seemed not to be using the crowd for concealment so much as borrowing visibility from the gaps between the people. Apart from the impression of a pursuer, David could make out very little. He couldn't be sure of the figure's build – it might have been as chubby as an overgrown infant or wiry enough to suggest it had no need for food – and it appeared to have nothing he would call a colour. He was reminded of the way sunlight faded the covers of books, except that the pallor looked more reminiscent of the moonlight that had seized him in the field the night he'd invoked Newless. The follower dodged into view again, keeping its distance from Kinnear while matching his pace. David thought of shouting to the bookseller, but he was too far away. He'd taken a step after Kinnear when he became aware of holding the paper plates. "I need to speak to him," he said and thrust the plates at Rex.

"What do you want me to do about it?"

"Whatever you think you ought to do for Andrea." Since Rex hadn't taken the plates, David planted them on the nearest table. "This can't wait," he declared and dashed uphill.

He was dismayed to find he'd lost sight of Kinnear. His skull felt as brittle as ice by the time he located the bookseller almost at the top of the street. Did someone else flicker into view between two people on the pavement lower down? All at once venturing closer felt like a threat of meeting face to face. It wasn't as though David had any reason to care much about the bookseller. If he didn't try to prevent the man from coming to harm he would be responsible for it, and how could he bear himself then? He saw Kinnear turn a corner onto the main road and sprinted after him.

He was afraid to hear a screech of brakes or the thump of metal against flesh. When he reached the corner he let out the little breath he had. The bookseller was waiting at the traffic lights, and nobody appeared to be near him. "Mr Kinnear," David shouted. "Len. Len Kinnear."

Kinnear met him with an expectant look. "Go on then, what was it?

Remind me and I'll kick myself."

"I'm not telling you the title. I mean, it's still gone out of my head. It isn't why I'm here."

Why exactly was he? Recalling how he'd tried to warn Norville and the street preacher seemed to leave him even less to say. Or was something else stealing his words in a bid to render him powerless? The lights halted the traffic, and as he crossed with Kinnear to the bombed church David had a sense that the thief of his speech was among the pedestrians who passed him on their way downhill – no, not among them but behind each of them in turn. "What were you in such a rush to tell me, then?" Kinnear said.

David could only speak as much of the truth as he was able to utter. "I want you to stay away from where I work."

Kinnear halted at the foot of the steps to the church, inside which bedraggled pigeons were fluttering up through the hole where the roof used to be. "It's on the way to my shop, pal."

"I'm saying don't come in. Don't come anywhere near me again. I'm never going to write, and you trying to convince me otherwise drives me mad."

"Don't you want people to know what you're like?"

"It isn't worth knowing. You can't have much taste if you think it is." He was hoping to offend Kinnear, but the man looked vindicated. "I've had writers say worse than that till they empowered themselves and embraced what they are."

"I've got nothing to embrace except my girlfriend."

"See, right there you're talking like a writer. Why don't you give All Write another shot. Maybe being with other writers will set you off. We've even got a vacancy just now. Remember you met—"

"I don't want anything to do with your group." Either David's desperation lent him eloquence or his rage did. "I don't want to be associated with anyone like them or the stuff they write," he said. "No publisher worth anything would touch it, and that's why they have to publish it themselves. All you're doing is deluding them that it's anything but rubbish. They ought to be ashamed of it, not cluttering the world up with stuff nobody with any sense would buy. It isn't even worth space on the internet. You should be ashamed of encouraging them."

Kinnear's mouth had hung open during most of this. "Have you finished?" he said.

"If you've heard me at last I have."

"Don't worry, I've got no more doubts about you. You're a writer." As David searched for more words Kinnear said "Just not the kind we want to support. The kind that thinks they're better than the rest of us."

"I don't think I'm a better writer at all," David protested, but that wouldn't help. "I just think I've got to be better than the trash you have in your shop."

"You've got what you wanted." Kinnear gazed with sad contempt at him. "You'll not be hearing from any of us again," he said. "Specially not Frank, and all he wanted was to help."

David was afraid that could be an accusation, but as Kinnear turned to cross the road to We're Still Left he saw it had only been a parting shot. Why did he no longer feel nervous on Kinnear's behalf? At some point his sense of a threatening presence had faded, and now it was gone. Somehow this seemed to promise that Kinnear wouldn't stumble on the Newless blog, unless the hope was founded on that notion. As David made to head back to work he felt more than equal to confronting Rex and whoever else might need it. Then a thought overtook him at last, and he wavered, almost falling on the cracked steps of the defunct church.

He might have ensured that Kinnear wouldn't find the blog, but Emily already had. Indeed, David had shown it to her. That was why the sight of her had kept reviving his panic. He couldn't let the blog cause her harm, whatever might happen to him. He started as a blackened pigeon flapped up from the gaping church into the grey deserted sky, and then he found a reason to grow calmer. However he'd achieved it in Kinnear's case, he seemed to have gained some control over events. "Don't touch Emily," he whispered, staring at the hollow church. "Don't even go anywhere near her. She's to be left alone."

CHAPTER TWENTY-NINE

"*Cunts.*"

I thought that would catch the attention of the girls behind the bookshop counter. One of them looks like the cover of a novel, the kind that's droll about romance so that the reader needn't own up to feeling too much and just intelligent enough not to threaten any of its audience. I hope to see her makeup crack – her face has spent quite a stretch in front of a mirror – but her features set into even more of a mask while the humour deserts it, turning it dull. "Excuse me?" she demands.

"*Cunts,*" I say loud enough for several loiterers at the shelves to stare at me. "By John Updike."

Her colleague raises her eyebrows, or at least the skin above her eyes, which is occupied by a pair of whitish lines almost too thin and faint to be identified as hair. "Not familiar."

It sounds as if she wants those to be the final words, but I won't even make them hers. "Aren't you?" I say like an innocent. "I thought he was quite well known."

"Of course we know the author," Bookface says. "Just not that book."

"I expect you meet a lot of writers in your job. What's he like?"

"She means we know his work," Baldbrows says, and the skin above her eyes climbs higher as though in search of extra hair. "We've never seen him."

"You might be surprised how many writers you've met. Some of them mightn't make themselves known." I'm tempted to let them know who they have the privilege of meeting, but then I'd have to shut them down, and I've already made today's choice. "Anyway, we're talking about cunts," I remind them. "You'd think they'd have made more of a splash."

"We can look into ordering it for you," Bookface murmurs as if she's in church or a restaurant or somewhere else equally sacred, "but could you stop saying it now?"

"I wouldn't mind getting my hands on what I'm after, only I was hoping you could give it to me right away." I watch her and Baldbrows fail to be sure enough of my meaning to object to it, and then I say "I'm surprised anybody in a bookshop wants to do away with words."

"Words like that one we can do without," Baldbrows informs me.

"And we certainly don't want our customers to hear them," Bookface contributes.

"I'll have to be careful what else I ask you for, will I?" I let them have time to wonder if not dread what that might be while I give the street another glance. There's no sign yet of today's selection, but I know they pass the shop on their way to their car. "Am I allowed to say the en word?" I ask the guardians of language.

"We'd rather you didn't," Baldbrows says. "There's no need for it," says Bookface.

"I thought you'd say there was. I can say the whole word, then."

"No," Bookface says, and I'm sure her stubborn impervious mask is growing glossier. "That isn't what we said."

The other girl's brows seem determined to reach for her hairline. "So is there anything we can find for you?"

"*Ten Little En Words*. You surely must have that."

"It hasn't been called that for a long time," Bookface says as if this is a triumph to celebrate.

"Not since before any of us was born," Baldbrows is even happier to add. "Don't be so sure who was born when." Saying this doesn't quite restore my sense of myself – it feels not far from achieving the opposite – and as Baldbrows makes to leave the counter on my behalf I find some loathing to help me feel more substantial. "Never mind bringing me that one if it's changed its name," I tell her. "I've got no time for things that won't own up to what they are."

She appears to take this personally, and I'm toying with a question – maybe she and Bookface cunt with each other – when she reverts to her job. "I'm afraid that's all we can bring you," she says and looks relieved to be able to stay behind the counter.

"There must be some things that are too old to change. *Prancing En Word*, isn't that a classic?"

Bookface can't entirely keep her suspicion out of her eyes. "I've never heard of it."

"Would it offend you too much to look it up?"

I'm rather hoping they'll say yes, but Baldbrows only shakes her head while Bookface consults the computer. "It's by Ronald Firbank," she says and seems not far from disbelief. "We can order it for you."

"I'd like to have something in my hands." I glance at the street, but we've still a few minutes before today's terminations pass by. "Joseph Conrad," I say. "You must have his book. What's it called again?"

Both girls gaze hard at me as if they can find my intentions in my eyes. "He wrote a lot," Baldbrows says.

"You know the one I have to mean."

Each of them might be waiting for the other girl to speak, unless they're willing each other not to take the bait. Professionalism gets the better of Bookface, who says "You mean the one about Narcissus."

"The character who didn't know his reflection was him. You'd wonder how anyone could make that mistake." I'm so distracted by the idea that I have to bring myself back to the situation; it feels like starting awake, I imagine, if I ever fall asleep. "That isn't all the title," I object. "What's the rest?"

Bookface ensures that I hear her breathe through her nose, more than I hear myself do, but it's Baldbrows who says "I think you know perfectly well."

"I'm asking you to tell me. Or aren't you supposed to help your customers too much?"

Both girls look offended – I've begun to think they have just one expression between them at a time – but I'm threatening their image of themselves. "Has the shop told you not to say what the book's called?" I suggest. "That's a strange way of selling books."

"Of course not. *The En Word of the Narcissus*," Bookface mutters as if she hopes not to be heard.

"That wasn't too hard, was it?" I feel as if I need to carry on the argument so as to keep myself where I can watch the street and perhaps to keep my mind alive as well. "You can't suppress words," I point out. "It doesn't make the thoughts go away. More like it puts them beyond your control."

"I don't see what you're getting at," Bookface complains.

"If you don't spell the word out you can't be sure what it is, can you?" For a pause like a void in my mind I feel as if I meant something else entirely, and then I manage to regain myself. "Let's say niggler. *Ten Little Nigglers. Prancing Niggler. The Niggler of the Narcissus.* Don't you even like me saying that? Let's try *Ten Little Nibblers…*"

"Shall I show you where the book is?" Baldbrows tells me rather than asks.

"*The Nitwit of the Narcissus*, you mean. Not *Prancing Nitpicker* or *Ten Little Nincompoops*." Being ushered to the shelf would take me away from the street, and in any case I've exhausted their ability to amuse me, not that there was much of it. "*Or The Nonsense of the Narcissus*, are you saying?"

"If you don't want anyone to find what you asked for—" Bookface says.

"You'd like to see the last of me, would you? Quite a few have." I'm tempted to enquire if the shop has a complaints desk, although no doubt there'd be a warning on it against abusing the staff, which I'd say would be a provocation to complain about the notice. If the shop does have a grievance facility I won't be visiting it just now, but at least the question might leave the girls nervous, though nothing like as much as I ought to make them. I'm about to speak when the pair I'm awaiting pass the shop and vanish downhill. "Thanks for the diversion," I tell Baldbrows and Bookface. "You wouldn't think it, but you've been some use."

My quarries turn the corner at the bottom of the hill as I leave the shop. Are the shopgirls already forgetting me? I know they won't be able to describe me, and I think our encounter may seem as if they dreamed it, since their minds are too small to have room for anyone like me. I haven't time to reward anybody so insignificant for their lack of appreciation. They aren't the ones I'll be giving something to remember, though not for long.

I'm first into the lift at the car park, but I don't need to be noticed yet. There are better locations for action. "Oh, what's that smell?" complains the elder of my targets as she pokes the grubby button. "We don't like that, do we? Hurry up and let us out, lift. Someone's been disgusting."

"If you want a definition of disgusting, just listen to yourself."

She doesn't hear me say that. The lift makes a muffled row about reaching the third level, and I watch her grow nervous that it may break down. She isn't sufficiently worried to make it worthwhile to halt the impromptu toilet between floors, but I enjoy her discomfort with the stench of urine. The moment the doors stagger open she lurches between them, so desperate to take a breath that she blunders towards the low concrete wall above the street. A little more impetus would tip her over the edge for a three-storey fall onto the pavement, but suppose that isn't fatal? She stumbles to a halt well short of it and gasps "Be careful."

I'm amused to think she isn't talking only to herself, even though she doesn't know I'm close enough to touch. She veers away from the wall like a dumpy vessel taking another tack and heads for her car. I'm in the back seat by the time she unlocks the door. She lowers her ponderous bulk into the driver's seat and eases the safety belt across her midriff as though she's wrapping a delicate package. "There we are," she murmurs. "Safe now. Soon be home."

I could contradict most of that. I don't need a safety belt, and they won't for much longer. There's no point in drawing attention yet; I'm not even in the mirror. I stay unobtrusive as she starts the engine and coasts down the narrow ramps to the exit, where the post that swallows her ticket with an expressionless slit of a mouth holds up its arm like a warning she's too unimaginative to understand. She drives up a side street and then swings across town to the tunnel under the river. None of this is any use; she's going far too slowly to be in sufficient danger. Even the tunnel keeps her to forty miles an hour, and she's boxed in by vehicles in front and behind and in the adjacent lane. Nothing bad enough could happen here, however much I'm tempted to find some way to bring her babble to an end. "Now we're under the water," she drivels. "Not underwater, or anyway I'm not. You are, though, aren't you? Underwater inside mummy to keep you safe."

Is this how mothers are supposed to talk to their contents? How do they speak to something they've got rid of without even bothering to take a look? Perhaps they try to keep it inside their heads, but they ought to know it won't stay there; you can't trap anything that way when you don't know what it is. You've lost your chance to shape it, and it's someone else's turn – who else's but its own?

The far end of the tunnel is in sight now. Emerging into the open may be a little like being born, as if I'd know. The car leaves the buried light behind and heads for the tollbooths under the clogged black starless sky, and I wonder if mummy will address the toll collector with the excruciating coyness she's been using. She only thanks him for taking her money and thanks him again for turning it into change. She drops coins one by one into the hopper beyond the booth, a constipated process that aggravates my detestation, and I occupy my time with grimacing and waving at the attendant through the rear window to prove he can't see me. The toll barrier lifts its arm at last to signal the start of the race, and the car follows dozens of red lights onto the motorway. All that red looks like a warning or an omen, but mummy doesn't notice any more than she's aware of me. "Nearly home now," she's busy droning, "and then we'll see what daddy has made us for dinner."

She can imagine that for another few minutes, because there's still a speed limit on this stretch of road. Brake lights flare raw as injuries – more traffic is streaming up a ramp to join the race – and then all the vehicles compete to gain speed as a sign like an eye crossed out with a single black slash sets them loose. Mummy remains in the inside lane, and the car speeds up so gradually that I ache to shove her foot down on the accelerator. "Everybody's so impatient, aren't they?" she croons as if she senses how I feel. "At least you aren't, little one. You take your time and come out right."

"It's your time, true enough. At least you got that right. Better babble while you can."

Her head twists an inch in my direction. Does she think she heard something? I don't want to be apparent quite yet, and I imitate the darkness in the back seat until a queue of traffic for a slip road forces her into the middle lane, where all the cars are travelling faster than she seemed to want to drive. She's trapped into matching their speed, and the vehicles rushing past her in the outer lane make her visibly nervous. "We don't like this very much, do we?" she complains. "We'll be glad when we're home."

"Here's something you'll like a lot less."

She blinks at the mirror, but perhaps she's just checking the traffic behind her. I give her a glimpse of my silhouette against a glare of headlights. I wag my head and shake my hands on either side, wriggling my fingers to frame the face she can't distinguish. "What was that?" she gasps, and the car swerves a fraction. "What did mummy see?"

"Blushpuss, will you use your name and not that puky word. I'll tell you mine."

I'm suddenly aware that I've been using her nauseous name for herself. Even if I meant the use as an insult, the realisation feels like owning up. "What is it?" she pleads in a voice almost too small for a child's.

I can't tell whether she's asking for my name or unable to determine what's happening, unless she hopes the question will somehow make it stop. "It's Lucky Newless," I say and frame my blank head with my outstretched fingers in the mirror.

She lets out a cry that sounds desperate for breath. The car wavers as she treads on the brake. Perhaps she didn't mean to – perhaps her nerves took over – and the car speeds faster as headlamps blaze behind it. It nearly strayed out of its lane, but it can't retreat into the inner one, because too much traffic has raced onto the motorway at the junction. "Blushpuss, that's our name for you," I tell her. "You never read about yourself, did you? Too late now. You kept wanting your colleague to make a name for himself and never saw your own moment of fame."

"Who are you?" she begs as though I haven't told her. "What do you want? Don't hurt me. Don't hurt us. I'm going to have a child."

I'd like to let her know how little this helps her case – how it stokes my loathing – but if I enjoy the delay much longer she'll be able to slow the car down. "Call the police," I urge so shrilly it must pain her ears. "Tell them there's an intruder in your car. It's your only chance."

Panic or confusion or an inability to think for the stridence of my voice makes her rummage one-handed in the bag on the seat beside her. It's enough. As she closes her hand on the phone I sidle through the gap between the seats and lean my face into hers. Her hand is still in the bag as she cowers away from me. I hardly even need to grab her other hand to swing the steering wheel awry with all her helpless weight against it. The car swerves into the outer lane, to be greeted by a falsetto chorus of brakes. We're travelling so fast that before the nearest vehicle can run us down we smash into the central barrier.

The car actually stands on its nose for a moment, and then crashes on its roof on the far side of the barrier. Throughout all this Blushpuss provides such a soundtrack that she might be screaming for two. Her row and the sounds of grinding metal and smashed glass are lost in an enormous trumpet-blast and an eruption of light, all of which announces the giant truck that sweeps the car and its contents into oblivion. "There's some acrobatics for you. There's a special ride," I tell Blushpuss's passenger as I merge with the night beside the road.

CHAPTER THIRTY

As David arrived at the agency he saw his face gliding to meet him. Was he early enough to be first for once? He was gazing at his features plastered to the window like a poster issued by the police when he heard Andrea's cough. He could have thought the sharp bark was summing her up as she appeared from behind the counter. Whatever expression the sight of him provoked, she'd withdrawn it by the time she reached the door. She shut him in before she said "Making up for yesterday, David?"

"I just thought I'd be as early as everyone else." As casually as he could manage he said "Is anyone else here yet?"

"You've beaten them at last. Since you're capable you might want to keep it up."

He'd been hoping everyone was safely there, and his unease made him retort "I don't think I've all that much to make up for."

"You abandoned your post, David."

"I wasn't alone out there, was I? There were supposed to be two of us. Did you realise Rex decided he was only there to tell me what to do?"

"He knows about promotions. That is his profession, you know."

"He needn't worry about the competition. I'm not a writer." As Andrea gave him a look that hadn't time for patience David protested "That's why I went after Kinnear from the writer's group, to tell him not to bother me here any more. I thought that's what you wanted."

"Don't try and be clever with words, David."

"I'll say one thing if you don't mind."

"Please keep it brief. As long as you're here there's plenty of work to be done."

"I expect there would be even if I weren't." Despite her cough, which sounded like an admonition too fierce to need language, David said "Rex didn't do too well at selling, did he? Bill told me nobody came in while Rex was on his own out there, but you saw they did when I was back on the job. And I went without my break because I'd chased Kinnear, remember."

Andrea gazed at him without speaking and then past him. "Perhaps you'd like to let your colleagues in, David."

He turned to see Bill at the door and another workmate at the window. She was wearing a handwritten holiday offer where her face should be – at least, the poster on the inside of the pane obscured her face. As David hurried to open the door his lips were shaping Emily's name, but the woman outside the window was Helen. "Not interrupting, are we?" Bill said.

"What do you imagine you'd be interrupting?" Andrea said.

"We don't see the pair of you together much. You could have been catching up on old times."

Well short of the end of this Bill visibly regretted having begun, and tried to compensate with a smile that looked as though he'd forgotten the technique. "Aren't we all here, then?" Helen said.

David was able to wonder if Emily was behind the scenes until Andrea said "All except our new mother."

"Won't she be," David said and swallowed, "coming in?"

"I've no reason to think that. Why, have you?"

"It's just that I thought she was usually here by now. You haven't heard." This sounded ominously unlike the question he'd intended, and he was quick to add "You haven't heard from her."

"Which is why I'm assuming she's on her way."

"I'm sure she is," David said and tried to be. He had no reason to think otherwise; he'd wished Emily the opposite of harm. As he managed to capture the nervous hanger in his locker he thought of looking up the Newless blog, but that felt too close to inviting the worst. Surely Emily had to be too concerned with her new state to offer any threat to him. He hurried out to the counter in the hope of seeing her, only to find Andrea's gaze waiting for him. She seemed to think he'd left before they'd finished talking and to expect him to know what to say, but when her silence failed to prompt him she said

"You haven't been home, then."

"No," Bill said as if he had to demonstrate his irrepressibility, "he's just been to take his coat off."

"There's too much cleverness round here for my liking," Andrea said and spiked her remark with a cough.

Bill covered his smirk with his fingertips as if he meant to stuff his words back in, and Helen poised her head at an enquiring angle. "Why wouldn't David have been home?"

Andrea couldn't quite seem to be ignoring the question as she told him "You still haven't brought in your photographs."

David had the unwelcome notion that they were all acting out the traits the Newless blog had magnified. "I'm at Steph's," he said. "I won't be leaving her alone while she hasn't got a job."

He saw Bill not entirely hide a grin and Helen give her head a tilt like wryness redefined as Andrea attempted to pretend her briskness was simply professional. "Will you sort those brochures out, please," she said, no longer looking at him.

He was surprised how satisfying the task felt at first – the Stanley knife even sharper than her coughs, the metallic tape around the parcel snapping apart as if flinching away from the blade that had sliced it. Distributing the brochures onto the racks let him keep an eye on the street, but nobody came to the door until Andrea unlocked it, and nobody did then. David took his place at the computer terminal nearest to the window and found several queries waiting to be followed up. He needn't be reminded of the Newless blog, but did he have to be quite so aware of the empty seat beside him? Of course Emily's condition must have made her late for work. He tried not to glance towards the door too often, since this put him in mind of summoning somebody else. He was making himself concentrate on selecting seats on a flight for a customer – a diagram exposed the innards of the aircraft, and a pair of rectangular slabs turned red as David chose them – when the door opened. "Em—" he was eager to start saying as he raised his head.

He didn't finish. The newcomer was a lanky white-haired man who was toning down his tallness with a stoop. He pinched his flimsy silver spectacles between a finger and thumb to pull them low on his nose while he squinted at the brochures in the racks. As David emailed the customer about the seats the man veered towards him at a clip that suggested his posture was urging him. "Can you spare a moment?"

"Longer than that," David said, only to wonder if this was excessively clever.

The man sprawled into the seat opposite him. "What it is, I want to give the wife a bit of sun at Easter."

"Anywhere in particular?" David said and promised himself that Emily would show up before he'd finished dealing with the customer.

"Nowhere that'll break the bank. Let's be honest, you have to watch the cash these days. We don't have too much in the coppers."

"In the, I see what you mean." David was conscious of Bill's surreptitious grin beyond the empty chair, and tried to let neither distract him. "About how much are you looking to spend?"

"Name me a place and then show me the damage. I don't want you thinking I'm stringy."

David glimpsed how Helen tilted her head to catch the meaning as he heard Bill not entirely stifle a sound. "We've some cheap deals on New Zealand just now."

"Let's be honest, by the time we went all that way we'd be coming back. That'd be a turnip for the books."

David was aware that Andrea had laid down the phone on the currency desk. "Well, that's not very helpful," she complained. "Dead."

"What's that?" Helen said.

"I've just tried ringing Emily but it says her mobile's not in use, and nobody's answering at her house."

"Maybe she's somewhere you can't reach her," Bill said, adding "The tunnel."

"Where can we take her that's closer?"

For a moment David was confused enough to fancy that the customer was asking about Emily. He had to drag his mind back to his task before he was able to say "How about Cyprus?"

"They split that down the middle, didn't they? Greeks on one side and turkeys on the other. We're a bit past going anywhere there could be trouble."

Even if Emily was under the river, would her phone be described as not in use? "There's been no trouble for a while," David was hardly aware of replying.

"You're saying everything's humpty-dumpty there now."

"I didn't quite say that." Could the man be some kind of test arranged by David's employers? He had to dismiss the idea as deranged in order to ask "So does Cyprus appeal at all?"

"Let's be honest, both halves think they're right. I'd better keep the wife clear just in case."

He was being nothing else but honest, David was almost goaded to protest. How long before Emily left the tunnel? "Greece, then," he said. "There'll be sun in the south."

"Will there for certain? That's the crook of the matter." The lanky man leaned forward like a conspirator. "On top of that her workings aren't too sturdy," he confided. "We'd better not risk anywhere the food's that different."

Once Emily came out of the tunnel, wouldn't Andrea's missed call show up on her mobile? "There's Malta," David said more desperately than professionally. "They've stayed pretty British."

"They've bandaged that about, now you mention it. So you're saying they'd do us a good English dinner."

"Some of the hotels do." Shoving his chair back felt like taking action, but by the time David reached the racks he was peering through the gaps between the posters on the window in the hope of seeing Emily. He grabbed a Home Abroad brochure and showed the lanky man the Empire Remembrance Hotel. "We've got customers who go back every year," David said as he retreated behind the counter.

"Let's be honest, that looks more like us." The man brought the page within inches of his face. "I expect the exchequer can survive that," he eventually said. "Put us in for a week over Easter."

Suppose the accommodation was fully booked, or the flights were? How many more of the man's verbal antics would David have to endure? He'd typed just the first syllable of the name of the hotel when the phones on the counter and on the currency desk began to ring in chorus. He could have imagined he'd triggered them somehow, and he nearly grabbed the nearest receiver. As he made himself continue typing, Andrea lifted the phone on the currency desk. "Frugogo Bold Street," she said. "Andrea speaking. Hello?"

Why should David be concerned that she'd had to say all this to prompt an answer? He glanced away from the computer just too late. Andrea was swivelling her chair to turn her back to the rest of the shop, and she'd lowered her voice. She might almost have been crouching around it, and he couldn't hear a word over the clatter of the keyboard, where his fingers felt as if they were growing frantic. "Here's your trip if you want it," he said.

He hardly cared how uninvolved he sounded. He was acutely conscious that Andrea had slumped lower in her chair, as though whatever she was hearing on the phone had dragged her down. When he pivoted the monitor to show the lanky man, a shiver passed through the screen. Surely his nerves were the reason, not some furtive activity inside the computer. "That looks like the ticker," his customer said.

David wondered if the man was mangling language as some kind of joke. When he typed the man's name and his wife's – Jerry Barnes needed to be spelled out as Jeremiah, and Deirdre couldn't just be Dee in the paperwork – he felt he was trying to regain control of words. As he turned the screen for the customer to check the information David was aware that Andrea had stood up, but when he glanced towards the currency desk she wasn't there. He charged Barnes' credit card and printed out page after page, which hadn't finished slithering into the tray of the printer when Helen saved her work and hurried into the staff quarters. As David collected the pages he murmured to Bill "What's going on?"

"Looks as if that call upset the boss. Helen's gone to see."

The smell of hot paper caught in David's throat. When he handed Barnes an envelope with the documents in he found it hard to speak. He might have liked to prevent the customer from saying "Let's be honest, I expect we're lucky to get this."

"I'm glad you did," David said without even remotely feeling it. Apprehension had clenched around the core of him. Barnes had scarcely left the shop before David said "Had we better find out what's wrong?"

"I'd leave it and see if they want us knowing," Bill said. "Could be a women's thing. If it's boyfriend trouble we're best staying clear."

Might Rex have been on the phone, or might the call have been about him? David felt as if he was attempting gingerly to disentangle his mind from a fear he'd been afraid to define. He hadn't produced any more thoughts worthy of the name when Bill said "It's all right. Here's Helen." David saw him take back his first comment as soon as they saw her face. His mouth tasted like desiccated paper again, and he had to leave speaking to Bill, who'd lost his grin by the time he said "What's happened?"

"It's Emily." Helen tilted her head to meet the knuckle she used to dab her eyes. "She's dead," she told him.

"Good God, no. No, no." Since none of this had any effect Bill said "It was never the baby."

"That's gone too. They were in a crash on the motorway." Helen squeezed her eyes shut and widened them before adding "That was her husband on the phone. I think Andrea is nearly as upset as he must be."

"Well, there's a revelation," Bill said, which was his excuse to revert to a hint of a grin. "She's human after all."

Helen straightened up her head to gaze directly at him. "Some things you shouldn't say even if you think them."

David felt as if he were observing all this across an unbridgeable distance from inside the cage of his thoughts. How could he have been responsible for Emily's death? He'd done all he could to achieve exactly the opposite. Or had wishing her the best brought her the opposite to prove to him that he couldn't direct events? He had a sense that he'd overlooked something crucial. His head was aching with the notion, which made the computer screen appear to throb like a dark heart, by the time Andrea came out of the staffroom.

She took up her position at the currency desk and stared out through the glass. Her gaze was so fierce that it might have been designed to parch her eyes of tears or simply to warn the staff not to speak to her just now. David could have thought it contained an accusation, which was one reason why he stumbled to his feet. "Can I have a few minutes by myself?"

Though Andrea didn't look at him he heard a trace of sympathy in her voice. "Go on, David."

He fumbled out his phone on the way to the staffroom. As he sank onto a chair he saw Emily's upturned coffee mug gaping round-mouthed at him from the plastic rack beside the sink. He bruised his elbows on the unyielding surface of the table while he read the first words of the latest entry. He was able to believe it didn't involve Emily even once he read a sentence halfway down the second page: There's no sign yet of today's selection, but I know they pass the shop on their way to their car. He still managed to hope that her death was no more than a tragic coincidence until the car took to the road, by which point he could no longer deny the identity of the driver.

He didn't know if the fluorescent light overhead began to throb as he read to the end. Perhaps just his vision did, but it felt as though his pulse had strayed outside him. He covered his eyes with his hands and ground his elbows against the table. He would have to go out soon and face his colleagues, and pretend he knew as little about Emily's death as they did. He was wondering if he should splash his face at the sink to feign tears, because his knowledge was so dreadful that it didn't let him experience grief, when another section of the entry he'd just read caught up with him. He scrolled back through the text and found the paragraph, and as he read it once again the silent thumping of the light grew more defined. "That's what you're doing," he whispered, "that's what it's always been about," but the realisation felt like being shut into a maze that was his mind.

CHAPTER THIRTY-ONE

David was at the front door when he heard wheels speeding through the darkness of the park. No doubt they belonged to a skater, but they put him in mind of a car on the motorway, not to mention a mobility scooter. Opening the door crumpled several copies of a free newspaper, and he had to resist leafing through one in search of deaths about which he already knew far too much. A muffled orchestral march paced him upstairs, signifying a funeral or an inexorable advance, unless it meant both. When he stole into Stephanie's apartment he was greeted by the aromas of her lamb and apricot tagine, one of her Moroccan specialities. She should have offered to include that in Andrea's promotion, he thought, and felt his lips writhe into such a grimace he could almost taste its bitterness. He padded down the hall between the holiday postcards, which felt even more remote from him than the views they showed, to say nothing of the jokes on some of them. The kitchen door was open, and Stephanie was at the cooker with her back to him.

She looked disconcertingly vulnerable, especially the bare nape of her neck. Perhaps this was because she didn't realise anybody was behind her. David hadn't managed to decide how he needed to feel by the time she turned and saw him. "David," she said with a start that she tried to disguise with a smile, and then her mouth grew uncertain. "David?"

"What are you asking?"

"How long have you been there?"

"Not long enough for you to lose your sleep about, but I don't think that's what you wanted to know."

Stephanie replaced the lid on the casserole and put her hand over her heart, covering the name on her apron. "Why were you looking like that?"

"Can't I look? Maybe I'm looking like I really am at last."

"David, what's happened? I can tell something has. Don't try and keep it from me."

"You think that's going to solve it, do you?" As Stephanie gave him a reproachful frown David said "You could be right, more than you realise. Someone died at work."

"Oh, David." Her frown vanished as her eyes widened, and she reached for his hand. "I'm sorry," she murmured. "Will a drink help?"

"No need to apologise," he said and moved out of reach to find a corkscrew in the utensils drawer. "I expect a few glasses may help me blab."

Stephanie slid a bottle of Pinotage out of the rack and stood it on the table. "So what on earth happened?" she said as David levered up the cork.

"You haven't asked me who yet."

"I assumed it was a customer from the way you said it."

"None of them this time. One of the personnel. Which would you like it to be?"

"I wouldn't wish anyone dead." Not quite as forcefully Stephanie added "I don't believe you would either."

"That isn't how it works. I've found that out at last." David poured two enthusiastic glassfuls, dotting the table with red drops. "You didn't know you'd shacked up with an idiot," he said, "or maybe you've been too polite to say."

"David, I truly don't know what you're—"

"You don't have to keep saying my name. I still know who I am." He handed her a glass and clinked his against it none too gently. "Absent friends, is it?" he said. "Absent something, anyway."

"When are you going to tell me who it was?"

"Who do you think deserved it most? The bitch you don't like me calling a cunt, do you think it ought to have been her?"

"I don't think any of them deserve us to want them to come to harm, David. I don't think anybody does."

"It wasn't her, maybe you're surprised to hear. How about Bill and his imbecile grin? As long as he thinks everything's a joke it's time for it to be on him, don't you agree?"

"David, I can see you're upset, but I don't understand why you need—"

"Well, it wasn't him either." David took a gulp of wine and kept hold of the glass. "What about the bird brain? Always cocking her stupid head as if that's all she's got in there. Time that was stopped, wouldn't you say?"

"I wouldn't, and if she gets on your nerves that much—"

"I should tell her, are you saying?" David said and downed another mouthful. "Maybe I will."

As Stephanie made to speak he saw a thought overtake her. "Does that mean it was Emily? But you said she was going to have—"

"She isn't any more. They're both gone." He saw Stephanie wince at his brusqueness. "Don't worry, I'm not going to rant about her," he said. "It doesn't matter what I say about her now."

"It very much does, and I hope—"

"I've already said I won't say anything bad."

He was urging Stephanie to wonder why and ask, but she let some sympathy into her eyes. "Do you want to tell me how it happened?"

"Something made her crash her car."

This wouldn't prompt Stephanie to ask what had, and David was on the edge of saying someone was responsible when she said "Is that all they know?"

"The police say it looks as if she was using her mobile on the motorway, in the outside lane. Her husband says she never used it on the road, wouldn't even touch it if it rang."

"I suppose being pregnant can change you."

"I'm just telling you what the police say. That doesn't mean it's the truth."

"Then what do you think is?"

He'd been hoping to catch himself out – to leave no option except speaking – but he felt his words desert him, not so much fleeing out of reach as being borne so far away that they were beyond his grasp. He could only make another dogged bid to trick himself. "I think there'll be one less to annoy me at work."

"You said you wouldn't say anything bad." When he only gazed at her, willing her to sense how much he couldn't utter, Stephanie said "What's making you like this? However upset you are—"

"Are you really sure you want to know? You'll like me even less than you do at the moment."

"You mustn't tell me how to feel, especially not about you. I want to know everything about you, David. Whatever it is, we can work it out together."

She reminded him of his parents. Perhaps that was one reason he'd been drawn to her, and he had no idea how useful it would be. "Then you have to read that blog," he said.

He'd feared he might be robbed of the ability to say even that, but it was out now, past denying – at least, by him. Stephanie looked confused and not far from saddened. "The one you said was using your title, you mean? Why should I want to do that?"

"I can't tell you. You need to see."

"Put the glass down for heaven's sake. You'll crack the stem if you hold it like that." As David managed to relax his grip and plant the wineglass on the table Stephanie said "Let's have dinner first, shall we?"

"Can't you turn it down?" He could tell she hoped to coax him away from his obsession. "I thought you wanted an explanation," he said. "In that case you'll have to look at the blog."

"Can you honestly not tell me otherwise?" When David shook his head, which felt like an attempt to shake more words out, Stephanie sighed. "All right, if it bothers you so much I'll look."

She seemed distracted, perhaps uneasy. Once she'd transferred the casserole to the oven she turned the heat low before she fetched her laptop. As she opened it on the table and inserted the jack of the lead David was reminded of Frank Cubbins. Was it too late to tell her he'd changed his mind? He mustn't do that to protect himself, and he had to believe she wasn't at risk. "What was it called again?" she said, not very much as if she wanted to know.

"*Better Out Than In.*"

"But you don't think it is." When David had no answer she typed the words, and he watched her across the table as she was confronted by the site. "What do you want me to see?" she said.

His mouth was almost dry enough to destroy his voice, and he took another gulp of wine. "Can you see the link about not needing a menu? Read what that entry says."

He watched her face grow puzzled as she read, and then it filled with disbelief and tried to stay incredulous until it covered its expression with a blankness he'd never previously seen Stephanie adopt. He saw her come to the end of the entry, but he'd taken several breaths before she looked at him. "Are you trying to tell me you wrote this, David?"

"I'm not, no. I didn't see it till the first time I read it."

"Then what are you—"

"Just look at some more. Read as much as you can."

He swallowed as she found another link, and then he reached for his glass. He had no idea which entry she was reading now, and her face gave no indication how it made her feel. She'd clicked on a third link before she said "How many of these am I expected to recognise?"

"You ought to be able to figure out a few. I know every single one." With a sense of relinquishing his last chance to keep her affection David said "Look at the latest."

He could see when she read past the encounter in the bookshop. From attempting to tolerate or at least understand the barrage of uninvited language, though the task was a visible strain, she began to look as if she would very much prefer not to comprehend what was in front of her, on the screen and perhaps across the table as well. For some moments after her eyes stopped moving she didn't speak. "Was that meant to be Emily?" she said as though she hardly wanted to be heard.

"I'm afraid it was. The others from work, they're on there too, and some of our customers are." Now that he was able to talk David found it hard to finish, though perhaps he was simply trying to fend off Stephanie's disquiet. "The couple he calls Daft and Pathetic," he said, "their names were Pat and Daff. They came in to book a holiday but the husband kept pretending he didn't remember places they'd been. I don't know if you saw, but he had a heart attack at the airport when he couldn't find their passports. Guess who stole them or hid them or just made it so the fellow couldn't see them. I'd forgotten about him and his wife, or I thought I had. They didn't even end up booking their holiday through us."

Perhaps he'd babbled at such length because he was afraid to learn what Stephanie was waiting to say. "Tell me none of this was anything to do with you, David."

"I can't." This sounded too close to wanting to be silenced, and he said even more fiercely "It has."

"What are you trying to say?" When he didn't respond at once she said "Or are you trying not to?"

"I told you I didn't write any of it. You must know I couldn't have." He was dismayed to wonder if he'd convinced her of the opposite. "All that about the motorway," he insisted, "it was posted last night when I was here with you. Go on and check."

He was silent while she did, but it left her looking uneasier still. "I wouldn't want to know you if you'd written it, but then who—"

"Suppose I didn't need to write it? What if I only had to think?" As Stephanie parted her lips and then pinched them inwards with her teeth he said "Or suppose it was more like the other way round?"

"You've lost me, David, and you're making me feel as if that's what you want."

"That's the last thing I do. It's hard for me to say all this, you know." With what he hoped was inspiration David said "He gave it away at the bookshop, if he was ever really there. Didn't you see what he told us?"

"I can't say I wasted much time on it."

"Not the stuff about titles, but maybe that's where all that was leading.

I didn't realise what he'd said at first myself. He says if you suppress your thoughts that just lets them get out of control, and that's what has been happening with mine."

He hoped Stephanie was grimacing only at the blog. "Are you saying you could ever have thought any of that about Emily?"

"That's exactly what I wasn't saying. I wished she wouldn't come to any kind of harm, and look what happened to her."

"Then you can't think there's any connection, and as for the rest of it—"

"It wasn't just Emily I wanted nothing bad to happen to. Remember Luther Payne? He was the case that was ruining my mother's sleep."

"I do remember." As if she'd seen how to bring David back to reality Stephanie said "And I remember how you wished he'd have an accident or something worse, so that doesn't prove your point at all."

"But it does, Steph." However unwelcome his triumph felt, David had to say "I kept wanting him to be dealt with and nothing happened. He wasn't killed till I wished he'd be left alone because my mother would have felt responsible if he'd been harmed. It isn't what I wish that makes these things happen, it's what I can't admit I wish. Most of the time I can't even admit how I feel about these people."

"Think what you just said. You aren't the only one to feel responsible."

"Yes, but my mother wasn't. Only I am."

Perhaps Stephanie's observation had been a last attempt to put off saying "Do you think you need to see someone?"

"Maybe you're right and I need to see Mr Newless."

"I hope you're just playing with words now." With a decisive movement that looked like a bid to take control, Stephanie shut down her computer. "I mean someone you can talk to about this," she said.

"I just did, and you don't know how hard it was. I don't think I could do it again."

Stephanie unplugged the laptop and folded it up. Perhaps this gave her time to think, or only to prepare to say "You want to know how all this looks to me."

"That's why I've told you everything. We've seen what happens when I keep things to myself."

"I've known something was wrong for a while. I'm glad you've told me at last." She rested her hands on the lid of the laptop as if to reassure herself the contents were safely shut away. "If you really think all this can't just be a series of coincidences..."

"You must have seen there's too much to be."

"All right, I did." She reached across the laptop to take both of David's hands in hers and gripped them hard. "Then even if you aren't aware of it," she said, "you have to be writing this. Maybe that's why you've been insisting you aren't a writer, because you don't want to believe it. But however nasty all this is, you didn't do these things, you only wrote about them. It must have something to do with that drug you took."

"If that's what makes sense to you."

"Doesn't it to you?" Her grasp felt like a plea rendered physical. "If you want to consult someone," she said, "I could come with you if you like. If you find it hard to talk about I could maybe help. I could say what you've said to me."

He saw how she was endeavouring not to let her distress prevent her from helping. He couldn't just reject her aid, however little it could achieve. "Let's see how it works out," he said and felt more alone than ever.

Stephanie hesitated before releasing his left hand so that she could top up the glasses. She did her best to sound amused, but it came out wryer. "This was meant to be a celebration."

"Can't it still be?"

"I've got a job."

Perhaps this wasn't quite an answer, but it had to be enough of one. "Well done, Steph," he cried and held up his glass until she met it with hers. "Tell me more."

"It's a new place. Mediterranean fine dining. Mick's wife recommended me. I'll be the sous-chef, but they're paying more than he did."

"I can see how happy you are. Just stay like that and we'll forget everything else for now. Let's have your celebratory dinner," David said and almost managed to believe in his own enthusiasm. He watched her bear away the laptop as though all that it brought to his mind could be kept at a distance, and vowed he would forget while they were celebrating her luck. She wouldn't like to know what he couldn't help thinking until he suppressed it. If she weren't so determined to dismiss Lucky Newless, perhaps she would be grateful that he'd made it possible for her to find a better job.

CHAPTER THIRTY-TWO

Once he was certain that Stephanie had gone to sleep David felt safe to lie awake without being afraid to disturb her, but then he had to think. What had he achieved by showing her the blog? She didn't believe how it worked, and he hadn't even established that nobody could see it unless he drew their attention to it in some way. All he'd done was distress Stephanie on his behalf, however much she'd striven to make tonight into an unspoiled celebration. He had to realise she would no longer feel at ease with him unless he sought some form of treatment, but how could that help him in the circumstances? At least he'd proved he could talk about the blog and what it seemed to represent, all of which felt like breaking through a mental barrier. Perhaps talking was the start of a solution, even if his listener didn't accept what he said. Or could Stephanie be right after all? Was it possible that some effect of the drug had lain dormant in his mind all these years, only to be triggered when he was forced to reach deep into his brain at All Write? Might he indeed be producing the rants on the blog and forgetting every time he had? In that case, wouldn't therapy help after all?

He didn't quite believe it. The explanation was too facile and left too much unsolved — how he would have had the opportunity to write all the entries, for instance. The one about Emily had been posted before he'd even heard of her death, and that was true of too many of them to be dismissed as coincidental. When Stephanie grew restless next to him beneath the quilt he felt as if his doubts were troubling her, and he made his hand relax on her midriff; he hadn't been aware that his arm had grown so tense. As her sleepy fingers slipped between his he tried to match the rhythm of his breaths to hers, keeping them shallow so as not to risk wakening her, though she must be used to his breaths on her neck in the night. Perhaps she found them comfortingly familiar. He was attempting to share the peace she'd achieved, however temporary it might be for both of them, when he felt a chill breath on the nape of his own neck.

He had to stiffen his whole body to restrain a shiver, though he'd realised what the icy intrusion must be – a draught through the window. He heard the wind rouse the trees in the park as he blinked at the dim bedroom. Beyond Stephanie's silhouette a sliver of light through the curtains petered out on the quilt, well short of her dressing-table and its mirror, which framed a feeble image of the window. As far as David could make out from the reflection, the curtained window was shut tight, and if he went to check he might well disturb Stephanie. He was reaching to draw the quilt over his neck when he glimpsed movement in the room.

Had the curtain stirred? He thought he'd seen the scrawny strip of light across the bed grow restless. No, its edges hadn't shifted; that wasn't what he remembered seeing. It had darkened for an instant, but not because of any restlessness of the curtains. A shape had crossed it – a shadow that his memory suggested had been as thin as an insect. However fanciful he wanted to believe that impression was, he couldn't avoid recognising that the intruder was behind him.

The realisation seemed to let it take shape in the mirror, though not much. He was able to distinguish the hint of a looming figure crouched beside the bed, unless it was on all fours. Its head was lowered towards his. Although it had no face that David could see, he sensed that it was watching Stephanie as well as him. He felt its dead breath on his neck again before he heard a whisper that might have been the night wind finding words. "So here we all are. Aren't we sweet," it said.

The voice was so close that David could have fancied he was hearing it just inside his head. He was struggling not to shrink away from the unnatural presence at his back in case that roused

Stephanie, which was one reason not to speak, but he had to answer. "What do you want?" he mouthed.

"What you think."

"You mean what I don't." David felt as though speaking was the only way to fend off dread, together with a kind of nightmarish mirth at the grotesqueness of the situation. "We can talk, then," he said barely loud enough to feel his lips move.

"So long as you keep me interested. That'll be an experience."

"We can't talk here."

"Why, I thought you wanted her to know all about us. Don't you even know what you want yourself? Maybe that's always been your problem."

If the breath on David's neck had grown colder still, he was afraid that meant the intruder was gaining more substance. Perhaps the deranged conversation was lending it to him. Were there the beginnings of a face within the silhouette in the mirror – the glint of eyes and teeth? All this brought David closer to panic. "I can't talk properly like this," he mouthed. "If you want to hear what I have to say you'll have to come with me."

The only response was a silent breath on his neck. He flexed his fingers cautiously and set about easing them from between Stephanie's. He was nowhere near freeing them when she clasped them more firmly. "Don't," she said.

He could have imagined she was warning him not to accompany the intruder. Her voice was disconcertingly clear, on the edge of wakefulness. "Go back to sleep," he murmured. "I shouldn't be gone long."

He squeezed her hand and let it go, and was inching to sit up when she turned on her back. "Where are you going?"

"Just for a walk. I can't sleep."

Her hand groped out from beneath the quilt and fumbled at the air. She was searching for the cord to switch on the light above the bed, and David was terrified that it would show her they weren't alone. If she saw Newless, what would have to happen? David reached for the cord, only to miss it in the dark. His mouth was parched with alarm by the time he captured the cord and swung it out of Stephanie's reach. "Leave the light off," he whispered. "You don't want to wake yourself up."

"I'm awake now, David. I'll come with you."

"Please don't." He was almost too panicked to come up with a reason. "I want to be alone," he said, "so I can think."

"I'll only lie here worrying about you if you go out."

"There's no need to worry. I'll only be in the park. Just close your eyes and maybe you'll sleep," David urged and risked glancing past her at the mirror. He appeared to block her view of anyone behind him, but how long would the figure remain in its crouch? In desperation he said "I'll take my phone and you can call me if you need to."

"I may do that if you're out long." While this might have been meant as an admonition, it sounded more like a plea. "Just remember," she said, "you don't have to be alone with your thoughts."

"I'll remember," David promised and swung his legs off the bed so hastily that he lurched towards the intruder. The idea of touching Newless made his innards clench with dread. His face almost collided with the insufficiently detailed head that had risen level with his, and then the figure dodged aside. "Don't keep me waiting," it breathed, "or I'll have to make my own amusement."

As the last word reached David the intruder was no longer in the room. Was Newless demonstrating how swiftly he could be somewhere else? David dressed as fast as the dark would let him and tiptoed across the room. He was inching the door shut when Stephanie said "I'm still awake."

"Try not to be," David murmured and turned away from closing the bedroom door to feel a cold breath on his face in the darkness of the hall. He had to welcome it, however violently he shivered, because it meant he was keeping Newless away from Stephanie. "Let me move," he muttered into the face he sensed only inches from his. "You heard where we're going."

He was reaching for the light-switch when he faltered. Suppose

Stephanie hadn't stayed in bed? Surely his voice was too low to be heard through the door, but then he mightn't be able to hear if she moved. He made himself advance along the hall, where every pace felt like venturing into peril, not just because of the darkness that refused to give way to his eyes; he was aware of a figure in front of him, matching his progress at less than an arm's length. When he both heard and felt its whisper he was even more unnerved to realise that it was still facing him. "Keep talking, then," it said. "That's why I'm here."

"You want to talk as well, do you?" The prospect of establishing contact had begun to feel like risking his own mind, but David had no idea what else to do. "What about?" he demanded, not far from some kind of hysteria.

"I ought to thank you for the entertainment in there. It's what you do best, you should know."

David managed to find anger in the midst of his dread. "What is?"

"Not being honest. Can't you even be honest about that?"

David stumbled to a halt, having sensed that more than the intruder was standing still in front of him. "Are you going to open the door?"

"I'll let you see to that. I'm not your doorman."

"Then get out of my way or I can't."

At once David was afraid that Newless would take him at his word and return to the bedroom. He had to be reassured by feeling a frigid breath on his cheek as he ventured forward to grope for the latch. He'd scarcely twisted it and begun to pull the door inwards when a shape darted out through the gap. While the figure was his own height, the gap wasn't even as wide as his little finger. He had to make himself open the door all the way and step onto the landing, which was deserted. "Where are you?" he said and was dismayed to hear a plea in his voice.

"Right by you. Where else would you want me?"

The answer seemed to engage his senses, so that he felt a breath as cold as malice and was able to distinguish a form at the edge of his vision, though it was almost too thin to glimpse. When he turned to confront it he thought for a nervous moment that it had gone in search of amusement elsewhere, and then it appeared to regain such of a shape as it had. He could make out no more than the suggestion of a presence, so insubstantial that it put him in mind of a childish sketch of bones. Or was it more like an elongated foetus? By the time this impression caught up with him he was already protesting "Don't you want to be seen?"

"Maybe you'd better remember what happens to people who get more of a look."

The voice had risen above a whisper, but David wasn't sure how closely it resembled his. "What about people who hear you?" he had to ask.

"Those as well."

If this was a threat, David couldn't allow it to deter him. As he made for the stairs he said "I'm giving you the chance to speak up for yourself."

He was halfway down the sleeping house before he heard the voice beside him. "Dishonest as ever."

Did Newless know all David's thoughts or only those he'd acted out? Even those were caricatures, David told himself, and surely that should mean Newless wasn't so closely in touch with him. "You must want to talk to me," he said, "or you wouldn't be here."

"Keep thinking that."

David couldn't tell if this was a response to what he'd said or what he'd left unspoken. He hurried downstairs, hearing his own footsteps and a similar but thinner sound if not just an impression of one. As he reached the outer door he was aware of restlessness beside him, impatience so intolerant of delay it felt worse than childish. "You go first," he felt grotesque for saying as he opened the door.

A solitary car passed along the main road, and once the lingering whisper of wheels trailed away the night was silent enough to have frozen the wind. Beyond a line of mansions split into smaller dwellings a police station showed lit windows but no other sign of life. For a wild moment David imagined taking Newless in there to accuse him. What would the police see except a madman? "Come in the park," he said.

The trees beside the paths were so still that he could have fancied they were inverted, rooted in the soil of the thick sky. Alongside the park a mass of unlit buildings that had been erected as an orphanage was now a disused hospital. David was trying not to be distracted by thoughts of uninvited birth or of a child without a family when the vague shape beside him snickered, a pinched vicious sound. "You must have been anxious to see me," Newless said, "to use that bait."

"Which bait? I don't know what you mean."

"Your bedmate. Staidfanny." With a titter involving no audible mirth Newless said "The hole you try and stop up."

"Don't call her that," David said, only to feel he should have been quicker to protest "I didn't use her as bait at all."

"What else do you think you were doing, showing her me? Did you honestly believe it would get rid of me somehow?"

They were in the park by now. The face leaned close enough to David in the gloom beneath the trees to add to the chill on his skin. When he twisted his head towards it the face stayed out of plain sight, though there didn't appear to be much of it in any case. "Maybe I did," he said and felt pathetically timid. "All right, I did."

"Then you failed, because I'm here. And Staidfanny didn't help."

The branches entangled with the darkness overhead put David in mind of the state of his thoughts, and he could only retort "I told you not to call her that."

"You must tell me how you think you're going to stop me."

"Can't you hear how infantile you sound?" Having said this, David found no reason not to add "Try acting like an older brother."

"Maybe you should hear how you sound yourself," Newless said and sniggered. "I'm no brother to anyone."

The darkness seemed to be lending him more substance –

letting him own up to more of himself. "What do you imagine you are, then?" David said.

"Don't you think I'm what you think?"

"That's just words." David felt too close to madness for saying "Tell me about yourself."

"What would you like to hear?"

A face loomed at the edge of his vision, and he tried to believe that only the night made it look so imperfectly formed. With what he took for inspiration he said "Where are you when you aren't on the blog?"

"Waiting to be entertained. Where else am I going to be?" Too immediately for David to answer that, Newless said "Let's go back to the question you asked me to begin with. What do you want?"

"You to stop doing what you do."

"You wouldn't deny me my fun." With a laugh that left any amusement behind Newless said "Mustn't deny yourself either."

"I can do without it. I don't want any part of it."

"You think that's what I meant, do you?" When David didn't speak Newless said "Let's see if we can get to the truth. I asked you once how you're going to stop me."

They were in the depths of the park, where the lamps on the distant perimeter road only made the path less visible. Through the trees to the left, dim inversions of the lamps dangled in a lake. Each time David passed one of the remote lights it seemed to flicker as if his companion had drawn on its energy, which must mean Newless was blotting out the light – was gathering more substance. It made David yet more desperate to find some way to take control. "It depends what you are," he said.

"What you think."

"You already said that. Maybe you aren't so good with words after all."

What could he achieve by antagonising Newless? Perhaps at least it would hold the creature's interest – would keep him there while David tried to grasp how to deal with him. "Don't say you're jealous," Newless said.

David did his best to laugh, though it sounded too reminiscent of Newless. "Why on earth would I be?"

"Because you can't be me however much you'd love it."

"And what would I be if I were?"

"Can't you even admit that? I'm everything I say and everything I do."

"So am I," David retorted and tried another laugh. "In fact, so's everyone."

"And what a poor show you all are." Newless might have been imitating David's attempt at mirth. "You most of all," he said. "You aren't half of what's in you, and you know why, don't you? Because you had me as an excuse."

"So tell me what you think I'm capable of."

Another light beyond the lake went out as the face leaned closer, and David glimpsed teeth bared in a mocking grin. "You can't even be honest about what you want to know," Newless told him.

"Then you'll have to tell me what it is."

"You're really hoping I'll be stupid enough to give you some tips on how to finish me off. Anyone who didn't know you might think you've no idea how to do away with people you don't like."

"I'd better learn from you, had I?"

"If you've got it in you, you could do worse."

David felt as if he was playing deranged word games with himself and losing his way in a maze of language. "Why don't you try being honest for a change," he said. "You don't think I can destroy you, do you?"

"I know you can't. Go on, tell me how you can."

It wasn't just a maze, it was a hall of mirrors made of words, and David heard himself say "Tell me why you think I can't."

"Because you already failed. Mind you, it was a pretty feeble attempt.

I'd like to see you try it properly."

David did his best not to hope too soon. "Try what?"

"What else is it going to be except telling all the truth? Saying what you really think in front of everyone. You gave it a go tonight but you missed the point. Or more likely you didn't want to see it, knowing you."

David had to struggle to conceal his eagerness. "What point?"

"You can't just say what you think of people. You have to let them know."

David imagined how they would react at work: Helen jerking her head askew as if he'd hooked it by its haughty eyebrows, Andrea bidding to spike his observations with an officious cough, Bill making haste to don his humorous mask. "Who are we talking about?" he said.

"You decide who you have to mean. I'd start close to home."

"You're saying if I tell everybody everything I don't like about them you'll go back where you came from."

"I've been there too often." Teeth glimmered in the darkness beside David's face. "I don't think you've got it in you to keep me there," Newless said.

They'd reached a bridge across the elongated lake. The black water meandered between the trees as though searching for the stretch of road where Stephanie lived. As David halted in the middle of the bridge, all at once anxious to see where she was, a dank chill rose from the water. It felt like an adumbration of the state Newless had hinted at – a threat of glimpsing somewhere so barren of light and warmth that it consisted purely of a yearning for sensation, for any token of existence. Could he condemn even Newless to that? Perhaps Newless had the measure of him, and David was no more able to consign him to such a place than to tell people what he didn't want to admit he thought of them. As David tried to find the strength to do all that if he had to, Newless said "Well, there it is."

David wasn't sure why this made him more nervous. "What is?"

"What brought me to you. You can't still think talking about your pests at work did." When David remained silent, Newless seemed to take his version of pity on him. "Staidfanny," he said.

At once David saw her. Perhaps the insidious voice had delayed his doing so. She was at the bedroom window, just visible by the light from the road. She looked tiny as a vignette framed by the entire night, and even more isolated by the distance to the bridge. David knew she was trying to distinguish him in the park, and he snatched out his phone almost without thinking. "Can you give me a few moments?" he felt worse than absurd for asking.

"You want a private word, do you?"

"I don't need that." If he sent Newless away he might be sending him to Stephanie. "Don't you want to stay with me," he urged, "now we've met at last?"

"We'll have to find out, won't we?" At least this didn't bring the face looming towards David, which lent him a little reassurance until he grasped that it was watching Stephanie. "Fascinate me, then," Newless said. "Keep me that way if you can."

David had to hold the phone close to his face, blotting out Stephanie in order to find her number. He heard the bell start to trill in his ear, but not the phone in the faraway apartment. The bell had rung four times when Stephanie disappeared from the window so abruptly that he could have thought she'd been dragged back into the unlit room. He wasn't far from crying out by the time he managed to discern that he hadn't been left alone on the bridge. Was the dim figure scrawnier than winter twigs, or had it begun some unnatural growth? He had to welcome its presence by his side, but that needn't entail making out how much more there was to it now. The bell finished shrilling, and Stephanie said "Where are you, David?"

"In the park. I said I would be."

Before he'd finished speaking she reappeared at the distant window, shading her eyes with the hand that wasn't holding the phone to her tiny face. "Where?"

"On the bridge."

She leaned minutely forward – at least, the distance made her movement seem little more than microscopic. "I can't see you."

"I can see you. Can you now?"

He was waving his free hand above his head as widely as he

could. Stephanie hadn't answered when the figure beside David started imitating him, making some kind of extravagant gesture in the dark. Might the antics mean that Newless was losing patience with the conversation? "I think I see something," Stephanie said.

"Then it has to be me," David said, fervently hoping so. "Anyway, you know where I've got to."

"Are you coming back now?"

"I've only just got where I am." He yearned to keep hearing her voice and watching her at the window, even if none of this was for the last time, but he was afraid to bore Newless. "I'll be gone for a while yet," he said.

"Then why are you calling, David?"

"I saw you and I didn't want you to be worried."

"Oh, David." If this was affection, he felt as though it was out of his reach. "Don't you think I am?" she said.

"No need to be. You can hear I'm all right, can't you?"

"I'm not sure what I can hear."

He had to hope Stephanie meant him. Newless had snickered at David's question, but surely she hadn't heard that. He didn't want to think what happened to anybody who became too aware of Newless, and he was about to end the call for fear of endangering her when she said "What are you actually doing now?"

"Just trying to sort out my thoughts. I promise that won't do any harm."

"I don't like to think of you trying out there all by yourself."

"Honestly, you shouldn't let it bother you." David glimpsed a restless movement near him and was afraid how much impatience it might betray. "See if you can't be thankful instead," he tried saying.

"Thankful for what, David?"

"For how things have worked out. For your new job." There was no mistaking the restiveness beside him now. "You could even thank me," he said, "if you like."

"I'll thank you for coming back to me."

"I will as soon as I can." He could tell she didn't simply mean returning to the apartment. "You try and catch up on your sleep," he said.

"I'll do that when I know you're coming back."

"Be sure I am, then," David said almost passionately enough to convince himself, and watched the tiny isolated figurine's hand sink away from her face.

She was lingering at the window, shading her eyes while she peered into the night, when Newless said "Not enough. Nowhere near."

"What isn't?"

"Can't you be honest about that either? What you told the ungrateful cunt to do."

"Don't—" David started to protest, and then he wondered if he had an insight. "You want to make her do more, do you? No, you want to make me."

"You mean you don't want it."

"The point isn't whether I do. We're talking about you." David's thoughts were developing almost too swiftly for him to articulate. "There isn't a lot to you, is there?" he said. "Not much more than words."

Newless gripped the low railing of the bridge as if to demonstrate he could and loomed towards him. "Quite a few people would tell you the opposite, but they can't tell anybody anything."

Stephanie's window was deserted now. David hadn't noticed when she'd left it, and his rage at having had to leave her anxious made him fiercer. "They may be dead, but you didn't really kill them, did you?"

Newless thrust his face at him without making its features clearer. "Then let's hear who you think did," he said, and his eyes glinted like his teeth.

"They killed themselves. That's as much as you could make them do. No wonder you have to rant like that every time. You've got to exaggerate to impress yourself."

The rudiments of a face encroached on the edge of David's vision – a dark shape not quite so featureless as a silhouette. "You'll be impressed," Newless said, "when I've paid Staidfanny a call."

David was overwhelmed by a loathing he lacked the words to convey. "What do you think you're going to do?"

"You won't know till I've done it. You never have. Not so unimpressed now, are you? You won't even know when till it's done. Have fun waiting and trying to guess what she's earned herself."

"She's safe from you. I'll never think of her that way."

"Now who's nothing but words? You can't even admit you've condemned her. That's why you're here."

"Then I'll admit it. I'll tell her everything if that'll keep her safe."

"It won't," Newless exulted, and David felt a snigger like frost sprinkled on his cheek. "You'll never be able to tell her enough. Now you know it you won't be able to stop thinking about it. You'll want to and that's why you'll fail."

David's abhorrence came close to choking off his speech. "You're relishing this, are you?"

"You wouldn't deny me my amusement. That's what keeps me alive."

"Alive," David tried to scoff. "I wouldn't call you that. You couldn't even open the door when we came out here. I wouldn't say there's much to you at all."

He had a sudden sense of being close to an edge far more perilous than the low railing. He had to use exactly the right words, or was it that he mustn't use the wrong ones? The uncertainty felt capable of robbing him of breath. "Wait till your cunt finds out how much," Newless said and leaned more of a face around David's.

Was there something David mustn't even start to think? "All you keep doing is telling me to wait," he said as if he had to be quick to outdistance his thoughts. "You can't show me to my face. You're just words in the air."

He was terrified this might send Newless to demonstrate his powers on Stephanie, but all he could do was carry on his mockery without knowing whether this was the right approach. "You can't touch me, can you?" he jeered. "I can't see anything worth seeing either. Maybe there isn't really anything to see."

Before he could take a breath Newless reared up in front of him, between David and the rail, which David was gripping in both fists. "Tell me this is nothing," Newless said like a wind from the black lake.

David saw eyes no less empty than the sky and in some sense as remote. Otherwise the face that blocked his view of Stephanie's apartment was too close to his own to distinguish, though he had the impression of an image in a distorting mirror. A shiver shook him from head to foot, and he barely managed to speak in order to head off his thoughts. "Still not impressed."

Newless lurched forward and wrapped his arms around David. "Now tell me I'm not here."

"Maybe you are," David gasped and tried to think no further. Could he do what he'd realised he must to keep Stephanie safe? Was anyone worth that? His doubts made him embrace Newless as if this might squeeze them both out of existence. The body felt like bones imperfectly covered with flesh, and so did the arms that clasped him. Too fast to reflect or to take back the action he toppled himself and his companion over the railing into the lake.

"Let's see who comes out." He wasn't sure which of them said that as they fell. He was dismayed that the thought had been put into words, and even more distressed to realise what he'd done his utmost to avoid thinking – that the disgust he felt was at himself, not Newless. Could this destroy Newless only as long as it stayed unacknowledged? These were all the thoughts he had before he struck the water. It felt like being seized by ice, and drove the breath out of him. In a moment he was underwater, clutching his companion to him as the scrawny arms hugged him, and he couldn't have said whether he or Newless was dragging the other down to the bottom of the lake. He had no more time for words, and the breath he attempted thoughtlessly to take felt like swallowing the dark.

PROLOGUE

"Was everything all right for you?"

"Surprisingly good."

"Don't take too much notice of him, will you? He just says these things. We thought his saginaki was delicious, and so was my lamb shank, and Alan's aubergine was especially tasty, wasn't it, Alan?"

"Indeed it was, and I'll second Susan's comments. As we say, don't mind our son too much. He has an image to maintain."

"Does anyone object if I speak for myself? Maybe all your dishes are the next best thing to the authentic article. Pass everyone's verdict on to the chef so long as you don't forget mine."

"You can tell her if you like," the waiter says to David's parents. "When there's a birthday she always brings the cake out herself."

"Oh, does she still do that?" David's mother says and blinks at David. "There isn't going to be a problem, is there?"

"Not for me."

"I think Susan means with you, David."

"Not as far as I'm aware of. It's hardly only up to me." When his parents look reproachful David says "Do you think I'm the kind of person to spoil a birthday treat?"

"We used to think we knew what kind you were."

"I'm sure we do really." Nevertheless David's mother says to the waiter "Better tell her she's got all the Botham family here."

As the waiter heads for the kitchen David's father murmurs "I sincerely didn't know who the chef was when I booked."

"I did when I said I'd join you," David says.

His mother gazes at him. "I hope that means—"

"I've already given you your birthday present, mother."

She seems anxious to believe she doesn't understand. Neither of his parents has found any more to say by the time Stephanie appears from the kitchen. The candles on the cake she's bearing lend her face a glow, which is one reason he's put in mind of an actress. Her face is a little too carefully composed, an aspect of a performance. It takes on more life as she begins to sing the standard birthday ditty, and David wonders if she'll be paying the copyright owners a royalty; would Frank Cubbins have warned her she should? Placing the cake in front of his mother doesn't require Stephanie to look at him. As his mother blows the flames out Stephanie leads the cheers and applause, however equivocal David's may be. She's still facing his parents when she says "How's everyone?"

"We're doing well," David's father says, "and you certainly seem to be."

"And you deserve it," says his mother.

"Everyone should get what they deserve," David contributes. "Is that what we're saying?"

There's a silence apart from the churchy murmur of diners until Stephanie looks at him. "Don't you think I have?"

"I never said that, did I? More like the opposite. You were the one with the problems about how you were helped."

"You're still keeping that up, then."

"It must be your talent that got you the top job in less than a year," David's mother says, "but wasn't David some help?"

"We aren't talking about that, Susan." As his mother makes to respond Stephanie says "And I wouldn't want to ruin your celebration."

"Now you're sounding like David," his mother says as if this is a hopeful sign. "You won't ruin anything by telling the truth."

Perhaps Stephanie realises the Bothams have had quite a lot to drink.

She's visibly making allowances as she says "I think I'd rather leave it if you don't mind."

"I thought you didn't believe in having any secrets," David reminds her.

"I must have learned my lesson." All the same, he has provoked her to say "I'm afraid this was how we ended up carrying on."

"How was that?" David's father seems to feel expected to ask.

"I got to sample his new personality before it went public. You were testing it out, were you, David? Perhaps I should have felt privileged."

"I should think it can be difficult to live with a writer," David's father offers.

"Maybe not as hard as being one," David's mother insists.

"There's nothing easier than being myself," David says, "now I know who I am."

His parents are eager to argue with that, but it's Stephanie who says "Then it shouldn't be too hard for you to tell Susan and Alan what they really want to know."

"I don't find it that interesting to talk about," David says, "to tell you the truth."

His mother takes a fiercely audible breath while his father looks as if he's wincing from a blow in the face. Stephanie regains her poise before David can glimpse any other reaction, a professional performance that puts him none too favourably in mind of Andrea. "Have a lovely birthday, Susan," she says. "If you'll excuse me, I'm needed in the kitchen."

"We hope we'll see you again very soon," David's mother calls after her, and murmurs "Did you honestly have to say that, David?"

"Yes, I honestly did."

"Well, I don't think I understand you." Even more reproachfully she says "And I want to understand."

"We both do," says his father.

"I know you do. That's your job."

"It has nothing to do with the job," his father protests. "We had you.

We brought you up."

"We're still your parents. We still feel responsible for you."

"Then don't. Only I am," David says and finds he can manage to add "But of course you're my parents. That's why I'm here."

"We just want to know why you've changed," his mother persists. "Was it having so much death around you?"

"Susan only had her clients' deaths to cope with, and she's over those," his father says. "You had the girl at work and I suppose Stephanie's boss as well."

David hears them training their expertise on him. "I haven't changed."

"David, you have," his mother says low but passionately. "Sometimes you seem like nobody we know."

"Maybe you should have known him." As David sees doubt that could become suspicion in his father's eyes, he adds "This has been me since before I was born. I couldn't own up to it, that's all. Now aren't you going to cut your cake?"

His mother transfers three slices to plates and passes one to him. It's as delicious as he would expect from Stephanie: light sponge, icing with a citrus tang, cinnamon in the cream. Perhaps thoughts of the chef are making his mother almost wistful enough to voice them. He's beset by memories himself, not least of how Stephanie gave him the ultimatum of seeking psychiatric help after his night in the park. Even if he'd convinced her that he'd missed his footing on wet leaves on the bridge, he hadn't been able to hide the consequences that had overtaken him. Being hurtfully honest was the only way he could be sure of saving her from worse.

As soon as he has finished his helping of cake he stands up. "I'll leave you to enjoy the rest of your birthday."

"I enjoyed this part as well," his mother tries to assure him. "I'm glad. I just need to get home now and work."

He's afraid that if he stays much longer he'll have to hear them talk about their clients. He doesn't want to think about those – to need to deal with his views about them. He kisses his mother and hugs his father and insists on paying the bill. While he's at the cash desk he hears his mother murmuring "Do you think there's anyone else?"

For a disoriented moment he wonders if she has his mental state in mind, and then he realises she's talking about Stephanie.

"I should think so," his father seems to regret having to say, "after nearly a year."

David hopes Stephanie has found someone else, if only so that he can forget about her. When he steps out of the Sunshine restaurant the sun is setting beyond the roofless church. As the crimson glow sinks through the arch of an unglazed window it looks as if the void within the walls is drawing the sun down. He's passing We're Still Left when the last of the sunlight goes out, and he almost collides with a man who's emerging from the bookshop. It's Len Kinnear.

At first he seems determined to ignore David. He makes to move a display of second-hand books from the pavement into the shop, and then he stares at David. "It's you, isn't it," he declares.

"I don't know who else you think I could be."

"I mean it's you that's writing for that rag. Mr Nasty from the north."

"That's one of the things they call me."

"I knew it couldn't be anyone else. Recognised your style of rant from the first time I met you. So you've decided you're a writer after all."

"I had to be honest. It's the only way to live."

"Still too good for the rest of us, I suppose, now you've made such a name for yourself."

"More like too bad."

"That's what you're trying to be, is it? Must be a chore, having to think that stuff every week."

"Not just then."

"I hope you're not complaining. Think yourself lucky you've got a writing job that pays. In fact I'd say you were a few kinds of lucky."

"Which do you have in mind?"

"There aren't many bloggers that get picked up for print. Lucky for you it's a new paper that wanted to get noticed. Only there's better ways to do that than slagging everybody off and everything as well. I keep wondering how much of that stuff you really think."

"All of it, believe me, and that includes what I said about your writers' group."

He mustn't hold anything back. Kinnear lifts a carton of books off the trestle table and gives him a parting stare. "Watch out you don't get a brick through your window with that kind of talk, and maybe a bit more."

"If I do I'll know where to find who's responsible," David says and heads downhill.

The route to the station takes him past Frugogo. He considers crossing to the opposite side of the street, though what would this avoid? The window of the agency is almost covered with posters for holiday offers, but he's just able to make out the staff through the gaps. Helen sees him first, and looks away at once, tilting her head in that direction too. Bill takes back his automatic grin, and then Andrea notices him. She leaves the racks of brochures and strides to the door as if she means to move him on, presumably demonstrating how she won't let his presence trouble her. As she shuts the door behind her she coughs a warning. "Revisiting the scene of the crime?" she says.

"I didn't know there'd been any here."

"What would you call how you spoke to everyone?" Before David can answer, if he has any reason to, she says "You make a living at it now, do you? Are we supposed to call you Lucky Botham now?"

"That's one of my names."

"It's the one you seem to want the world to know. I'm afraid I know it so I know what I don't want to read."

"I thought you liked your men unrestrained. How is Rex, by the way?"

"I won't discuss my personal relations with you, David. I'll call you that if you don't mind."

"Maybe I ought to. Shouldn't you call your customers whatever they tell you?"

"If you plan to book a holiday through us, and obviously I hope you do, I'd rather you didn't use my branch."

"You've got enough business even without me here to help you, then."

"We're doing satisfactorily, thank you," Andrea says and emits a cough that sounds decidedly final. "Now I must get back to work."

"Then there's two of us."

She can't know why he accompanies this with a dry laugh. As she turns her back he imagines helping her into the shop by propelling her through the pane of glass. So long as he envisions the spectacle and feels the elation it brings, it won't take place. Surely he needn't write about it to make sure; he can't think even *Print* would publish that. "Keep your head up, Helen," he calls as Andrea opens the door. "Don't be niggardly with your sniggers, Bill."

He's almost at the station when he hears the evangelist ranting in the distance. The preacher should be safe; he was in one of the first instalments of *Bad Thoughts*, though how long can the effect be trusted to endure? As David makes for the ramp down to the station he's accosted by a woman selling the *Big Issue*. "You'd be better off with *Print*," he tells her. "That's where you'll find the real truth. Just read Lucky Botham's *Bad Thoughts* and maybe you'll find yourself."

She seems not to understand that much English. David marches vigorously enough for two men down the ramp. A slot in the top of a barrier swallows his ticket, and a further slit returns it to the world. On the escalator and the platform he's as alone as he ever feels these days, and he even has a carriage to himself on the train. "Still in there, are you?" he mutters. "That's where you'll be staying. If I can't get rid of you, at any rate I can keep you where you'll do the least harm."

He has to believe that, otherwise the sense of constant infestation would be unbearable. Often it very nearly is, not least because he knows that in a way it's himself. The train speeds out of the tunnel into a larger darkness that the lights of houses alongside the track hardly seem to touch. Soon he's at the station where the lamps above the car park line up plots of shadow beneath the vehicles. The artificial glare displays how flawless his car looks now that the scrape on the door has been repaired and painted over — as flawless as innocence. He could almost fancy that the accident never happened, that none of the repercussions of the last year did. He has no right to think so, and as he drives home past Dent's house the empty windows and the For Sale board seem to send him a rebuke.

He has braked in the middle of the deserted road and is about to back into his drive when Mrs Robbins comes out of her house. With a bag of garbage in either hand she can't help reminding him of a parody of justice. He lowers the window to call "Always more rubbish."

She lets the lid of the bin drop with a slam and scowls at him. "I think that's your speciality, Mr Botham."

"You'll have to explain."

"All the things you've been writing. Everybody knows it's you."

"I wouldn't want it any other way. I don't mean to hide what I think."

"You won't make many friends round here like that."

"I haven't got too many elsewhere either," David says, though the amount of support he's attracted in the paper and online has taken him aback, not to mention the tone, some of which makes Newless seem restrained. "So can I ask what you've read of me?"

"Not a word. I've been told about it and that's more than enough. I don't think you'll find it round here."

"I should think Slocombe's stock it. He doesn't like to be told not to sell anything."

"I hope he's got more sense than to offend us that pay his wages."

"We'll find out," David says and shuts the window. He feels as if not just Mrs Robbins has prompted him to drive to Slocombe's Open All Hours. He parks in front of the stained concrete parade and skids on an abandoned greasy chip from Ho's as he makes for the general store. In the dull colourless light from the street the magazines and packets of food in the window look more forsaken than ever. As David steps across the grubby threshold Slocombe lifts his head to peer across the counter. His broad flat face seems almost as squashed as the crumpled canvas hat pulled down nearly to his exaggerated eyebrows. "What can I get you today?" he says.

David can't see *Print* among the publications spread across the half of the counter unoccupied by sweets. "You can tell me if you're selling me."

"Selling you." In case this isn't sufficiently incredulous Slocombe says "We sell to people, we don't sell them" and for good measure adds "Hello?"

When did he start saying that? Perhaps he learned the usage from a younger member of the family. David can't think of a verbal habit that infuriates him more, but he says only "I don't mean me personally. I was hoping you sold *Print*."

"Print."

"The weekly that's been surprising the trade with how well it sells."

"I know what it is." Apparently Slocombe is too affronted to bother echoing any of David's words. He yanks his hat an inch higher and squints under the brim at David. "Are you the character that writes for them?" he demands. "Someone said they lived round here."

"I'm one of them."

"One of them." Slocombe makes this sound like quite an insult. "Well," he says, "you won't be finding yourself in here."

"May I ask why?"

"Why." At first Slocombe seems to find the question too outrageous to answer. "They showed us a copy," he says. "We might have taken it till we saw what you did."

"And what are you saying I did?"

"Did." The word appears to be another source of outrage. "If you have to think that kind of thing about people you should keep it to yourself," Slocombe declares. "Even better, don't think it at all."

"I give you my word you wouldn't like it if I did."

"Word." Slocombe frowns as if his brows can squeeze his puzzlement to nothing, and then he abandons trying to understand.

"You've been giving us too many of them," he says. "Maybe you'll upset so many people you'll be made to stop."

David can only vow not to let himself be silenced. "If that's what you want, maybe you should stock the magazine."

"That won't be happening." Slocombe has grown too impatient to waste time with an echo. "Now if you want to buy something, this is still a shop," he says. "Hello?"

"I shouldn't keep saying that," David advises him and hurries out of the store. For a moment he wants to turn and dash back in. He's afraid that he didn't sufficiently confront the shopkeeper, and he feels urged to be quick. Surely it's imperative to write whatever he needs to write; that's the only way to deal with the situation. "Home now," he mutters as he climbs into the car, and hopes the words aren't required to keep him together. Surely they can't be, but as he drives home he feels drymouthed enough to be running a race.

ACKNOWLEDGEMENTS

Jenny was there first, as always. Some of the book was written on the balcony of our accommodation at the delightful Roulla Apartments (where Eleni's hospitality is famously splendid) in Alykes on Zakynthos. It also went to the World Fantasy Convention in Brighton and the Festival of Fantastic Films in Manchester.

My old friend Keith Ravenscroft kept me supplied with good things, not least the fine French Blu-ray of my favourite horror film. "Maybe it's better not to know…"

This novel owes some of its form to the example of my friend Steve Mosby, author of a number of excellent crime novels, some overlapping into horror. If you haven't read him, give yourself a treat.

FLAME TREE PRESS
FICTION WITHOUT FRONTIERS
Award-Winning Authors & Original Voices

Flame Tree Press is the trade fiction imprint of Flame Tree Publishing, focusing on excellent writing in horror and the supernatural, crime and mystery, science fiction and fantasy. Our aim is to explore beyond the boundaries of the everyday, with tales from both award-winning authors and original voices.

•

Other titles available include:

Thirteen Days by Sunset Beach by Ramsey Campbell
The House by the Cemetery by John Everson
The Toy Thief by D.W. Gillespie
The Siren and the Specter by Jonathan Janz
The Sorrows by Jonathan Janz
Kosmos by Adrian Laing
The Sky Woman by J.D. Moyer
Creature by Hunter Shea
The Bad Neighbor by David Tallerman
Ten Thousand Thunders by Brian Trent
Night Shift by Robin Triggs
The Mouth of the Dark by Tim Waggoner

•

Join our mailing list for free short stories, new release details, news about our authors and special promotions:

flametreepress.com